The Madam

The
Madam

a novel

julianna baggott

ATRIA BOOKS

New York London Toronto Sydney Singapore

ATRIA BOOKS

1230 Avenue of the Americas
New York, NY 10020

This book is a work of fiction. Names, characters, places and
incidents are products of the author's imagination or are used
fictitiously. Any resemblance to actual events or locales or persons,
living or dead, is entirely coincidental.

ISBN: 0-7434-5457-X

First Atria Books hardcover printing July 2003

10 9 8 7 6 5 4 3 2 1

ATRIA BOOKS is a trademark of Simon & Schuster, Inc.

For information regarding special discounts for bulk purchases,
please contact Simon & Schuster Special Sales at 1-800-456-6798 or
business@simonandschuster.com

Designed by Jaime Putorti

Printed in the U.S.A.

This book is dedicated to

Mildred Holderfield Smith Lane, my grandmother,

and to her mother, Ella, the matriarch and madam.

Acknowledgments

I would like to thank my grandmother—who was raised among show people, nuns, hustlers, and whores—for her willingness to share with me the particulars of her astounding life. This is a work of fiction, but it never would have been created without my family mythology, which has been so lovingly handed down. I thank her for her permission and for her patience with my endless, often intimate questions.

I want to thank my father for his tireless research of hosiery mills and railroad switching yards and for finding an elephant on a Miami dock. He also gave me the landscape of his youth, mountains and coal ash, and I'm grateful.

I would like to thank my mother for never burying anything, not even our ugliness, and for her exuberance, her adoration of storytelling, and for passing that love on to me.

I couldn't accomplish anything without my husband,

David. I would still be fishing for my keys without him. I thank him for his inexhaustible patience and well-timed rowdiness. And I want to thank my kids, Phoebe, Finneas, and Theo, for understanding that it's just a job, that we could just as believably run a fish shop and have to wash our hands with toothpaste to get rid of the stink and forever be discussing the special on herring or sea bass.

James Quisenberry—thank you for all of your intelligent and thoughtful explanations about the business and history of coal mining. It was a wonderful education. And I thank the other miners who, once they heard the title and subject of the novel, chose not to be acknowledged here. They, too, were brilliant with detail.

And I want to thank all of my readers: David Teague, Marisa de los Santos, Elise Zealand (as always!), Blake Maher, Jim Loscalzo, Rachel Pastan, Fleda Brown, and Kirsten Maxwell. And thanks, Tom, Gary, Ray.

Thank you, Greer Kessel Hendricks, for your keen eye, your trust, for your faith in me and my work. So much more than an editor to me, you are brilliant and fabulous in every way. Thanks also to Louise Braverman and Suzanne O'Neill, and my sincerest thanks to Judith Curr.

And thank you, Nat Sobel and Judith Weber, for sending me down this curious, astonishing road.

I would like to thank my ancestors—hustlers, yes, but poets, too. I know it was in you; how else can I explain its presence in me?

Part One

1

*B*efore there can be a murderous heart, or, for that
matter, before there can be a whorehouse, an orphanage, a dank trunk with rusted hinges, there must first be a
hosiery mill. And a woman within it—Alma. You must
imagine her as a young mother, thin, cheerless, her hair
frizzing around her head. She stands in front of a smoothed
pedestal, curved like a flexed foot, fitting each toe seam to it,
pulling stockings on and then, quickly, off again. It is like
dressing and undressing a thousand women's bare legs.
Sometimes she thinks of their legs, the future bodies that
will stretch and wear thin the cloth, their fine, soft hairs and
broad calves. Sometimes she sees thousands of legs —pale,
dark, thin, fat—the endless churn of days swaggering toward
her as anklebone and soft knee. She doesn't want to be here,
righting stockings all her life, the wet air, shivering from the

livid machinery, spiked with the acrid pinch of dye vats catching in her nose each time she breathes. She has no interest in moving up to mending, looping, to stir yarn at the dye vat, to sit like the old pallid men in the corner with their magnifying glasses counting threads. *Who would?* she hisses to herself. *Who would ever desire this?* And it seems to her that a person should desire something.

It's spring, the sun only musing about heat, and it should be cool enough, but the factory is kept hot, intentionally humid, so the threads won't snap, wad, gum up the machines, or simply spin out to whir blankly. The factory is one giant roaring room, the winding machine's high-pitched whine, the great clacking cams, the unending ruckus of the beating machines, and the women bow to them, their fingers fidgeting and smoothing around insistent needles. Despite the oil, the gears grind corrosively, a damp rustiness that smells of blood. When Alma looks up from the hose and the upturned wooden foot, her eyes tear from the dust and the whole wide factory before her tilts and quivers. The room seems fragile, like it could shatter, but then the tears plop to her dress front and the factory is as it should be, churning, thunderous, massive, an immovable train with a million pumping engines. The noise is so loud it seems that it should send the workers rattling into their machines. But it doesn't. Some scuttle up and down the alleys, coughing, coughing, their lungs nicked by barbed cotton dust. Others bend to their fast hands. The dust and humidity are so thick, Alma feels like she can't breathe. She's heard of the bigger mills where clouds billow in prep rooms as workers beat and claw out the raw cotton, the lint flying up from openers, pickers, cards. But in this factory, too, when she walks by to go to the bathroom—a foul room with its slimy floor and thin partition—and looks back to her station at the end of the long room, she sees nothing but stirring bodies caught in a white haze, the workers moving like ghosts.

Here the air is choked by whiteness. It's the opposite of the world outside where the steep mountains empty into the valley, its city shuffling in black dust from the coke oven fires and coal mines up in the mountains, a thin mist that grays the streets, the buses, dimming everything from her paint-chipped porch rails to the university's white pillars. The dark dust swirls in the Monongahela, teeming with catfish that rake up slow silty clouds. It's worse in winter when each house heats up from its coal-burning stove, each chimney pouring smoke and ash. Perhaps you can see her days, the blur as she moves from white cloud to dark, from lint to ash to lint.

But Alma can feel things shifting. She knows nothing of atoms. She can't. She's a woman in a hosiery factory in Marrowtown, West Virginia. It's 1924, nearly summer. Atoms are still the matter of physicists' dreams, dim stars with the skies just beginning to ink. But if she did know of atoms, she would say she could feel the restlessness of them, like schoolchildren at the end of a long spring day. She's aware of the vibration of everything—not just the factory's thrumming hive, but in some minute invisibility all around her, inside of herself, a small electric charge.

She's always felt that she's known a bit of the future, nothing specific—more a feeling, an inclination. And she can tell—does she hiss this to herself as well?—that the future holds a change, an abrupt one, like the two wide factory doors that swing out just before the end of the shift—as is happening now, Mrs. Bass lifting the heavy latch—and suddenly the dark factory of hunkered sweat-stained backs is swimming in sun. Mrs. Bass walks up the stairs, her knotty backbones poking out of the thin cloth of her work dress. She sounds the whistle, a hollow rise of air. The machines wind down, but not all the way—a kept purr, and it's as if the purr is in Alma's chest, locked in her ribs.

The night shift stands in the open doorway, men and women spitting their tobacco juice, their orangy ambeer, in bright sluices. Mr. Bass sits at his little table because it is the end of the week. He looks mannerable in his pressed white shirt with a starched collar that seems to catch the sharp knob of his Adam's apple each time he clears his throat, a habit that draws attention to him, his tally sheet, his shiny hair parted straight down the middle. Alma stretches her back.

"How many gross you got there?" Mrs. Bass has snuck up on her. Mrs. Bass is a cankered woman, slightly older than Mr. Bass, it seems, bent, with big thievish eyes behind small glasses, ferretlike with snapping buck teeth. Like Mr. Bass, she shouts, because she is nearly deaf, having lived her life amid the drumming. She doesn't seem to trust anyone and asks even this simple question as if expecting a lie.

"Eleven, ma'am," Alma tells her.

"You sure there? You count it twice?"

"Yes," she says, although she only counted once. It is eleven sacks, though, stuffed tight. That's the truth.

The old woman writes it down, the last on her list, and scurries to the little table and Mr. Bass with his tray of money, his pencil stub.

There are two lines now, one to get in, one to get out. The night shift jaws in the doorway. Some are coal miners' wives; Alma can tell by that ashen, obdurate look of having breathed so much dust your skin grays, and yet being willing to breathe more. Threadbare, worn by the burden of toughness. She recognizes one of the women from her school days. Tall now and angular, the woman holds onto the boniness of her childhood. Alma remembers her as one of the girls with the sticks, who'd run after her until she fell, and then lashed her arms and legs, red, tender. The sticks were sharp, some pulled from trees, still green, pliable, snapping whips. It happened twice, and then she stopped going to school. It was her mother's fault, and her mother said there was no need for Alma to suffer for her mother's passions. The woman nearly catches her eye, but Alma looks down quickly and then away, across the factory, as if she might have left something behind at her station.

Alma feels herself slipping away into her childhood skin, the nigger lover's daughter—for that's what she had been called for years. She had felt like an ugly, ruderal child. On her mother's farm, its sweet peas shriveled on their curled stems, suffering from the atrophy of her mother's dismissal of love, all of the crops, corn, tomatoes, yellowed and sun-bleached, she was a cast-out child, an oddling who learned on her own how to trap and skin and boil wild rabbit and squir-rel. She recalls that those squirrels, wiry and quick with their sharp teeth—like Mrs. Bass—gave her bad dreams. She pre-ferred the rabbits. Even here in the factory she can still have moments like these, of bone-deep memory when she sinks into her girlhood and feels forever fastened to that delicate skeleton. She tries to remind herself that she is a wife, a mother. She will go home to Henry's back, pained from switching rails all day, hooking and unhooking heavy metal clasps, and the pressing needs of her three children: Irving, outgrowing his shoes; Willard, with his oversize head and fat hands, talking about God, sweet, slow-witted Willard; and her girl, Lettie, who has started with the bad dreams, calling out in her sleep about water and a hand. Sometimes Alma is afraid of her children. She was raised in a sullen house, her parents silent. Her mother's kind of silence was stern, proud; her father's, ashamed, even before there was a humiliation. Alma was never loved lavishly. Even Henry's courtship, although lusty, was reserved. She remembers only once in a guttural whisper that he told her she was beautiful. And that was enough for her. In fact, it might have been all she could have endured.

The Madam

But the children, as infants, clung to her while crying, and then they fell asleep, creating a patina of sweat that she dared not break for fear of waking them. And even now, older knobby-kneed kids, they rush her with wild attention. Willard, nearly the size of a man, will sometimes race to find her seated in the kitchen—when she least expects him—and he'll bury his face in her lap, kiss her hands. Lettie, now ten, is a river of emotion, winding, quick, a dipping whirl, a surge strong enough to carry Alma away. Irving has grown distant, and yet he can throw a hungry glance and her knees give, her stomach clots. Often she senses a need in them so deep it seems they want to swallow her. She imagines them, hands joined, circling, and it's not her children but a giant mouth. She fears disappearing into it, into herself, into the house, its rooms rented to noisy boarders—show people—a troupe working for the Tremont Theater, a variety act. The sign reads: DANCING BEAR! SINGING PARROT! ACROBATICS, CHORUS GIRLS, AND COMEDICS! THE GREATEST PERFORMERS OF THE WORLD! 10 CENTS, PLEASE. But they're a lousy bunch. The bear is even a shuffler, small and old with an arthritic hip. And who can afford a show these days?

This is her life. Better than her childhood, sacred by comparison, but still she is desirous of the change she feels. She is here to turn stockings, but it can't last too long, not with her heart charged as it is, not with this buzz of change around her.

Her shift waits for its money, says, "Evenin', Mr. Bass,"

9

each one, as he tallies up and hands out bills and change. The woman in front of her is antsy, a blonde who's already taken off her apron. She's looking around, her soft neck craning. She spots Mrs. Bass, who's now sweeping up between the rows. Alma doesn't know the blonde's name. She doesn't want to.

The blonde leans down, says, "Evenin', Willy," in a breathy whisper.

Mr. Bass looks up, and then his eyes cut to his wife, sweeping now in a dark corner, a small puff of dust collecting at her manly shoes. "Evenin'," he says, shy all of a sudden, soft around the edges of his face. He takes his nub pencil and changes her eleven into a fourteen in one quick, mincy stroke, and counts the money out in her hand.

She glances at Alma, smiles, almost apologetically, but too, with a sense of deep exhaustion. Alma looks at her own shoes, square-toed and uncomfortable. Each pregnancy widened her feet, but she's never admitted it, a certain vanity, and so her toes are forever pinched. She wants to tell the woman to look somewhere else if she wants an accomplice. *Don't apologize to me.* But really, she's got nothing against the blonde. She hates Mr. Bass—even now, before she knows so much about men—in his clean, starched shirt, his sharp Adam's apple, the pale razor-nicked skin of his neck. What about Mrs. Bass, his ferretlike wife? She's taken care of, of course, better than most, but she's not twenty feet away, and sweeping her heart out, short angry stabs at the dust and knit-scraps that she'll pick out of the heap while he flirts,

cheats. No wonder Mrs. Bass doesn't believe anybody when
they tell her how many gross at the end of each day.

Mr. Bass watches the blonde walk out the door. Coughs.
Straightens. Turns back to Alma, all business again. Six dollars and sixty cents for the week. It's always disgraceful. This
small amount, never enough. She isn't angry, exactly, but
there's a tightness of oiled parts, as if her heart is a motor, its
gears tensing in the air. She stuffs the money in her apron
pocket.

The heat of the day is dropping off. The other women talk
and laugh, jostling together, all hips and elbows from where
Alma has stopped behind them. The blonde's with them, too,
no longer breathy, loud now, her voice clanging. Alma also
sees the coal miners' wives, a somber clot trudging up the
mountain to their company housing. She can hear the dulled
clamor of her mother's voice: *You aren't a coal miner's wife,* her
mother would say, *and you should be glad of that. I got you out,*
meaning she married an epileptic who wasn't allowed in the
mines, a sacrifice for her daughter. Miners are her mother's lesson. She always pointed them out to her as a child, knowing
many by name (although she'd never talk to them) and others
by the way their skin, sometimes too pink from scrubbing,
held onto the coal around their wide fingernails, the switchers
with their missing fingers, and the ones who'd been in an
explosion mottled with blue scars, what the doctor couldn't
dig up still trapped beneath their skin. The women she
claimed to know by their worn look, weakened by worry of

the alarm whistle, and babies, babies, clinging all over them. Alma was supposed to have learned to feel a gush of relief, a contentment, even more than that, a steam of pride—for what? Her mother marrying a man she found pathetic so her daughter could know a different kind of poverty? Alma never felt pride, and her mother didn't either, although she tried. But no. And Alma doesn't feel it now. The road ahead rolls downhill, and the slipping golden light is collecting in the soft dip like it's a basket the women are walking into.

She looks into the tall grass of the field beside the road, the mountains' blue outline filling up the sky. The grass, noisome with crickets, frogs, cicadas, has a pitching scream to it, a screeching chorus, but her ears still ring, the factory's din filling her head. The world is muffled as if everything were trying to sound out under a wrap of cotton and coal dross. She can just barely make out the rinky-dink plinking of the gypsy carnival. She knows she should march on to her own road, her hedgerow, step into her house next to the neighbor's field of cows—beautiful bow-bellied cows with udders so full she sometimes can see the droplets of milk pearling on the teats—to be the woman inside of her work dress, her skin, the one with fingers worn from righting hose, a mother, a wife. But she cannot take another step, although the women ahead of her look lovely, dusted still in some coal-choked sun, everything touched by the filigree of ash. Bouncing bet bob in the field—pinkish white clusters, and, too, the new ones, their green tongues just beginning to twist into a bloom.

She turns, walks into the tall grass, to take the long way home through the carnival, even though she knows that Henry will walk into the noisy house before she does and not find a thing cooking. Maybe because of it. Wouldn't it be nice if he needed her as much as she needed him? And, too, perhaps most of all because she's dreamed up the cows, their wide girths pitching as they balance on their hooves, their bodies' rock and sway, their twitching tails. She's spent too much time gazing out the kitchen window at them, their pinbones shifting hips, barrel, unlocking hock and knee, their delicate dew claws, the constant chew and chew, the way her own mind works at something, like a memory—her run-off father, for example, his clipped tongue. Sometimes, even in winter with the windows shut tight, she can hear the cows low in the field, their sweet cries, the hollow tink of neck bells each time one shifts her weight or lifts her heavy head. It is too much like her own life, fenced, servile, the shuffle from barn to sky and back again.

But she is outside now, alone. She feels the clatter of machinery in her chest begin to whir, the ground is so lit with its tamped singing, and the plinking music grows louder until she can see the carnival's strung lanterns, until she's walked through the small clutch of trees, stepped over a sagging fence, and she is there, in the shuffling crowd. It's a small relief, a valve's steam tipping up its metal cap.

She takes it in: the striped tents, the painted signs— MULE-FACED WOMAN, RUBBER MAN, a charred pig turning on

13

its spit. A faded painting on a wooden door of a half-man, half-woman, one side with its thin moustache and suit, the other with its lavish eyelashes and glittery dress. The entire whirling spectacle puckers, fades, puckers again, a clatter-roll, cawing, as if the earth here were plowed, revealing furrows of gaudy light that climbed right out, as if from a grave, and shook loose the dirt. She feels something close to jealousy, a surge of need. She feels the way she did as a child, wanting, and her mother, her father, their large bodies and voices, the importance of their lives teetering above her; the carnival is like this, its bright colors, its hawkers in bow ties, its giant clicking wheel.

The paths around the run-down exhibits are worn, muddy, pocked with small puddles and cart ruts. But the rain is good. It washes away the soot. It pulls the ash from the air and pins it, wet, to the earth. She would like to see the Mule-Faced Woman. She always wants to, but there's never enough time or money. She's only ever been to the carnival this way, over the fence walking home the long way from work. It's almost as if she's discovered a new world here. It smells foreign, too. Not any one smell by itself, but all of the smells mixed together—the charred pig, the sweet candy, the metal, liquor, bodies, dung, hay, even the smell of her own body, the cling of oil, dye, cotton and coal ash, yes, always that. Mixed like this, it smells like no place she's ever been before. It makes her think of China or Persia, or some such place you only ever hear stories about. *Byzantium,* the word forms in her mouth; it seems dizzy with glitter. She's told Henry about the carnival many times. She's said, "We should go someday. Take the whole family. It's got lights and music and all kinds of people the like you've never seen before." She imagines the kids running through the crowd, the strung lanterns turning their faces red then blue then red again.

But Henry never wants to go. It costs money to go anywhere. "Not to mention," he says, "this here house is a damn carnival. We got a bear. What else do you want?"

Henry doesn't like the bear. He acts jolly enough around it, rubs its ears as he walks past, but he takes offense to it living in the house, she suspects, powerful and kingly with its brushed fur, the way it sometimes lords around downstairs, a yawn showing its large white teeth, imposing, as if it's the man of the house. He's jealous of it, she can tell, and afraid of it, too. He is actually a fearful man. Sometimes he's afraid of Alma—she can sense it—and then he hates her for making him afraid, and the hate makes him strong again. She catches herself worrying over Henry. She knows only her mother's failed attempts at domesticity and love. Her marriage to Henry is subtle, complicated, like paper that's been balled up again and again, and now when she tries to figure it out, to smooth it open, it's impossibly wrinkled, and whatever may have once been written on it is now illegible, lost.

She walks up to the eight-legged calf steeping in a jar of formaldehyde. She always pauses here, staring into its whiskered face, bulging eyes, its egregious body, calcified in a shocked expression of horror. It makes her recall her baby born early, dead, a hateful association, but there nonetheless, each time she sees it. The doctor said the baby must have had something wrong with it, and she wonders what it looked like. The doctor wrapped it in a bloodstained sheet, the small clot of its bones, and she imagines a soft rubberiness of arms and legs, the cord at its navel snipped and bloody. He told Henry to take it away so as not to give her a shock. Henry was scared of her then, too, scared of her growling with pain, scared of the blood. She wonders if the baby would have been a shock, if it had too many arms, too many legs, like the calf. She looks at the calf's proud owner, his lumpy cheeks shiny with pride, tapping the glass with a little stick, saying, "Lookee here. Lookee here. Marvel of marvels!" It's been so many years since the dead baby. It had been her first, and now Irving is twelve. Could it be fourteen years? She was just a girl, herself, then, just seventeen.

Today she's got the money to see the Mule-Faced Woman, but there's a line—a soldier missing a leg, a boy sitting curled around his crutch, and there are two fat sisters, twins maybe. But then the tent flap opens, and a tartish girl with a primped mouth says, "Next show starting. Come on in." The line files into the dark tent, and Alma follows along. The girl holds out her grimy hand, and each person puts a nickel in it, which she, quick, shoves in an apron pocket.

At first it's so dark inside that Alma can't see a thing. Slowly her eyes adjust and there's a row of ten chairs, a tiny curtained stage.

The girl walks like a woman, and Alma wonders if she is a woman, only tiny. She hobbles, one leg longer than the other—in evidence by one shoe's built-up heel. Now Alma can make out her high breasts and compact hips.

The girl-woman speaks in a voice so tinlike it seems as if she's talking into a can: "This here is a woman of a grotesque nature. Her mother a woman. Her father a mule. A cruel fate. This show is not for the weak of heart nor the weak of stomach. I beg of you: Leave now if you are frail by nature." She pauses.

Alma imagines the sex in a horrid flash, a woman and a mule locked together, the mule's penis, large and heavy as a club. She pauses, trying to think if it's possible. Mules can't usually mate, isn't that right? Does she mean a donkey? Shouldn't it be the Donkey-Faced Woman? Alma blushes, wonders if the other people there have imagined the sexual act, too. The audience fidgets, but no one gets up to leave. Alma tries to direct her attention away from the dark theater. She hears a barking dog, its clinking chain, a woman's peal of laughter, a heavy woman by the deep sound of it, and the repetitive punctuation of a sharp ring, perhaps a shovel striking rock.

The girl-woman sighs, heavily, shakes her head, like she's an executioner doomed to this sorrowful task. "Well, then, I suppose I will have to show the horrible truth of the Mule-Faced Woman." Nickels clicking, she pulls back one side of the curtain, revealing a woman's long legs in a knee-length skirt and high heels. It's the normalcy that makes Alma tighten with fear. The girl-woman takes time tying the curtain back before she moves to the other side. She pulls the second length of hanging cloth slowly, staring out into the audience. A sharp gasp rises up. The small crowd begins to stir and whisper. The Mule-Faced Woman has an immense jaw with large squared teeth, wide nostrils, oversize eyes. She is reading a book. She looks up at the audience, takes a handful of peeled nuts from an oily sack on her lap and eats them. Her skull is sloped, misshapen. She is grotesque, Alma agrees, but what is most shocking is her refinement. She is dainty, almost, reading her book, a leather-bound edition now tattered. Alma never reads books. One of the boarders is a reader: Wall-Eye, the parrot trainer. Once she snuck into his bedroom, while he was performing at the Tremont Theater, to run her hands over the books on his shelf. She thought of stealing one but didn't. She is aware of the university in town. She has imagined its cool corridors, walls packed to the ceiling with books, and the men who sit in wingback chairs reading them. Women, maybe, too. She is sure there are women who've read more books than she would know how to count. She has always wondered what they contained, all those pages, each lined with words. She imagines they hold secrets about the entire world and how it works. How plants unfold, and seed. How people should think and talk. She supposes they know why some babies are born dead, some born like Willard, a little slow to focus and bat, some

born looking like mules, and some born healthy, pink, kicking. Alma doesn't have time to read, although she is proud to
know how. She doesn't have time to eat nuts from a paper
sack. She decides that the Mule-Faced Woman doesn't have
such a bad life. She gets to idle in the hurly-burly of the carnival, only has to recline in front of strangers. There are worse
things by far. In fact, Alma looks up and down the two rows
of five chairs each: the fat twin sisters harumphing to each
other madly; the man with the missing leg, his boy now
clinging to him, arms wrapped around his neck; a bloated old
man, his wife praying now, head bowed—whether for the
Mule-Faced Woman or her own soul, it's impossible to tell.
And Alma, herself, in her factory work dress and apron, her
hands worn from righting hose, her hearing still dulled from
the factory's rigorous chorus, rapid eternal detonations, the
awful dust, a wife who doesn't understand love, a mother
afraid of her own children. She wonders what the Mule-Faced
Woman sees each night from her little stage and lights, the
world and all its calamities paraded before her, a lurching
sideshow act. Alma imagines herself on stage, maybe under a
banner that reads THE NIGGER-LOVER'S DAUGHTER, for that is
the way she still thinks of herself, unshakable. She and her
mother, living alone in the old farmhouse, had been a lesson
to learn by. This is what it'll get you, skinny as a bone, the
daughter in a shambling, feed-sack dress, the mother's skittering, nervous hand raised to cover her riddled teeth—indi-
gent, hungry, alone. Alma would sit there on stage in her

blue factory dress and stare out at the horrified crowd. Her hands begin to shake. She is alarmed, stands up too quickly; her chair tips and clatters to the ground. She hurries out the door. She's late, after all. Henry's probably making his way up to the house by now. She picks up her step.

Two gypsies, white women draped in gauzy scarves, are smoking cigarettes outside a tent. One reaches out and grabs her arm. "You need your fortune read, honey. You look all but lost in the world." The other bobs her head, a chin dimpled like a crab apple.

She says, "I'm sorry, but I don't have time. I've got to get home to my family."

The women shake their heads in grim unison. And Alma isn't sure what the sighs and the wagging heads mean, whether they're saying, "A family to get home to, that's what I wish I had," or something else, as if that is just what is wrong with the world, a family to get home to. The woman releases her arm, and Alma springs forward, stumbles over a dip in the path, but catches herself. She jogs now past the strong man, all fat bulk and jeering, the line of lanky boys, the heavy hammer and its high bell. She climbs back over the sagging fence, the grass, and now she can hear it all. Her ears have opened up, and the earth is still screaming, still igniting the charge of her heart as she walks swiftly back to the road, a blue-tinged bowl, now empty.

2

Once she rounds the tall hedgerow, the house appears. It's large, so large and old it's begun to sag into itself on one side, crippled by its bandy wall. It's almost time for the show people to be heading out for the theater, if they are planning to warm up at all, but their two cars sit stalled in the yard. She can hear Mr. Eddie at the piano—a player piano with its switch off—and Nettie croons off-key, too high and warbly, in the parlor. Alma stands in the yard a minute. The farmer is calling in his cows. They shift in the dusk, large bodies working themselves uphill.

As soon as she walks up the porch steps and opens the screen door, she knows that Henry is already home. Amid the noisy mommick, she can sense his humming presence. He knows she's sidestepped through the carnival. He'll be angry,

21

perhaps a short rage, perhaps a smoldering coal that will last all night. He'll sleep curled away.

Nettie is singing: "I say a blond-haired woman make a poor boy leave his town. I say a blond-haired woman make a poor boy leave his town. Oh, but a redheaded woman make him turn his cover down." She is near forty, with low-swaying breasts, no brassiere. Her cronies sit on the love seat, their full rumps squared by the handles and their hips pressed together. One puffs a cigar. The other, a consumptive, most likely, a lunger, rattles with a coughing spree that ends with her tonguing spit into a handkerchief, which she stuffs back up her long, tight sleeve. Willard is behind the love seat, his face chubby, his mouth green from candies, his wide smile showing his stained teeth. He is looking at his older brother Irving, tall now, long limbed, who is motioning from the corner, telling him to poke the ladies through the open rectangle between the seat and its back. Willard obliges. He always does what Irving tells him to. He pinches at the fat beneath the ladies' dresses with his stumpy fingers and thumbs. One woman hoots— Fancy? Or is it Dancy? Alma can't ever tell which one is which, even though one has dark hair and the other is fair. The other woman reaches behind the love seat and clips Willard's ear with the palm of her hand. Alma doesn't scold anyone. She feels invisible, and would like to remain that way for a while. She simply takes it all in. The wallpaper faded, water-stained, bubbling in places, the calendar pictures of waterfalls and the Last Supper, framed and hung, the dark spots on the wood floor, the rag rug worn near through its nubbing, the dark whirring of flies, the ceiling-hung fly strips blackened to uselessness, and there is Wall-Eye with his parrot on his shoulder, sitting calmly in a chair near the door to the kitchen, waiting to be fed. He's the first to notice her.

"Is dinner soon?" he asks. He may or may not have been looking at her. She can't remember which eye is the good one, left or right, as confusing for her as it is with Fancy and Dancy. And it seems like nothing is as clearly labeled as it ought to be. She shouldn't feel so lost, so disoriented in her own house.

"Yes, soon."

Wall-Eye says, "I need to eat or I'll have no energy to perform." He's thin and bookish, the kind of weakened soul who gets pale if he doesn't eat on time. He stares off in his cock-eyed directions, the shoulders of his suit jacket covered with bird shit from the parrot, who every once in a while joins in with Mr. Eddie's chorus, screeching, "Redheaded woman! Squawk! Redheaded woman," as if the parrot has more to say about the immediate goings-on in the parlor than Wall-Eye. "Do you think Sir Lee will come soon with a liquor run? We've run dry, you know."

They are a troupe of drunkards. "He should come any day," Alma says, deflated, tired now. What she felt in the carnival, displaced, an inching toward some sense of freedom, foreignness, is gone. She retains only a nervous register in her chest.

She walks to the kitchen. It billows with heat. Flies and steam. The insects seem to ride on the wet air, motors sputtering. She's relieved to find Henry like this, asleep, head resting on his arm laid on the table. He looks small to her, like another one of her children. His lunch box yawns open with its crumbs and pathetic, bitten-down apple. A collection of flies circles the brown core. He has spent his day arranging train cars, the bursts of air from the brakes, the heavy locks, coupling metal to metal, load after load of coal. Her love for him can be simple, as simple as that work. She doesn't want him to wake up.

She notices the boiling pots on the stove, the lids jiggling, a wincing of metals. Henry must have started dinner. He knows only to get the water going. Alma lifts the lids quietly. A burst of steam. There's nothing inside but bubbling water. She walks to the icebox and pulls out two cabbages wrapped in thin towels. She is always pleased by the heft of the cabbages. This is true, she supposes, of anyone who knows real hunger. There are too many flies, a constant buzz. One, polished wings and eyes, lathers its arms, a quick rubbing, while balanced on his thread-thin legs with backward-cocked knees. She chooses not to slap it. There would be no point to it. She thinks of the expression "Kill a fly here and ten thousand come to its funeral." She would say it aloud if there were someone to hear it. She has a momentary wish

company. She doesn't like to be alone, and yet it seems she
ways is. Sometimes she feels lonely even when she's in a
illed room, even when she's in bed with Henry, and she
thought he'd cure her of lonesomeness. It seems to her a sickness. She feels infected, like she belongs in a sanatorium
along with Fancy (or Dancy?) the lunger, to scrub this stain
from her soul, something she imagines to be lodged in her
electric chest.

It's the bear that wakes Henry. He comes in quietly
enough, sits across from Henry. He puts his paws on the
table, waiting, like a gentleman, another boarder—but more
polite, actually—for his food to be served. He's wearing his
bow tie, a bright red, and an oversize fedora with a matching
band. He eyes the apple core, but he knows better than to
reach for it. He's a well-trained bear, delicate, refined. And
old, too. He looks especially frail today, his chest sunken, and
an extra huskiness to his normally labored breathing. His
eyes are weak. He sniffs at Alma with his flared nostrils, a
polite inquiry as to how she's faring. But it's his scent, most
likely—fur, dung, hot breath—that shakes Henry from sleep.

Henry looks up, a momentary dullness, a small surprise
to find himself here. He glances around, his face wet, red
cheeked. His bristled hair lifts off his forehead stiffly.
seems to choose not to address the bear, although he's
ously disgusted. "Where have you been off to?"

Alma pats down the curls around her face, t
loosen the steam-tightened coils. She keeps he

25

him. "Mr. Bass wanted to show us girls a[...] they're thinking of buying." She says as little [...] not because she wants to keep the lie simple, b[...] they have become grudging with words. Some[...] seems each utterance is a gift, and neither wants [...] more than the other is willing to offer. It's a balance, [...] trying to be stingier than the other. "He thinks the mach[...] might replace some of the ones they got and they might b[...] able to turn out more hose this way." She thinks again of the [...] gears of her heart, not shiny, but oily and dark, racing. Actually, she doesn't like to lie. This is before she understands that Henry is a capable liar, the kind who can hold onto one inch of the truth within a lie, just enough to believe it as long as it is coming out of his mouth, long enough to feel guiltless.

"That so?" Henry answers.

"That's so," she says, quartering the cabbages with chops of a heavy knife, dropping them in the pots. She was afraid of him when they were first married. He hit her once for looking a certain way at a friend of his who'd come to drink, a hard slap that left a red mark on her cheek. But then she killed his dog, accidentally. It got into rat poison that she'd set out. It holed up under the porch, and she found Henry cradling it, a yellow lab, heavy and limp in his arms. When he looked up at her, he was scared, like she'd done it on purpose. He realized that she could kill him as easily, a carelessness with poison, a meditated oversight. He never hit her

again, but still he likes to yell a bit, sometimes, to stomp and
carry on the way he thinks a man should, and she allows him
this, because, in truth, she would have killed the dog on purpose if she'd known it would have given her this power.
Perhaps someone is born murderous. Or perhaps they learn it.
Or perhaps life draws them to it. She isn't sure.

Henry is shaking his head. He hasn't believed her story
about the shiny machine—and he's right; Mr. Bass is too
cheap for new machines and would never ask the workers for
their opinions. Henry stands up. He's about to say something like "Well, Judas priest, Alma, why not a little more
attention here at home?" He puffs his chest. But then the
bear, who assumes in Henry's standing that he's no longer
interested in the apple core, paws it and pops it into his
mouth. Its teeth look yellowed and a bit worn down but still
huge. Henry turns his attention to the bear. He starts in.
"Why, when a man comes home from a long day, does he
have to have a bear looking at him? I ask you that. And then
stealing his food? Goddamn it! Where is Bucci, that little
bastard?" He calls for Mr. Bucci, the bear's trainer, an Italian
acrobat, but there's no answer, not even a shuffling of feet
from upstairs. "I want this bear out of my kitchen!"

The bear gives out a weak moan, stands, and lurches. He
looks like he might roar, but instead he waddles and then
drops to all fours and walks out of the kitchen. Henry and
Alma stand there, listening to it struggle upstairs, limping on
its arthritic hip. She turns back to her pots. The cabbages are

now softening, shining, becoming translucent. And the kitchen is quiet a moment, except for the constant hum of wings. There's a small feeling of victory, like Henry has won his kitchen back, and everything hushes while he waves his imaginary flag. She doesn't look at him. She's stopped giving in to these domestic flares of pride. *It's just a kitchen,* she wants to say. *It's just a show bear. This isn't the Merican Wars, and you're not your heroic brother giving up his life in some battle.* She knows that he feels like he should have had a more exciting life. He's told her a million times about his brother's letters from Veracruz, how he pulled bananas right off the trees to eat.

Lettie appears, walking in on her hands—the Italian gave her lessons. Her feet swagger in the air. Her hands slap the floor.

"Stop it," Alma snaps, no patience, Henry having worn hers thin. "You'll turn into a show person." She can hear her tone, too harsh, too quick. It isn't the way a good mother would chide a child.

Lettie flips to her feet. She's a nervous girl, a tomboy, yes, but still sensitive, so easily stung by almost anything Alma says, it seems. Her pinched eyes tear up easily, as they are doing now. She's breathless from tromping around on her hands. She sings out, "Sir Lee's here! He's got boxes! And Irving is running the runners! And Mr. Bucci's bear is sick. He told me it's been moaning." And she runs out of the room, which is still steamy, buzzing, sweltering.

"Well, she's given us the news, I suppose," Alma says. She

thinks of Irving. He's too wild. Sir Lee is liable to jerk on the brakes just to make him fall off. He is a snake that way. She hears the bear padding around overhead—above the low buzz of flies, its heavy moan. She looks up at the ceiling. Henry does, too, but then they ignore it. They can't do anything about a sick bear anyway and aren't in a habit of taking time to talk about things they can't fix.

"Well, thank the Lord Sir Lee has showed up!" He turns to Alma. "Where is your money for the week?"

She wipes the sweat from her face. Her hands are red and puffed, her wedding band a thin choker. She's tired. Her bones ache deep within them. She opens her apron pocket and begins to rummage. *Don't take my money*, that's what's in her head, a chant. She hands Henry five bills and the change, keeping a hidden dollar for herself. But she feels defeated, not so much because they have to pay for liquor—she understands profit—but because she has to hand it over this way, to Henry. He asks with his hand out, and she must fill it.

Mr. Eddie keeps at the piano, but there's more bounce to it now. He's playing a rousing fanfare, in fact, with all the flourishes, celebrating the prospect of getting drunk.

Nettie waltzes into the kitchen. "Well, you heard? I've got to get me some liquor to clear my pipes!"

Alma wants to tell Nettie not to drink too much, that she'll be too swimmy-headed to go on, but she knows Henry would chide her for it.

As if she knows what Alma's thinking, Nettie says, "It's medicinal! You know that!" She saunters out the back door, Henry following close behind.

Alma adds the pink meat to the pots, lids them, and opens the cupboard. She lifts a shiny flour sifter hiding a canister of sugar. She unscrews the canister lid and pulls out a liver-pill bottle, a small pinky-size cardboard tube, filled with her tightly rolled bills. This is where she hides her money. She takes the extra dollar from her pocket and rolls it between her moist palms, then stuffs it into the liver-pill bottle, capping it. It feels so good, this little ritual of roll, stuff, cap. It's a secret indulgence, a comfort, her money hidden away, its quiet existence. She works fast, not wanting anyone to come bustling through. She's learned to hide money in the kitchen, in with the sugar and flour, the things that men are too proud to pester with. It makes sense to hide money in food. She can sometimes taste hunger, the empty bloat and lightening head.

She pushes the liver-pill bottle so it sinks among the white grains, then tilts the sugar to count the bottles—16, which is not bad, not bad at all. *A woman needs her own money,* she says to herself. She thinks of her mother, briefly, alone in her country house, her father in the dark hat that shaded his eyes. She thinks, too, of the black man, the Prophet—had her mother named him that? Had he been born with a name like that?—because she can't ever just think of her mother or her father without thinking of him, his strong back, his beautiful hands, the way he smiled so kindly. She would have loved him if her mother hadn't. He was easy to love. He died of a head wound, after her father had already disappeared, despairing, humiliated, an epileptic with a missing tongue tip, a bruised skull, his wife in love with a black man. One day they were all there in the house. The black man never came back, nor her father. She misses both of them. Sometimes she wonders if the Prophet isn't gazing down on her from heaven, if her father, closer, isn't watching, hidden out in the trees, circling the house, his hat dipping from a window that has just held his full face. Can she remember his cheeks, the exact huffing deep red shade of flush, his front teeth, one overlapping the other? Memories slip. Yesterday, perhaps, she could still recall a certain mole, but today it's been rinsed away, wiped clean from his hand, by what? Simply the erasure of time? The bear moans again from above. It's a deep, soulful moan. And all of the sudden she wants to cry. She's not sure why. She isn't the tearful type. She often wishes she were softer, more like other women she's heard of, prone to crying fits. She pauses there with her hands on the sugar can. She wonders if she is forgetting something this very moment, something small, precious, inscrutable, unimportant except to herself, one of the mind's trinkets, and she is mourning the loss of it, unwittingly. She doesn't know if she's thinking of the black man or her daddy—is he dead now, too, having finally splintered his skull till it could no longer mend itself, an irreversible rupture?—or her heartbroken mother, now all alone, or that feeling again that her heart is a clacking machine, that it's stirring the air around her and that things are going to change, or that they may never, that her husband will become unreachable, wordless, that her children will swallow her whole. She feels for the bear and for all of us here bolted to this earth. She doesn't cry, though. She holds herself for a moment, squeezing the meat of her arms until the skin is pinched and there's an ache. She stiffens. Tells herself to put the sugar can into its spot under the sifter, close the cupboard, walk out the back door. And then that's what she does.

Now outside without the steam and the electric fidget of flies, Alma feels lighter, too light almost, air-filled, lacking an anchor. It's Sir Lee. He makes her uneasy. Henry, Nettie, the boys, and Lettie shift in the yard. Sir Lee lifts himself from his car parked in the yard. He walks toward everyone like a drunken ship, broadest at his belt, shiny and black as a stretched eel. There's enough light to see the sweaty gleam of his face, the buckle of his nose, a moustache, its thin curved line above his narrow upper lip. She once saw him throw a heavy rock at a stray cat picking through her garbage. He hit the cat square in the head. It went slack, blood trickling from the knock and from its tiny nostrils. He took it with him when he left, hefting it into the backseat, saying it would make a good toy for his dogs to tear up.

She turns her attention away from him to the yard, uneven, grass worn to dirt, upturned rocks. The wash line is naked but for two wide, thick-strapped slips that belong to the oversize, aging chorus girls. One has a faded brown bloodstain on its skirt. She doesn't like having other people's wash strung in the yard. She will remind the girls to hang their clothes in their rooms with a towel underneath to catch the drops. For now, the white slips sway brightly in the near dark.

"Hey there, Mr. Henry Holfer. Miss Alma." Sir Lee tips his hat where his whole body seems to come to its dented point. "I have some good stuff for you today. Angel teat, I tell you. No hospital alcohol in this batch!"

"Good to hear," Henry says. "We don't intend to scrub down the floors with it."

Irving circles Sir Lee's polished car parked in the side yard. Irving's hair is cropped so close his white head glows beneath the fuzz. Willard's hair is darker, thicker, like a slick leather aviator's cap. Willard follows his brother around the car, doing what he does, running a hand over the tires, the glossy handles. He pauses to look at himself caught in the chrome. His face, odd enough naturally— exaggerated by fat and reddened by heat—is further distorted in the rounded mirror. He looks up and glances around the yard until his eyes fall on Alma's face. "Look at me here!" he shouts, and she smiles, nods. She wonders what he thinks of his reflection, if he sees himself as different. She doesn't think so. They've never told him that he is.

"Still a working man, Henry? Still slaving away? For the railroad? Is that it?" Sir Lee asks the same thing each week, and Henry is always forced to admit that he's still holding a job, as if he's weak because of it.

"Yes, yes, the railroad."

Nettie sidles over to Delphine, Sir Lee's girlfriend, who sits in the passenger seat. Sir Lee swats Nettie on the rump as he passes by, and she lets out a weak squeal. He hoots and grins, pitching back and forth, back and forth even as he's standing in one spot. Delphine is young, with a sweet face cupped by her bobbed hair and pretty painted lips. She's spent time in New York City; Sir Lee told Alma that. And Delphine talks in a different way, clipped, almost rude, as if she's got little time for you, but Alma likes it. It's exotic. There's a sadness about her, too, something worldly and jilted.

Nettie's leaning against the car, dipping into Delphine's window. Delphine nudges Nettie out of the way to keep an eye on Sir Lee, takes a sip off a flask, and then lights a cigarette, agitated, while Nettie prattles on.

Lettie's pinched eyes fix on one face and then another, standing close to her father. Alma wonders if she's the one who taught Lettie this nervousness. Alma was an anxious child, too, and she feels childish now, in fact, like she shouldn't be here, as if she's too young to be buying liquor, running this house, wife-and-mothering.

Henry says, "What you got for us?"

Sir Lee whistles and a boy about Irving's age pops up from the backseat, out Sir Lee's door, hurrying to the rumble, where he pulls a tinkling crate box up and out, his shoulders shrugged and back swayed to keep it up.

"Put it under the sink in there, boy," Sir Lee says.

"Yes, sir," the boy responds. He's skinny and freckled, with a tight, tensing jaw. His hair is blond and cowlicked, his lashes full but pale, and he has an underbite that makes him look like a mean little dog. Sir Lee always has somebody to help him. He never carries in the boxes himself, and wouldn't have Delphine haul them in unless it suited him to, but has it always been this boy? He seems plain after all, like he's just appeared and will disappear when he's no longer needed. Alma almost asks about him, but doesn't. As he scrabbles past, she sees a rash, swollen red marks on his arm. The marks sicken her, make her own arms ache where she was pinching them in the kitchen.

"I sure do like this car!" Irving shouts out.

Delphine says, "Sir's got a business dealing for you. It sounds real good—"

But Sir Lee cuts her off. "Shut up and let the man do the talking."

Delphine shoots smoke out over her head, exasperated. Sir Lee pulls out a piece of paper and starts to look it over as if he's reading it.

"They've got trunkloads down in Florida, and you can buy a trunk. Cheap."

Alma doesn't know what he's talking about.

Henry says, "What's inside these trunks?" He stuffs his hands in his pockets. It's an old habit that Alma recognizes, a self-restraint, as if he'd reach out and grab the paper if he weren't held back.

Sir Lee leans his head forward, over the wide girth of his belly. "Hard to say, exactly. By law they're selling it to you sealed, but it's unclaimed goods from a ship of rich folks. Jewels, most likely, precious heirlooms. Now I'm not telling this to everybody. But how do you think I could afford to buy that fine automobile you see before you?" He hands Henry the paper, and Alma catches a glimpse of a detailed map, a thick paragraph of wording. Henry looks it over.

Lettie pipes up. "Where's Florida?"

Sir Lee bends, trying to fold the deep chords of fat. "It's a magical land far away with mermaids and root-beer rivers." Alma can barely stand Sir Lee so close to her daughter, his hot breath in her face. "You all should go and get you a trunk."

"Do you have to go there yourself?" Alma asks. "Or can you just send for one, by post?"

"Oh no, you have to go yourself. The post is too risky. You need to go and ask for Jake. It's an inside job, see?"

And there is a shift in Alma. She recognizes the moment. Sir Lee swaying in the yard, the lilting slips on the line, the boys rounding the car. Dark settling. She is suspicious of the trunk, of a man named Jake, the inside job, everything that slides from Sir Lee's mouth, but she can't help but sense the momentum of change, a turn in the current. *We'll have to go and get it. All the way to Florida.* She has never been anywhere. Not anywhere. Her heart pounds loud and fast. It throbs in her ears.

"I would like to go there," Lettie says.

"I'd like to have a car like this one!" Irving shouts out.

"Well, if your daddy plays the hand that's dealt him." Sir Lee pulls the corners of his mouth back into an expression that's more grimace than smile. His eyes flash like darting minnows.

"Thanks for telling me about it, Sir Lee. I sure do appreciate that."

Sir Lee holds out his hand, and Henry shakes it. Sir Lee holds it out again. "For the liquor," he says.

Henry is embarrassed. Sir Lee always flusters him. He pulls out the bills Alma gave him; before handing them over, he smooths them on his thigh because they've been clenched in his fist.

"If you need a little loan," Sir Lee says in a low voice, rocking in, "for the trip down and the trunk, you let me know. I'll give you enough to tide you over. Low interest, because I consider you a good friend. You've got good sense, Henry. You know a deal when you see it. You got a real head for business." Sir Lee rocks back to the car, goosing Netty on the way. She squeals, but it's perfunctory. "When you go down, ask for Jake. And get out of the railroad, once and for all." Sir Lee hitches his pants before getting into the car.

Delphine waves wearily, her hand white and wilted like a handkerchief. They pull out of the driveway and turn onto the road, lost from view by the tall hedgerow. And it's a relief. Alma feels as if she's been holding her breath. She turns to Henry.

"We can't go to Florida," she says. It's a test.

He claps his hands together, rubs them. "And why can't we?"

The slips flip up on the line. The breeze lifts Alma's skirt, fills it up around her hips. She laughs and presses it down.

Just then the back door slaps shut, and there is Mr. Bucci, ringing his small hands, his wiry, acrobatic body now stiff and hunched, his head cocked to one side. "The Great Realdo is dead," he says.

"Who's dead?" Henry asks.

"The bear," Mr. Bucci says. "My bear. The one who wore my top hat and could tap his feet in the show. He's dead now."

Lettie grabs her mother's dress, her fists wringing the cloth at her hip. The little girl starts to cry. "I told you," she says, as if it's now Alma's fault for not taking the girl more seriously and saving the bear's life.

Willard runs to his mother. He grabs her, too, around her backside. The two children weigh her down. It gives her a small panic, as if she's in water, about to drown. Willard cries, "Oh no—the bear is dead and gone to heaven!"

Irving says, "Quit. Bears don't go to heaven." He looks at

Alma, too, daring her to contradict his practicality. Alma doesn't. Lettie and Willard sag on her skirt. She loses her balance and takes a few quick weighted steps to right herself. She pats their heads. She says, "Shh, shh, hush now." It's what she's supposed to say, isn't it? Something gentle.

Nettie shifts her hips. "Well, how do you like that! I'll send one of the chorus singers to town to cancel the show tonight. Can't go on with a dead bear! I'm going to have me a drink." And she sidles to the door.

"How the hell are we going to haul a bear out of the house?" Henry says, walking inside. "It'll take four, five men." Irving follows him, stiff-chested like a man himself.

Mr. Bucci shuffles in behind them, saying, "The Great Realdo is dead," starting again, taking it from the top.

It's dark now. The moon is low in the sky. It's quiet, clouds clumping like piles of slag, heavy, gray, dolorous, but there is the unalterable promise of change like a high bell— not a gong, a high bell—one hundred bells, hand-rung, in a somber church. Her children are latched to her middle. "The bear is dead," Alma says in a whisper. She thinks of its soft fur, its large body gone limp. And now it seems a good thing, a necessity, an ending so that the beginning can truly begin.

After dinner and the scrubbing of plates, everyone heads upstairs. Alma follows and stands in the doorway to Mr. Bucci's room, watching the men for a few minutes. Mr. Bucci, woeful, a stammering hesitation to each movement.

Wall-Eye, a narrow book of a man, too fearful to touch the bear. Mr. Eddie, already drunk from his toddies. Willard, strong enough but too unpredictable to help, liable to drop his end for no reason. Irving, eager but too wiry. She knows that it will be up to Henry, most of all, to haul it out. The room smells of fur and shit—although the bear had been trained to go outside, it hadn't always made it—Mr. Bucci's sweet cologne, his gas burner, and, too, the cloying sourness of his grief. Alma leaves them to their work.

Now, Lettie kneels between the soft webbing of Alma's thin cotton nightgown stretched from knee to knee. Alma is brushing Lettie's hair, fine and knotty with matted gummy spots she picks at with the comb's first dense tooth. The little girl is trying not to cry, pinching snot from her nose, her head bobbing and snapping as Alma tugs. She hums "St. Louis Blues" to drown out the sounds of the men hauling the bear, but she can still make out the heavy body on the stairs, the fast thudding, the men calling out, "Whoa!" Mr. Bucci's sharp gasp. The front door opens, and she can hear them working the bear across the wooden porch boards, not as smooth as the floor inside, and then the body hefted down the porch steps. Finally it's quiet, and she knows that the men are having a sink drink in the kitchen and that maybe this will be one of those times that Henry lets the boys have a sip because they've acted manly in the face of adversity.

"Maybe now that the bear is dead, you won't have your bad dreams," Alma says.

"It isn't the bear I dream of," Lettie answers. "It's always water and a hand coming out of the water and I'm standing on a dock, but I'm a grown girl. I'm scared of the hand. That's what it is."

The girl's nappy hair is brushed through. "Well, maybe the bear was holding the bad dreams for you. Maybe now that he's gone, the dreams went with his breath, just like that."

Lettie looks at her sadly. "It wasn't the bear's fault."

And Alma doesn't know what to say to that. There's nothing to say, because her daughter's cheeks have gone red again, and anything will make her cry now. Alma feels useless. It's often how she feels with Lettie, who looks at her with such wanting, waiting for her to do something, to say something, and Alma has no idea what it is. She wants to ask her what it is she should do, because it seems sometimes that Lettie knows the answer somehow but refuses to tell her. Although perhaps what she needs most of all is the comfort that somebody might be in charge, even if it isn't the truth. Sometimes Lettie glares at her with a look that seems to say, *Don't you know what you're doing? Are you a mother at all?* And Alma would like to confess that no, she's still a daughter. She has no idea what she's doing or how she got here.

"Go on to bed now," Alma says, and Lettie scrapes her bottom lip with her top teeth, sniffs, and tromps out of the room.

Henry appears in the doorway, smiling. "The bear's out of

the house." He's sweaty, his sleeves rolled tightly above his elbows. "It's a good thing to be rid of that bear, I tell you."

Alma is brushing out her own hair now. She looks in the rippled mirror, rose-etched around its rounded trim. She is still a pretty woman: her full bowed mouth, her simple nose, her arched eyebrows and gusty hair, curlier with each pregnancy until now it nearly kinks around her face.

Henry shuts the door, pulls the straps of his overalls down, steps out of his boots. He sits on the weak bed, its coils sagging under his weight, the metal frame clanging against the wall. Outside, Wall-Eye is playing his bagpipes. His real name is something Scottish, although nobody ever calls him by it, and when he gets edgy Nettie offers him something to drink to calm his nerves. Then he gets boastful, talking about the old country, and soon the pipes come out. Tonight, no doubt it is the dead bear that has rattled him. Now Nettie is singing along. The two of them are out in the front yard. Drunk as she is, Nettie sounds as squeaky as the bagpipes. It's a mix that makes Alma think of lusty cats.

Henry lets out a raked sigh, slams the window shut. She knows he hates the noise and has probably thought of shooting at Wall-Eye and Nettie like his daddy used to do with crows in the garden. He'd pick up a shotgun in the middle of dinner and shoot it out the open window, a blast to make the heart stop, the gun smoke filling up like a small cloud hovering around the table. Henry had taken his small cash inheritance and moved over a hundred miles away. He hasn't got a gun.

"What if she won't take the children?" Alma is talking about her mother, the trip to Florida. Her mother has become unpredictable, a square-jawed woman who doesn't say much, and when she does, it's mostly to stand her ground.

"I'm a man, now, Alma. It's not like when I was a scared boy bowing and tipping my hat good day to her."

Alma remembers Henry, scuffing his boots on the porch, so mud-caked that her mother made him take them off before stepping foot in the house, and this seemed like a humiliation. He unlaced them and then shuffled in, his gray socks with their yawning holes curled up above his toes. He was shorter without the boots, smaller all over, it seemed, embarrassed and unprotected.

They both lay down in the bed next to each other. Henry stretches out with his hands behind his head. His body is long and muscular. When she touches him—which sometimes she does still, sometimes they roll toward each other to the sagging center of the bed—there's no give beneath his skin, just the hardness of his muscles. Not like her body, which has become a little wider, softer, her stomach stretched and scarred, doughy.

Alma says, "Nobody gives something away for nothing."

"We're gonna pay for it, Alma. I can borrow some money."

"From Sir Lee?"

"Unless you got a better plan?"

Alma doesn't say anything.

"Sir Lee's been good to us," he says. "We'll have to give a little something extra when we pay him back, but we'll be rich by then, so it won't matter."

"Do you think the trunks belonged to people now dead? Or is it stuff they just never picked up? Or stolen? He never did give a real answer."

"Between this boardinghouse and the freight yard, we barely make enough to cook up food for these sorry people. Something else has got to come along for us." There's a ferocity in his voice.

She rolls away from him, her hip pitching up, nightgown gathering in the dip of her waist. She knows that she'll go to Florida with him, but only because there isn't something else. It's just sweat and work. She wants to tell him that she gets to thinking about her life and she's hungry. It makes her feel starved for something. And she has no say in going, not really. She is his wife, and Henry is the head of the household. Even more so now that the bear is dead; even the way Henry lies on the bed, sprawled, feet spread, elbows cocked, seems suddenly larger, broader. As if he's trying on a new weight, a fierceness. He's entrenched, an immovable force, and yet it's a tenuous victory. He lifts his head at a creak on the stairs as if he's afraid the bear has come back to life to reclaim his territory, to take up the menace of his pacing.

Alma listens to the low moan of pumped air beneath the

high notes. She's seen Wall-Eye play before, his eyes shut, and he's almost handsome like that, his lips pursed, cheeks red. His face is in her mind so clearly, she feels like she could touch it. She loves Wall-Eye and Nettie and Henry and the bear and the children, Bucci, all of them, and they seem so pathetic, so sad, she'd like to wrap them in wax tissue like oranges sent from Florida displayed in the grocery window at Tersh's Market.

"Just let me do the talking to your mother. And if she don't take 'em, then we leave this place anyway. Give the children over to the Catholics, just temporary."

"No," Alma says, but she's already thought of it. She's already let her mind lead itself out to that possibility. She's aware, at the edges, that she's lying, that she could tell Henry not to go after the trunk. *I was just his wife. I had no say in it* . . . It's the story she will tell herself when she thinks back on how she could have done it, how she could have left her children. The truth is she killed Henry's dog. She has a certain power. The bear is dead, but it was only a show bear. She could resist this infiltration of Henry's virility, his lording around, but she allows only a small no. A thin, gauzy protest. She lets Henry go on.

"Just Willard and Lettie. Irving's old enough now. I was on my own by that age. The nuns'll teach 'em to read."

This time she only manages to shake her head. She imagines her children at this very moment. She can hear them rustling in the bathroom, where Irving is probably rubbing the dirty creases of Willard's neck with a washrag, and Lettie is splashing her own cheeks with water. They'll crawl onto their mattresses on the floor and sleep. What do they know of orphanages? What does she know, in fact? Very little. Perhaps it wouldn't be so bad.

"I've never been anywhere, you know that? A few train stops up the line and a few down. My brother went all the way to Mexico. In Veracruz, he pulled bananas right off the trees and ate them."

She could remind him that his brother got shot and died there, too, in Veracruz. She'd often thought of his brother. She'd met him, and he was fair with fine, wispy hair, the type of person who, when you hear is dead, it seems to suit him immediately. He hadn't been surely tethered to earth, in retrospect, and now he seems perfectly cast for the role of tragedy. But she doesn't say anything, because it's Henry's hopefulness that redeems him, that can possibly outweigh his burly show of toughness, the fact that he can will himself to believe that there will be something in the trunk to save them. It's beautiful, she thinks, the way he can wear hope like a hat.

He says, "I know I should feel lucky. I could work in the glass mill. I could have to pour tin. I could be underground, get buried alive in a collapse or like that cousin of mine, who got electrocuted." A rail hoisted to the cousin's shoulder tapped a live line and sent a current to the nail on his boot to the metal rail, and the man was pure electricity, his body a lit current. The other miners tried to resuscitate him, lifting his arms like boat oars, as they'd been shown, to open up his lungs and get his heart to beat again, but he was dead. He'd come to Marrowtown with Henry, both of them looking for work. But the railyard wouldn't take his cousin because he couldn't read. He was younger than Henry, and the guilt has stayed. "And take those people in Boston, twenty-one of them, who died when a tank car of molasses burst open just because it had gotten warm in January. Molasses poured from the tank in a black shining wave. It destroyed everything and pushed it into the river they've got there." Henry used to talk to her like this. He used to give long speeches, a burst much like the molasses wave that erased elevated train tracks and toppled cars, a great surge of talk, his eyes shimmering, distant. But it's become rare. They've both grown tired, stingy, unwilling. It reminds her of his dreaminess, his youthful desperation. Her own. "But I don't feel lucky. I don't."

The bagpipes rise to a new fevered pitch, and Henry jumps out of bed. He charges to the window and throws it open. He leans his whole body out and shouts, "Wall-Eye, if you don't stop playing that bagpipe, I'll shove it so far up your ass, your farts'll come out duck calls for the rest of your life!"

Henry turns back to the room. The bagpipes stop. Alma smiles at him, laughs a little. She loves his sudden bluster. He softens, just like that, to hear her laugh. He's standing there in his underwear, with his hair wild, his chest bare. He reminds her of when they were just two children, how he took her sweetly in the cornfields behind her mother's house. She looks at him and wonders when the last time was that they really stopped to see each other. He swings his head low, shakes it slowly, smiling, embarrassed now by what he must look like. He turns back to the window, looks out again.

"Come here, Alma. You can see the bear," he says.

And Alma walks over, stands in front of him. He puts his arm around her, and together they lean out the window. Wall-Eye has ducked back inside—Nettie, too. And there is a shining lump in the yard, black and wet-looking in the moonlight. The trunk exists. Their trunk, and now they will hurtle toward it. He wraps his arms around her waist, pulls her back inside, but doesn't turn her around. He tips her up off the ground. He rubs his face in her curly long hair, kisses her neck. She can feel the thick rise of his cock on her backside. He whispers, "Things are going to change for us. I can feel it."

And she says, "My heart's an engine."

But he doesn't say anything to this. His hands ride up to her breasts. She recalls the factory doors swinging open, the bright sun, the bouncing bet's smaller buds, their twisting tongues. She repeats it: "My heart is an engine."

3

The kitchen is blue, a dim milky light filtering in through the curtains. Alma finds herself dressed, wearing her one and only hat, usually reserved for funerals. She feels stiff but pretty. Dressed, like some women dress every day. She feels nearly dainty. She's wearing gloves and has written the note for the boarders in her best handwriting, neat, tidy, self-assured with no extra frills or curlicues. It sits propped by a half-fold on the table. She imagines Wall-Eye will read it first because he's the earliest riser. His one steady eye will glide over her words, and she doesn't want to be embarrassed by cross-outs and false starts. She worked hard on the letter, touches it now, scooting it just a bit so it's centered on the table.

Outside, Henry starts up the faulty engine, which revs, sputters, dies, then revs again. She opens the cupboard, moves the flour sifter—its curved metal wire grating against the cupped screen, just an inch, just enough to loosen a dusting of flour on the counter—and picks up the sugar canister. She pops it open and roots through the loose, sticky grains for the narrow cardboard tubes of liver-oil pill bottles. She lays them out one by one on the counter. She rinses her hand under the cold sink water, then taps each pill bottle on the table so the extra sugar drops off, and shoves them one by one down into her purse, all but the last one, which she clenches in her fist.

Henry calls out, "Alma! What are you doing in there? It's time to go!" He doesn't worry about the boarders waking up. They're a lazy bunch; even Wall-Eye stays in bed till ten in the morning, often later.

Alma caps the sugar, puts it back in the cupboard behind the flour sifter. The house feels resolutely empty now that she's taken her money. She feels conscious of her money, as if she's carrying a full pitcher of milk that she doesn't want to spill a drop of. She slides the straps of her pocketbook over her fist, her wrist, and down her arm till it's locked by the clamp of her elbow. She touches the note on the table again, wonders about the boarders. It will do them good, she thinks. They've taken her for granted for too long. Haven't they seen how hard she works? Haven't they seen her drag herself home from the hosiery factory to tend not only to her children but to all of their needs? And never once have any of them offered to help, not once. The bear was at least polite enough to sniff at her sometimes, to inquire how she was doing. She says it out loud: "It will be good for them." And she lets this conviction slip over to include not only the boarders but also Willard, Lettie, and Irving. She tries the thought on, that her children will learn something from being away from her, that it will help them grow up stronger. She likes it and nearly convinces herself that she's doing something useful by letting Irving fend for himself for a while and by leaving Willard and Lettie with her mother. Hopefully, with her mother. She sees the old woman's tensing jaw, the tight circular motion of her teeth grinding, even when she isn't chewing food. Her mother is a fractious knot of a woman, but fragile, too, broken and mended fiercely. She doubts that Henry will have the strength to take her on, and Alma will go with him to the door. She and her mother don't have that kind of arrangement. They only speak to each other when it's necessary, not to show affection, only to exchange information, because her mother has come to dismiss emotion as extra at best and dangerous at worst. And Alma despises being in her mother's house—monastic, whittled to essentials: peeling knife, thimble, ladle. But she'll insist on walking up. It will be harder for her mother to say no to her. It won't stop her, necessarily, but it will make it harder. Alma's thoughts turn to the orphanage, its dark doors and fenced-in dirt square for playing. The rowed children, a line of boys, a line of girls filing in from the yard, and the nuns, grim and pale, their bloodless faces clamped by the bite of their wimples.

Now she feels shaken. Her stomach upset, she wonders if she should try to go to the bathroom again. But she's already gone. She decides not to. It's nerves, that's all. She won't give in to it. She notices mud tracks on the floor. She keeps her pocketbook clenched in her elbow's hold, takes a thin tea towel, gets down on her knees, careful not to get her dress hem dirty, and she wipes up the dirt. When she lifts her toweled hand, she sees it printed there—the hollow of her cupped palm, fingers, thick pad of thumb, the absence of knuckles. It is a dingy outline of what has touched down and what hasn't. Filth and vacancy. She wants to be filled, suddenly, to eat, to have Henry inside of her, to roar like the hosiery mill. Change is not something distant like air vibrating around her. It's here, now, and her heart is pumping, the heady strum of pistons in her chest. She stands up, drops the tea towel on the table next to the note, the white note, the white cloth with her dirty hand print.

She walks out of the kitchen, through the parlor to the front porch. Irving is leaning over the porch rail. He straightens when he sees her, as if she's caught him up to something, perhaps some apprehension, some fear that he thinks he's too grown for.

"Well, I suppose it's good-bye for now," Alma says.

"I'll be all right."

She takes his hand and presses the liver-pill bottle into it. "It's got money in it." She hugs him around the neck, and then pulls back to look at him. He shoves it into his pants pocket, taking her word for it, and looks out across the yard, to the far end where there's a mound of dirt displaced on top of the bear's grave. Irving's being tough, but there's a quickness in his eyes, and she can tell he wants her to leave before he starts to cry. "Well, now, all grown up. Take good care of yourself and go to the farm if you find that you need something."

"I won't need anything," he says.

"Alma," Henry shouts out, "you are slow as molasses in winter. Good lord and Judas priest!" He's got his elbow hanging out the window like the nose of an idle hound.

She steps off the porch and walks quickly to the car. Willard and Lettie are pressed together in the backseat, their sacks taking up much of the room. They're quiet, sullen— washed, combed, preened, and quieted by the process, humiliated, maybe, like shampooed dogs. They're scared, two small boxed-up versions of themselves. Lettie, especially, her face has closed up, sewn and stitched, unreadable.

The earth is dry, the dirt loose. When they drive away, Alma loses Irving in an immediate cloud of dust kicked up by the tires. His body disappears first, then his long, bony arm, until all that's left to see is his pink hand waving over his head, and then that's gone, too.

The mill road is lined now with yellow bedstraw, purple loosestrife, tall, strong, wind-swayed. Each bushy head—the color hushed by the dusting of soot—rounded by lush petals, becomes a smear of muted color in the roadside grass, revolting against the gray anonymity.

Henry isn't giving notice at the railroad. Alma told him

to write a formal letter so that if things don't work out, he can get his job back. "How could you think like that, Alma?" he asked her. "It's just that kind of thinking that holds people back."

Alma, on the other hand, wants to give notice at the mill, and so that's the first stop. Ahead, she can see the mill, the hum of it rising. She braces herself; her innards tighten. Henry pulls up to it, and the whole building seems to be shuddering from the roar inside.

Alma gets out by herself. Henry keeps the car idling. He guns the engine now and then so its putter won't die. She doesn't use the two wide doors, but a smaller side one that leads to the office. The room is little, cluttered. It's hotter than the mill, which is kept much too hot, and it's as if this room is the heat source, not the machines and pumped-in steam, just this little room with its angry furnace of a woman, Mrs. Bass, whittled and exacting, at a desk stacked with papers.

Alma pushes gingerly on the cracked door. "Mrs. Bass? Excuse me for interrupting you." It smells of the mill—oils, cotton, dye—but also of Mrs. Bass, her own sweat, a deep, rank humidity gartering moisture, and the faint stench of something recently singed.

Mrs. Bass looks up. She motions Alma to come in with a sharp twitch of her head and snap of her buckteeth. Her eyes are dark, and she looks at Alma over a pair of circular glasses that sit too close to her eyes, magnifying them like fish in a bowl.

"It's not your shift, not yet. It's early. What do you want?" She speaks too loudly.

It's strange to think that Mrs. Bass could place her. She's never thought before that Mrs. Bass knew one person from another. She never called anyone by name "I'm not coming into work. I won't be working for some time. Maybe not ever again." This last sentence is for Henry's sake, although he isn't present to hear it.

"Is that so?" Mrs. Bass says. "Is that so?"

"Yes. My husband and I are going to Florida to get something that will"—she paused to think just how to say it—"help us with our money."

"Your husband's idea, I take it?"

"Well, kind of someone else's idea, but he thinks it's a fine one."

Mrs. Bass is a small, whipcordy woman. She takes off her glasses. Her eyes shrink. She squints at Alma, making her eyes reduce even farther to sharp, dark points. "Let me tell you something. Men are full of ideas. Their heads are filled up with ideas. Women live in reality, Miss Alma. Do you know what that is? The real world. How many children you birth?"

"Four," Alma says. She could feel a trickle of sweat crawl down her back. She knows it's catching on the cloth, staining the back of her nice dress. "One dead."

"Do you know how many children your husband's got?"

"Yes, three. Just our three."

"No. He has no children. He has only the idea of children."

Alma stiffens. "My husband is good to our children. He's not but once or twice even taken a hand to them." She's angry now. She lifts her chin.

"I didn't want children and so I didn't have them."

She wants to tell her about the whispery blonde who calls Mr. Bass Willy, and that perhaps she shouldn't be such a hard-edged woman. But she stops herself. It's none of her business.

As if reading her disapproval, Mrs. Bass answers, "Mr. Bass doesn't know anything. He only has ideas. Haven't you been listening, my girl?"

Alma takes two steps for the door and then turns. "I won't be working. That's what I come to say."

But Mrs. Bass has already put her glasses back on and is bent to her papers, showing only the crisp part in her black hair and the tight twist of her bun.

Back in the car, Alma shakes her head and says, "Now, now. How do you like that?"

But Henry doesn't ask her anything about what went on in the office. He pulls the car out and drives on down the road. He says, "You know it's all business, Alma. We're two businessmen, is all, doing business. I'm going in by myself."

She sighs, nods. She can smell the mill, its harsh dye vats and clouds of rising cotton dust. They keep heading away from the hosiery mill and end up passing the American, which smells, too, the heaviness of liquid metal, poured tin, smoke rolling out of its tall chimneys. Two men walk out in their cloth caps, their grease-stained towels draped around their necks, holding their long, thin tongs. They stare at Alma because she's a woman, dressed fine, passing by in a car midday. She refuses to look down. She meets their eyes because she should be allowed to be dressed and out in the world, pretty, without having to look down, shy. She isn't a girl anymore, but still she feels a nervousness just in staring at the two men, a small quickening in her stomach that recedes a little once they've passed them.

"Willard doesn't ever have a shit-tail anymore," Lettie says, from the backseat. "He keeps himself real clean. Does Gramma know that?"

"That's good, Willard," Alma says, distractedly. "That's real good."

Willard says, "I hear the dirty women drop their kids off to be orphans when they go off with their men and then come pick them up after the men are done with them, and the orphans get sponge cake."

Alma turns quickly. "Where did you hear such a thing?"

Lettie says, "Irving told us that. Because he said he heard you talking about an orphanage, through your door. He's a sneak. Is it true?"

Alma fixes her attention on the road ahead. "No one said anything about an orphanage, now. It's only if it becomes necessary. Only if necessary." The children know to be quiet now. The car bumps along the road, and Alma braces. She doesn't let her body jostle and rock. She stiffens. The air from the window hits her face in hot gusts.

Sir Lee lives on a switchback road, winding its way up the mountain. Henry's been to Sir Lee's a few times before, but not Alma. She's heard that the house next door lost its hold in the early spring rains and slid downhill, landing on the road beneath it, and, sure enough, there it is. A little box, one intact edge hedging out into the street, but most of it chopped up and left as rubble by the roadside. Alma wonders whether the people were inside at the time, if they rode it all the way down until it came to its shivering halt. And where are they now? Alma imagines them in one of the old flour mills or abandoned barns in Dellslow. She's always heard of the people who huddle up in the drafty, rat-skittering rooms. She feared as a girl that the farmhouse would burn to the ground, and then they, too, would have joined up, cooking over the open-barrel fires in damp, crumbling buildings.

Henry pulls up to Sir Lee's run-down cabin, parks amid chicken-wire rolls and jowering dogs, nipping each other. Sir Lee's shiny black car is parked in front of the door. She wants to tell Henry not to go in. The dogs make her remember the cat Sir Lee struck with a rock for his dogs to pull apart, the blood trickling from its tiny nostrils, its slack body no more than a sack. She puts her hand under her pocketbook's cloth bottom. She can feel the outlines of money-filled liver-pill

bottles. Henry steps out of the car, pushing the dogs back
with his boots. He slams the door.

"Where's he going?" Lettie asks.

Willard pipes up, "Florida! Ain't that right, Momma?
He's going to Florida."

"No," Lettie says. "Right now. Where's he going? What's
he going to do?"

Alma watches him knock at the door. Delphine opens it,
pulling a robe around herself. She's slatternly, her hair a
frowzy mess, her makeup faded so that she looks like she's
been soaking, an exaggerated blue-black of outlined eyes and
puffed red circle of lips.

"Sir Lee is a cutpurse," Alma says. "Your father's going to
get money from a cutpurse. You need money in this life. It's
your protection. You remember that, Lettie. A woman needs
her own money to protect herself."

They sit in the quiet car. Willard's breathing is always a
bit labored in his thick chest, like that of someone not quite
snoring but sound asleep. The dogs, fur-matted and beastly,
settle, curl up on dirt patches by the front door. Henry walks
out of the house now, smiling broadly. Sir Lee is at the door,
shoulders as wide as the opening, wearing only a T-shirt that
shows his massive, fatty arms that narrow into wrists, then
narrow again, almost delicately, into small, pale hands, tidy
and white as if stuffed into women's tailored gloves—his
trousers zipped but not buttoned, his face cast over in shadows. Henry walks to the car with his elbows up so the dogs

don't bite his sleeves. One snags his cuff, though, and he
drags it a bit, laughing before he shakes it loose and hops in
the driver's seat, breathless at the wheel.

"Not a problem," he tells Alma. "Just two men conduct-
ing business."

Sir Lee grins in his doorway, rubs his belly. Henry waves,
but Sir Lee doesn't see him. A bird has just shit on the hood
of Sir Lee's car, a great white splotch.

"God almighty!" Sir Lee turns on his heels, back into the
house, and then charges into the yard with a shotgun. He
shoots it off up into the trees, up into the sky. Henry's body
jerks at the crack of each shot. He puts the car in reverse and
jiggers out to the road, the engine a high-pitched whine. The
whole thing reminds Alma of Henry's daddy with the shotgun laid across his lap at the dinner table. She wonders if
Henry doesn't think of Sir Lee as some kind of daddy. He is so
big, so forbidding.

"Business," Henry says again, to himself now more than
to her. "Two men doing business." Alma knows how much he
likes the idea of being a businessman with things to attend
to, finances, and he's trying to hold onto it, shaken as he is by
the gunfire. She wonders, too, if we aren't all looking for our
fathers after they're gone, and our mothers, too. She looks
back at her children, just a quick glance over her shoulder.
Willard, his broad face calm and round as a pie, and Lettie,
with her cheeks already tear-streaked. *It'll be good for them,*
Alma tells herself, *to practice having me gone, because mothers and*

*fathers disappear. Sometimes they die; sometimes this life wears on
them until they are no longer the same. One day I won't be here for
them,* Alma thinks. *That's the way it is.* She plays this sentence
out in her mind until it loses its sluggishness, until it purrs as
easily as gossip.

Alma can feel Henry's anxiousness. His knees are jiggling.
His hands tap the wheel. She knows he wants to be cut loose,
can imagine what it will feel like to have all these little cords
that keep him staked down finally cut. It's nearly midday
now, and they haven't even started out, not really. They pass
an old wooden derrick. Once there'd been a pumper with its
slow nods, needling the earth for oil. They've struck a vein
and now pipe it underground to a central spot where it's
tanked and hauled to the Monongahela River to be shipped
off. Alma wonders how long before the mountains pucker
and sag, fall in on themselves, disgusted, bereft, exhausted.
She doesn't want to be here to see it. Her own body has begun
to ache and grouse. She glances up at the horizon, the range's
womanly curves. Stripped to a bare clutch of trees. She
remembers climbing as a girl, finding star flowers, trout lily,
hedge nettle. She wonders if you can still find those woodsy
blooms or if the loggers have erased them, too. It is a sad
sight, the mountain being gutted. It is a sign, to her, of lusty
greed.

Her mother's house is in the country, a one-bedroom
shack with a rusty tin roof. There's a wash line strung with a

set of sheets, and a tub in the front yard, a pair of mangy, baleful, bench-kneed dogs on the porch, one with a balding rump, too old and deaf to bark. She spots her mother on the porch, peeling potatoes. Henry kills the engine.

"This won't take but a minute," he says, meaning, *Stay put.*

"I'll stand back. It's better if I'm nearby, harder to deny me."

Henry pauses, nods grudgingly. He walks up nervously, and Alma hangs back. The old woman never looks up from the sharp knife. She nips off the potato's purplish white claw-like roots, digs the knife in to cut out the eyes.

"Hey there, Miss Narcissus."

"What do you want?"

Henry smiles sheepishly, a practiced look of boyishness, but she doesn't even glance up to see it. "Now, why would you say a thing like that?"

" 'Cause you want something."

Henry sets one foot up on the first step, his hand in his pocket. Alma imagines he's cupping his fingers and thumb around the fat C of money from Sir Lee, his money now, clenching and unclenching. "Actually, what we have here is a real opportunity. A trunk of jewels, from a sunken ship, in Florida, and the law says the trunks are sealed, and we're planning on staking our claim. But, as you see, we are in need of your assistance, running the boardinghouse, helping with Lettie and Willard. Irving is able to be on his own. He's no trouble."

Narcissus chips off the potato's peel with quick strokes. She wipes her nose with the ball of her hand. She looks up, seeing Alma standing a few paces back. She asks Henry, "Now why do you suppose they say 'Nutty as a fruitcake'?"

Henry squints at her. "Excuse me, ma'am?"

" 'Nutty as a fruitcake.' Why do they say that?"

Henry laughs a bit, says, "Well, on account of the fact that there's a lot of nuts in a fruitcake."

"Then why do they call it fruitcake?" Narcissus says.

"I don't know, Miss Narcissus."

"You are a foolish man, and I've had my fill of foolish men." She drops a slick, bare potato into a pot at the side of her seat. It slides from her hand as quick as a fish. She coughs. "I ran mine off, you see."

"Is that right?" Henry says, shaking his head. Alma knows that Henry has heard the story differently. "Well, let me tell you this: I am a man now, Narcissus, and I won't be called foolish. I will talk to you as a man talks to a woman."

Narcissus looks up at him, scoots the bucket of dusty potatoes out of the way, as if she's about to stand, but doesn't. She looks Henry in the eye. "Get off my porch, or I will take a gun from in the house and shoot you, the way a woman shoots a man."

Henry's foot drops off the step. His gaze drifts around the yard. Alma stares at her mother—her dauntless brow, proud knotted nose. She is a dry hull with a dark withered center still corroding, distilling to some essential core. Henry could pick her up and snap her over his knee, but there's a steeliness to her, and he knows where she keeps her gun. He knows, just as well as Alma does, that she'd as soon pull it out and shoot him as spend the rest of the day peeling potatoes, because when you've been cast out, as she has, you've got a certain freedom. You don't have to live in fear of being cast out. She's wild. He's afraid of her. Alma is afraid of her, too. He tips his hat. He bows, just a small nervous bow—not all the way, just half. He catches himself in it, tipping his hat, bowing, which is what he said he would not do. And yet he says, "Good day," just like that, a reflex of manners. He's embarrassed. He hates himself for it, hates that his wife has seen it. He skulks to the car, slams the door so hard the metal frame shimmies.

Alma doesn't say anything to her mother. What is there to say? She walks to the car, too, slides into her seat, shutting the door.

Henry is fuming. "She's damn crazy. You know that?" His speech growls to a mumble.

Alma is nearly empty. She can no longer muster those strong emotions for her mother. It's as if there's a knob and she's tightened it. She feels sorry for Henry. It's plain on her face. And he despises her pity. She knows it but cannot help herself. She pities herself, too, and the children.

Henry says, "It can't all be my fault. I can't be held accountable for everything. If the children cry, if it rains, if the car gets caught up in a tornado, if we never make it to

Florida at all. I haven't failed already. We haven't even left town."

But Alma knows he's saying that he thinks it *is* his fault and that he *is* already failing. But she won't say a word. She looks at him big-eyed. Tonight she'll let him make love to her in the car, where they'll probably sleep on the side of the road to save the money, and she'll say, *It's all right. It's all right.* And he'll have to take it. Her look will say, *But I love you anyway, despite your faults,* or even maybe—and she admits this only to herself—*I love you because of them.* But he can sense it, can't he? Her pity?

Alma realizes that there are two trunks. One is hers. It's filled with junk. A grave disappointment. But there is another trunk that spills over with jewels. It will make them rich. This is Henry's trunk. And it exists just as wholly as Henry exists. Just as wholly as she exists. For now it seems her choice. It seems she can choose the trunk. She can reach out and point to the future she wants.

They don't say anything all the way to the orphanage. In the backseat, Lettie sniffles and Willard hums, more a leak of music from his head than any real song. When they pull up to the orphanage, Henry says, "I'll go in. I'll do it."

"No," Alma insists. "No, no. I'll do it."

The orphanage is the way Alma remembers it, having passed by as a child on the way to town—the dark stone building with two separately fenced-in swing sets, a few sagging, nearly airless balls. There's a grotto of Mary, a once-white statue, pensive, burdened by soot, her arms down, palms open, surrendered to the elements, slouched and centuried, surrounded by weedy fields. There's a chicken coop, a bridge leading to an old wooden railed-in dock floating in the ill-tempered Monongahela.

Lettie doesn't resist. She goes weak. Alma has to pick her up and carry her to the dark mahogany doors. Willard heaves the two sacks of clothes over his shoulder. They ring the bell. Feet shuffle to the door. It opens and a nun appears. She's young, squat, her cheeks pink and dry. The door is heavy for her. She leans into it to keep it from sliding her out of the way. She actually grunts, pushing her weight into it, and she's a little fearful, shifty-eyed, as if the door could push her out of the convent and slam shut and there would be no one to let her back in, as it's her duty to answer the door.

"Good day. Can I help you?" She's trying to be gracious under the strain.

Alma looks back at Henry, who's staring off at the chickens. A breeze kicks up the front of his hair. "I would like to drop my children for a stay. We don't have anywhere else to leave them."

"You'll need to talk to Sister Margaret. Follow me." The nun puts her back to the door, taking small backward steps to push it the rest of the way open. Once inside, she seems so light she nearly skips down the shiny stone hallway, lined with boxes of old clothes and cans of soup. It smells of ammonia, but beneath that an old clammy mustiness. There's no sign of children aside from a slight stuffiness, the earthy smell of children's oily heads and pasty hands. There are pictures on the walls of nuns, famous ones, no doubt, kneeling in prayer, angels circling above, each with bright spears of light beaming from their heads.

The nun stops at another dark mahogany door. Alma's dress front is wet now with Lettie's tears and snot. The girl's cheek is pressed to her collarbone. She's pushing so hard that the bone is sore. Alma's arms grow tired. Lettie is ten years old, after all, a big girl, too big for this, and Alma tries to bend to put her down, but her daughter only clamps on tighter.

The nun knocks lightly. She lowers her head. "Sister Margaret? Sister Margaret, a woman is here to see you."

"Bring her in. Bring her in."

The nun turns back to Alma. She holds out her hands. "I'll take the children from here," she says. "You have to sign a paper. That's all there is to it. I'll take them to their rooms."

Willard says, "Have you got sponge cake? I heard you got it."

The nun nods. "Yes, we do, on Tuesdays."

Alma tries to pry Lettie loose. "I'm coming back for you. I'll be back, real soon."

Lettie, between sobs, mutters, "I want . . . to see . . . the mermaids. I want . . . to see . . . the mermaids."

"I'm coming back for you," Alma says again. "I am." But

67

Lettie doesn't ease up. She pinches the skin of Alma's arms, and Alma has to work, finger by finger, to pry her loose.

The nun's hands are quick, her grasp firm. Unlike how she seemed in her dealings with the heavy door, she's strong, like a winning wrestler. She worms her arms around Lettie's middle and finally pries her away from her mother, while bracing for Lettie's immediate arching. Alma says, "I'm coming back for you real soon. Real soon. You hear me?"

Lettie still arches. The nun turns a corner. Willard looks over his shoulder, the two sacks on his back. He smiles and nods. Alma looks down at the polished floor. She brushes at the wet stain on her dress. She feels sick like she might throw up. But she wipes her face and turns the knob and walks into the office.

Sister Margaret is tall, broad-backed, lean, solid as a fender, but pretty in a flushed kind of way. The habit doesn't suit her. It looks too hot and itchy, too small. Her shoulders stick out stiffly, bulbous knobs, and when she walks around her desk—propelled by the balls of her feet—her hem is obviously too short, revealing her black-stockinged ankles and boxy shoes. It hadn't ever dawned on Alma before that nuns had legs, really. They seemed to glide around on air-filled bell-shaped skirts. The nun's ankles remind Alma of the carnival curtain pulled back to reveal the Mule-Faced Woman's ordinary legs, and, too, of the hose at the mill. She wonders if she has righted those very stockings, pulled them over the pedestal's flexed foot and ripped them off again—or if nuns have holy stockings made in Rome especially for them. The nun bows her head slightly and motions for her to take a seat. But Alma just looks at the chair, shakes her head no. It's too much to ask. She won't be needing it. She'll just stand.

The room is absolutely quiet. Nothing stirs. Jesus suffers placidly on a cross hung on the wall, his ribs protruding, his head lolled crowned with thorns, his side knifed. The desk is tidy—blotter, papers under a smooth stone paperweight.

"You're here to leave your children," the nun says matter-of-factly.

Alma nods. She feels dizzy, decides to sit after all. It's more ladylike than falling down. She takes a step toward the chair, but then lurches. The nun grabs her elbow and leads her down into the chair. Alma expects the chair to be unyielding, but its weak cane seat gives beneath her. The nun hands her a tissue. Alma takes it, realizes that she's crying.

"Do you think you're going to be sick?" the nun asks.

Alma shakes her head no, but then says, "Maybe."

The nun places an empty metal wastepaper basket in front of her. It makes a hollow gong against the stone floor. Alma feels childish. She feels weak. She wonders if the nun isn't looking at her in such a way that seems to say, *You made the wrong choice, men and the body and sex and all of that, birthing these children, and now you've failed, and you've had to come to rely on me. Here I am, having made the most holy choice, and I have to clean up after your mess.* Sister Margaret says, "It's difficult, I imagine. For some more than others. I prefer the ones that it's most difficult for."

Alma knows that it's supposed to be a compliment, but, in saying that she prefers Alma, the nun has admitted that she has preferences, that she is, in fact, judging. Alma went to school for only a handful of years. She remembers a snake that had accidentally slithered in, and how her teacher, long-necked and young, refused to kill it. Instead she had one of the boys trap it in a bag and set it outside to the field. She remembers the thin snake now, and the teacher, sitting at her desk, reading without moving her lips, and how she interrupted her once and the teacher looked at her in the same way she looked at the snake, not wanting to touch it, fearing its quick-tensing body, but wanting it to be saved nonetheless. Alma feels like a child, again, certainly.

"And you plan to come back for them?"

"Yes. Willard is slow, and Lettie needs care. She's easily upset at things. Don't expect much of Willard, and don't scold Lettie too much."

"I'll make a note of it." But she doesn't write anything down. She rounds her desk and sits behind it. She puts a paper on the wooden desk and slides it to Alma. "It's a simple form, stating that you've handed the children over into our care. You sign here." She points with the pen tip to an X at the bottom of the page.

Alma takes the pen, looks over the page as if she's reading it, but she isn't. Nothing sinks in. It is a page full of black lines and circles, not even letters. It means nothing to her. She signs her name, then looks out the small window. She can see the field, the chicken coop, the dock. The sky is a dingy gray, like laundry water, squared by the window frame. She glances at Jesus and then down at her own hands, palms up and open. She wants to tell the nun about the trunk, that this trip is necessary and they will come back rich. But in this tidy office, the trunk cannot exist, not even as an idea. It waits outside the boundaries of this reality. The trunk would be worse than imagination or a fancy; it would be a lie, because Alma doesn't really believe in the trunk, not really, especially not here. She wants to tell her that Henry believes in the trunk and that there are things that you do because you love someone, things you believe because they need you to believe them. She thinks of him at the bedroom window, just before he's told her to come look at the bear, these words come back to her: *He wears hope like a hat.* Alma could say, *You wouldn't understand,* because the nun hasn't ever been married, probably has never even been in love. But that would be cruel to say, and, she's quite sure, untrue. Alma believes that there are base emotions that play out differently in each life but are the same for all of us. Who better than a nun understands what one will do for love? She wants to tell the nun that she's in love, and, too, that she needs more than love. She's looking for something that may or may not be contained in a trunk, that may or may not even exist. She says, "Things are hard. I worked at the hosiery mill, a turner, and we run a boardinghouse. And we've got the children, and there was a bear—"

The nun raises her hand. "When will I see you again?" she inquires.

"Soon," Alma says, but she doesn't know. She feels broken, her mind fragmented. Her children—she wonders where they all are at this very moment. She could run from the room and start off down the halls, calling for them, her voice ringing out against the stone floors. She could collect them.

But no, it's done, the family splintered. Her legs are heavy. They feel boneless. She rubs her hands along the rough edge of the seat. She imagines her children's damp socks, their throaty winter coughs, the heavy breaths of their sleep. It's as if they've been attached to her by ropes but now the ropes are slack—and she's gone slack as well. She longs for the warm, broad hand of her own father resting on her head. She can't imagine reaching Florida. She can't imagine finding her way home. Things will never be the same. She knows this much. The children are no longer holding hands. They no longer circle her. They are no longer a giant, open, turning mouth that can swallow her whole. They have disappeared, scattered. She can feel an itchy tear that has pearled on her chin. It quivers. She wipes it with the back of her hand. "I'll be back soon," she says, in a hoarse whisper. "Soon."

4

A ticket-taker walks up to the billing. DANCING BEAR! SINGING PARROT! ACROBATICS, CHORUS GIRLS, AND COMEDICS! THE GREATEST PERFORMERS OF THE WORLD! 10 CENTS, PLEASE. It's raining, and he can't keep the umbrella propped over his head while trying to hammer. He lets the umbrella drop, its spidery metal legs curled up, the black cloth catching rain. The thin board and nails are slick, but he manages to dig one nail in, pounding it till it's flush, then another and another, until all four corners are tacked down. CLOSED, the sign reads. It's tilted, as it should be, a diagonal across the poster. It's final, and although he feels for the sorry show folks with their dead bear and joyless, lead-bottomed chorus girls, it's a good thing to put an end to something. There's little in his life that is so certain as this: CLOSED. He wipes the rain from his face, picks up the umbrella, dumping and shaking out the pooled water, and ducks back inside.

Irving wanders the empty house, room after room. He can still smell the parrot, even the bear. He wanted to go with them, to be packed up in Nettie's trunk, to be folded and tucked away in Mr. Eddie's bag, as small as a doctor's satchel. His cheeks still burn from where he let the paunchy old women pinch him. The house is cold, staunch in its emptiness. He walks to the kitchen, climbs up on the counter, where he kneels, hunting through the cupboards, but there's nothing. No one is here. He stands up on the counter in his boots and looks down at the bare table, its four spindly chairs. Everything in the house seems shrunken from this viewpoint. He misses Willard, his puffy body and large head, all rounded like a diver's costume. Sometimes Willard seems like he is peering out at Irving through the circular glass window in the diver's metal mask, dim and lonesome, like Irving is the only one who can truly see him in there. He wonders if Willard and Lettie are with their grandmother or in the orphanage. He should be with them, to watch over them. He can't stand the quiet, the hushed silence, the house holding its breath. He shouts, long and loud, stomps his feet until the cupboards jiggle on their hinges. Then he stops and it's quiet again, quieter it seems than it was before.

*　　*　　*

The Madam

Out in the yard, Narcissus hangs clothes on the wash line, glancing down the road for the return of her daughter and her worthless husband, although she doesn't expect them. And she's right. They don't come. The dogs shift in the shade. Then there's the cough, like a badger in her chest, like living with a weasel in the cage of her ribs—her daughter, young, in the yard, with a caught squirrel rasping in a crate. She coughs and coughs until there's a dime-size spot of blood on a white handkerchief, perhaps a sign that the animal is dying—the girl will crush its skull with a rock—or that she is dying; impossible to tell. She puts the handkerchief in her pocket, her body wrung out. She stiffens, pulls a damp old corset from the basket. She isn't sure how it got in with the other clothes. She hasn't worn it for years. It reminds her of her sagging stomach, low breasts, those shriveled adornments on her rib-slatted chest. It makes her feel like she is hanging up a confession, an admission of nakedness. But there is no one to see it, and it has to dry. There's no room in this life for any kind of timidity. She clips it to the taut rope. She coughs again, and beyond her, in the whispering yard, she hears a voice, a lank lisp, a hiss. Sin can multiply like mosquitos' skeins of eggs, a gritty scrim on stagnant water, a new breed always rising. The yard is filled with ghostly tongues.

Time passes like this, Alma staring down rows of corn, tilled earth lined by green shoots, their leaves unfolded, flopped and curling, full, each row ticking by too fast to count. And then it opens, a stretch of time yawning, something for her to remember it all by: a table, draped in a linen cloth, set in a field, a white woman and a black woman fussing over the place settings, a round cake, children running with kites, screaming. The kites dip, swoon. The girls are in dresses, the boys in knickers. Strings tangle. Two children, a boy and a girl, collide. The white woman calls out, comes running across the field, but everyone is fine. The children stand up. She brushes them off. Everyone is fine, and it is a sign that their own children are taken care of, even though she doesn't know if they've fallen, or if there's someone who will brush them off. But she needs to believe that they are being tended to, cared for. And it's not so hard to imagine, with Henry humming as he drives and the sun so warm on her face. It sure is something. The air is clear. She can see on and on. There are no mountains, and she feels at once exposed, unprotected, and yet also let loose. She wonders why anyone would ever build houses on the sheer side of a mountain and thinks back on the little house that slid to the road below it. She imagines all of the houses careening down the mountain till they pile up in the valley like rows of dilapidated boxcars resolved to live under the constant drizzle of ash. The car clips on. The fine air circles.

Willard has stolen sponge cake from the kitchen, a soft rubbery square, and as he looks at his book of knights on horses, emblazoned shields, he slips his hand under his pillow to pinch a bit and let it dissolve on his thick tongue. Every morning he makes his bed, pulling taut the white sheet and the thin gray wool blanket. He lines up to use the bathroom. He prays in a straight line in front of the podium and cross, a litany, a tick-tack repetition. He likes the orderliness, the lack of confusion, that you always know what's coming next. At twelve-thirty if he looks up from his lunch, usually soup and bread, through the windows of the dining hall, he can watch one of the nuns scatter seed in the chicken coop. Nothing sneaks up on him, not even his own body. He always knows when he should go to the bathroom, because he's told. In fact, there's usually a small line, and even when he doesn't think he has to go, he manages a compliant trickle that makes him proud. Everything seems to be marching toward a simple, common goal that, moment to moment, can be attained, held true. Most of all he likes the sponge cake and this time at night when he can look at the pictures in the book for a while before the nun, always the same one, always dressed the same way, stands up from her chair in the corner, where she prays in such a way it seems sometimes she's nodded off, and asks the boys to say their prayers and close their eyes. And then she turns out the light.

Lettie doesn't want to fall asleep, and so she watches the mouse. It doesn't scare her. It's tiny, unremarkable, easily overlooked, and yet she's found it, so perfect with its shiny, gray fur and pulsing ribs, skittering along where the wall meets the floor. She wants to declare it, at first, to send an urgent whisper down the row of beds, until each girl is wide awake, electrified by it. But she chooses not to. She wants it to be a secret. The other girls are all sound asleep by now anyway, their heads denting slab pillows. The nun is gone. The mouse flattens itself to fit under the crack below the door, and Lettie gets out of bed. She has to follow it, she thinks, to protect it, to keep it safe. If one of the sisters saw it, she's afraid they'd kill it or put it in a cage. She doesn't trust the nuns, the way they hide in their clothes—too secretive. The mouse continues to scurry close to the wall, but when another door appears, it slips again beneath the crack. Lettie opens the door. The room is nearly dark. She searches the floorboards for the mouse, at first only looking down. But it's nowhere to be found. When she looks up, she finds herself in a small chapel, a shining gold box on an altar, and Mary, again, she stands at every turn, her beleaguered smile, her obstinate gazing. Lettie is caught by her eyes, which seem to follow her down the aisle to the front pew, where she curls, yanking her nightgown down over her bent knees. Mary watches her, unblinking, and here finally Lettie falls asleep, so deeply that she won't hear the bell, an alarm to wake the nunnery for a search. She won't stir when the women shuffle nervously up and down the corridors, calling her name. And when the older nun, the one most in charge, finally finds her and carries her back to bed, Lettie will be dreaming of the dock, the water, the hand. The railed-in dock is nearby. It sits

on the orphanage's property. The plank bridge leading to it
floats in deep water, the wood weather-worn to a splintered
fur. How couldn't she dream of the hand with the dock so
near? And had she ever seen the dock before? How could she
dream up something that she hadn't seen? But the dream will
continue on in its doomed procession. She will be that grown
version of herself, able to bend over the dock's guardrail,
which is normally much too tall. She will be larger, and yet
not more firmly planted. She will feel like she's just been let
loose, as if she's been wearing wings that have been snapped
off, not from her back, oddly enough, but her chest, causing
her to lose her footing, to stumble and catch herself. White
flapping wings, that's what she will see first falling into the
water, a tattered flutter. But they will go under, become
balled and dull, twisting in the current, snaking. Her mother
will be nearby, Willard, too. But not Irving, no, he's never in
the dream. She will smell grass and the deep water, sul-
phurous, rusting the rocks at the bank. And cake, yes, sometimes she smells sheet cake. Distinctly. White sugar,
whipped icing. She will desire to be a little girl again, to
think only of the cake. But the hand will appear. It will be
demanding, white and knuckled, a man's hand, she thinks, or
a large angry woman's. She can never tell. She will ask, "May
I help you?" But she won't reach out. Her mother is never far
off. There's always cake and sweet grass. And the hand will
disappear eventually. It will go away, and when it does,
things will be better, even for the hand, which sometimes,

only sometimes, she realizes is attached to a body, an angry, flailing body that will become waterlogged, blue with all the water it's taken on, blue and swollen, but relieved at last of some dark restlessness. It will be better for the body when the hand goes under, and for her, her mother, Willard, everyone who stands just off, a clutch of women. She never wishes that the hand begins to swim, that the body rises up, its arms becoming strong and stiff to slap itself to shore. She will wish, as always, for the body to become a stone, to sink, but it never does. She will wait at the guardrail, staring into its splayed fingers, its open reaching. This time the hand will be connected to an arm, the arm to a body, and just below the blurred surface she will see her mother's face, the slow fanning of her hair, and Lettie will cling to the nun's broad chest.

5

*T*he sky still has some sun and the Miami docks are filled with trucks and men, and beyond them giant ships. Alma can glimpse the inlet, a deep, lurid blue. She has never seen anything so blue, nor so bustling. The commotion, a wild throng. The squat, heft, and pitch of bodies. Men haul tree trunks thick and heavy with green bananas, hundreds of them, mounted on their dark backs. They curse and call out, garrulous crowing amid the clatter of stacking boxes, drumming engines. It reeks of rot, seawater, fumes. The distant horn bellows, like a giant lung leaking air. Everything is lacquered in a wild profusion of light. Colorful sweat-stained shirts, the gleam of oranges through crate slats. Nothing dusky or diffused. Alma spots an elephant, huge, gray, flapping its ears. It is hitched to a wagon as if it were just a horse, but it is magnificent, if a bit saggy and worn-looking, its skin drooping around its thick ankles. Beneath its saddle, a yellow swathe of cloth billows like a skirt, gadrooned in a silky orange trim to prove its exotic past. "Did you see that?" she asks.

But Henry, dazed, doesn't answer. He slows the car, hunched at the wheel, looking around. He turns down a road lined with warehouses, winds to a back dock. The crowd, its bustle, thins.

Henry parks, walks off toward the warehouse door, a gaping square, unlit hole.

Alma sees a dog, its brown ragged head, at the end of the dock, whimpering, a bit of its leg caught in a trap. She heads toward the water, the dog, its bared teeth. She wishes she'd gone in with Henry. Perhaps they don't need to buy the trunk. Perhaps they can just turn around and leave the trunk intact, whole, the dream of it.

She begins to panic and runs to the warehouse door. Once inside she will ask if it's someone's dog caught in the trap. It's an excuse to see inside, to stop Henry before it's too late. She's breathless. Henry is there, talking to an old man with a loose waggle of skin on his neck that stretches from chin to collarbones where it's tucked into his buttoned collar. She asks about the dog, but Henry hushes her. It's disorienting, the lined boxes, trunks, the streaming light, the smell of something ravaged and left to sit, rotten fruit, dank mildew, seawater, and burned coffee. The man says, "It's a stray. Don't go near it. It'll bite ya." The old man turns to Henry, hushed, asks Henry if he has children, a family who might need this money for food. And Henry says no, that his wife can't have children. "It's why she goes so soft for dogs."

Alma totters out the door, the strong wind in her face, back to the car, and soon Henry appears, his arms stretched to carry the trunk, short and narrow, like a small casket. She thinks of dead children, her own, suddenly dead, each one pale and lifeless, cheeks sunken. And it seems true, what Henry told the old man. She feels childless, lost. Henry sets it down, kneels before it. Twists the latch, metal grating metal.

It gives a small, disgusted pop of air.

Moths rise up, flutter, and climb in the honey light.

6

He remembers the puddles, just like this, the slick sheen of gasoline, the colorful oiliness, shiny as a row of eyes with the lights of Cheva's Pool Hall reflected in them. This is the city at night with his father—Marquette Street lined with parked cars, and the door to Cheva's swinging open, the momentary hum of a ruckus rising up, light pouring in a rectangle that widens and then narrows to a glow that slips back quickly beneath the door. It isn't his mother's city, day-lit and caterwauling with crisp suits, women in gloves, the jostle, the fever of having a list, getting things done. This is louder, all of it broader, more wild, gusty. The men buy liquor at 1232, just an address, a blind pig, his father called it, and then they hitch their way to the pool hall, where they spike their drinks. A man pisses down the alley between Cheva's and a seedy bookstore–tobacco shop. His hand over his head, he leans against the brick wall. Irving looks away but can hear him groan and then shuffle.

Up the street he sees someone sitting on a runner, a boy eating chicken from a white, grease-stained box balanced on his bony knees. Irving recognizes the car as Sir Lee's, and the boy is the one who hauled the liquor into the house this last time when Sir Lee started in about the trunk and then Mr. Bucci's bear died.

Irving walks up with his hands stuffed in his pockets. "That Sir Lee's car?"

The boy is biting dark chicken off a leg, his lips and cheeks and chin greasy. "Sure is. I'm Smitty. His boy, and so it's part mine, too. He ain't my real father, but he took me in. One day, when he gets the word, he's going to California and he's taking me and Delphine right along with him. It's a fact."

The boy talks too fast. Irving is hungry and lightheaded because of it. He glances behind him at the glowing eyes of puddles.

Smitty says, "You Alma's boy? The one with the sister and the ding-witted brother?"

Irving doesn't like people to talk about Willard like that, but he doesn't want to start a fight either. The boy is wrangly, his arms pocked with bright sores. Irving figures he'd bite if headlocked, like he does that chicken. Irving says yes, that's him, all right. But he's wondering now why he's here. His father isn't going to stumble out the door like he did the last time when Irving was told to sit in the car and wait and wait. There are no children allowed in Cheva's, no guns and no knives either. He doesn't know where his mother and father are or how long they'll be gone. He should have headed out to the country. He'd have been there by now, even if nobody had stopped to give him a ride, and maybe his grandmother would have been cooking something up, the house smelling meat-seared, fat snapping unctuously. But that old woman is too proud. She'd have seen his arrival as some weakness in him, and he didn't want to have to explain himself. Not that she would have asked for an explanation. She wasn't the type to ask questions, but he'd have felt obliged to come up with something, and she would have seen right through it. He wishes he was with the nuns, now, that he'd been too young to fend for himself. He wonders if Willard and Lettie are eating sponge cake, deep tin pans set out for the orphans to pick through till their hands are gummy with sugar.

Smitty says, "Well, does your momma feed you?"

"She went south with my father to get a trunk."

Smitty laughs, a snort. Then he looks up at Irving, says, "I'll sell you some chicken. Do you got any money?"

Irving reaches in his pocket. "I got a bill."

"Well, I'll take it."

Irving has already uncapped the bottle. He hands Smitty a curled dollar and Smitty scoots over, giving up some room for Irving to sit on the runner. He hands him a leg, and Irving takes a bite. It's cold, but he loves how the flavor swells on his tongue, the way his jaw works the meat in his teeth. It all feels so good. It's a simple, comforting pleasure. The two boys don't talk. They curl over their chicken legs, elbows cocked. Irving feels deeply that everything will be okay. His mouth tells him that it's all going to be taken care of. There's chicken to eat, and he's going to be just fine.

Narcissus is cold. It's spring. The house should be holding onto its heat late into the afternoon. But despite the sun squares on the floor, she feels like she's freezing, a deep cold from her bones. She pulls her winter coat from the closet. There's the badger cough, clawing. She finds it hard to breathe, has felt like she was dying for a long time. Since the prophet, yes, since he was killed in his cell. No strong young man dies of falling and cracking his head on a jail-cell floor. That's a death for an old woman. It's the way she could die now. Alone, a fall, bleeding until the blood has all spilled loose and dried. It was the butt of a rifle. She knows it. She's been dying ever since, yes, but this is a different kind. This is an animal death.

She turns off the boiling pot of corn. She doesn't want to eat. She coughs, the creature clawing inside her. She goes to her bedroom mirror, warped and ghostly. She brushes her hair. She walks to her bed, the dogs clicking and rustling behind her, but realizes that she isn't really walking. Her legs are so stiff, her back so flexed, that it's more of a stagger. She's tired, the wool coat itself a burden of weight. How did she get so frail? She hasn't had the strength to tend to the farm for years. Each potato was the dirty head of a child who demanded attention, and she had no more time for rearing children, not even her own grandchildren, the oldest boy, the girl, the one in between who messed himself, could never learn to use the pot. How many times did she scrub him down? Too old now. And the yard talks to her, a nuisance of garbled speech. She prefers the house, but even here the earth is trying to take claim, the walls patched with glowing green moss. A vine of ivy roots, trying to find the kitchen sink's wet seal, winds its way through floorboard cracks. She would not be surprised to find her ceiling, rife with fault lines and peeling paint, replaced one day by a whitewashed sky. The dirt, pressing in from all sides, is snakish with sound.

She picks up the framed photograph of her and Chester, cursed, a damaged spirit, and her girl Alma. She takes off the velvet backing, pulls it out, the photograph too, and another piece of paper slips free. It's a pencil drawing, the Prophet, lean and tall, his dark thicket of hair and wilted smile. She can see him along with the other prisoners, working the field. Her husband in bed, his last fit so terrible that they'd had to hold him down. But now Chester lays there. He says, "You think I'm not the man of the house? You think I'm weak?" Once he dropped a bowl of soup on his chest, a bright burn, and he could not look at his wife. He wouldn't let her hold a cold rag to it. Alma stays out of the main room where her father is set up in an iron-post single bed. She runs her hands along the farthest walls. And when he starts up again, falling to the hard floor, his body beating sharply against the wood boards, Narcissus calls for help. She runs to the fields, to the officer with the rifle, overseeing the men. She yells, "He's having another fit. Can you send someone for a doctor?"

The law says, "You, there. You, boy. You in for thinking you're Jesus, ain't you? You think you're some kind of prophet. Go on in and save the man, if you're Jesus."

The Prophet runs into the house. By now, her husband has already bit the end of his tongue, and the tip of it lays in dust, blood pouring from his mouth. The prophet holds him down. He stuffs the rag in her husband's mouth, puts down a bundled blanket to keep him from bruising the back of his skull. After the fit is over, the body lays there limp, a restless panting.

She says, "Are you really a prophet?"

"No, I'm a colored man. If I was a white man, I'd be called a doctor." He isn't angry. "But I suppose I come from people who believe in what they can't see, and they do by it."

"What kinds of things they can't see?"

The Prophet asks her, "Was it a good tongue or was it evil?"

She tells him that it wasn't evil, but it never did him any good.

"Bury it, in that case," he says. "Bury it in the ground."

And so she does, while Chester is recovering, while his head is wrapped up, too fat for his hat. She takes Alma out to one of the gardens and they dig a hole. She can smell the sweet dirt. She unwraps the bit of tongue from a handkerchief and lets it drop. They cover it with dirt, and Alma doesn't ask any questions. The Prophet looks up from his bent back, his hoe, and nods. She's done the right thing. It's for the best.

Sometimes the Prophet comes to the house. She asks the law if the Prophet can come inspect her husband, to wrap his wounds and lay hands on him, and he does, while Chester twists in sleep, restless, on the edge of a fit. But once they step into the same spot in the kitchen, face-to-face, and she holds him, suddenly, she reaches out and hugs him like she's been missing him, and she starts to cry. She never loved her husband. It's loneliness, the break of it, how it can fall away suddenly, the open expanse in front of you is like a land you've never seen before, that reaches on and on. It reminds her of the way the Prophet described heaven while redressing her husband's bandages—the herald of trumpets, the chorus of angels, the blinding brightness. It is a place, yes, but a place the same way this emotion is a place, this overwhelming love is a territory, a landscape. He comes back every day until her husband is well again, well enough to know better. Chester finds the pictures she's drawn from her window, pencil sketches. He holds the pictures up to her face, and she simply looks away. He begins to cry from the back of his throat. He tries to yell at her with his stubbed tongue, but it comes out in growls and hisses. He wants to know what he's done to bring it on. He wants her to say that she loves him, but she doesn't say anything, although there is something almost like love, a tenderness. She doesn't allow it. She wants him to leave, if that's what he's going to do.

She buried the bit of tongue, and that's how she learned to bury herself, piece by piece. This is how she went on, until now, and she's already gone. She's already buried everything that was once alive in her, except the badger, the weasel, this cough. She presses the pencil drawing to her chest. She wonders if she will find the Prophet in heaven, if there is a heaven, if it will be the heaven he described, if it will be that land that once laid down at her feet. She wants to go, to let the ragged animal die, to put an end to the sibilant chorus tonguing dirt. She can feel a slow suffocation in her chest, a blanket over the animal's snout. She is waiting for horns and angels and light.

7

*A*lma is driving alone now. Henry is already ghostly. She tries to remember the heft of his arm around her, the meatiness of his chest. It is almost there, the physical memory of his body, but then gone, only the air in the windows, fluttering her dress. The trunk smells foul with its seawater, its mildewed books, and wet woolen dankness. She feels like she's hauling a dead body home. Henry is gone and she's got a dead body. It is as if Henry has died and this is his body, this moldering trunk with its rusty hinges. She thinks of her mother, after her father left, after the Prophet died, how she looked vacant, like an abandoned house, shutters wind-kicked wide open, a curtain lifting now and then, a reminder that there was once care, attention, a femininity, or even a simple practicality of keeping back some sun.

She pulls the car over to the roadside. She has to pee. She

leaves the car running and opens the two car doors on one side to block her from the view of a car that might happen to pass. She pulls down her underwear, a bit crusted from what's seeped from her, Henry's old juices from just the night before—they'd made love in the car every night on the trip down, falling asleep with their feet propped out the window—but it seems like weeks already. It seems like another lifetime. Because, from now on, she divides her life this way—before Henry stayed on in Florida and after Henry stayed on in Florida—and she's aware of this great rift, her life like two Bible parts: first the old, meaning her mother and Mrs. Bass and the factory, as loud as a child's squalling mouth, her children growing into these bigger, fuller bodies, Henry, of course, her life steeped in his shadow; and second, the new, so far just a long road and a car and a trunk that smells like death itself.

The piss hits the hard dirt and sprays up on her shoes, and the puffed and pinched bare spots of her feet where there are cutaway holes below the thin buckle straps. Her legs are bare. It is too damn hot for stockings. She's unclipped them and rolled them down her legs. She's alone now. Who will see her? A farmer maybe in a field? At this distance, she's a woman, squatting at the roadside to pee. She's a dirty woman, traveling alone. Someone to be pitied for more than her lost hose. And goddamn it, she doesn't care anymore what anybody thinks. It dawns on her now that she's no longer the nigger lover's daughter. It is as if that girl, with all of her worthless, nagging fears and all of her dreamy desires, has lifted up and out of her. She feels different now, no longer as attached to this world. She feels loose, wild, like she's spinning away from the things she's always known and loved, and she likes it. She doesn't pull up her underwear. Instead she lets the air dry her soft patch of hair. There is no farmer in the field, and she's stopped looking out for one.

Even as she was standing there on the Miami dock, she knew that the moment would last only briefly here, in this world, and too, that it would go on to live in her mind forever. She watched herself, the wind pressing her dress against her thighs, for example. A clot of gulls startled, and their wings lifted them, *het, het, het,* into the sky. The setting sun poured on Henry's back; he was washed in gold light, his skin brassy as he kneeled there before the trunk. In fact, he didn't look like himself as much as he did a movable statue of himself. There were only a few men, shirtless and distant, still loading a truck bed. The old man from the warehouse shuffled out the large opening and then quickly disappeared back inside. Henry lifted the lid, and it blocked Alma's view of his expression. A gray coat sleeve flopped over the trunk's lip. Henry stood, heavily. He looked past the woman in the wind-pressed dress, his wife, past the stray dog struggling in the trap, out to the ocean. He closed his eyes, tilted back his head, a pose that seemed to say he was drinking the ocean, one lusty gulp after the other, but maybe he was crying. There was a hitch in his breathing. She knew that it didn't matter whether he was actually crying or not, because she would decide that later. When it suited her that he was crying, he would be crying. And when it suited her that he was lustily drinking the ocean, he would drink. Alma wasn't a woman on a dock. She was watching a woman on a dock.

This is how it happened: Her hair whipped around her head. She walked over to him. She looked down into the trunk—a woman's wilted hat, a moth-bitten wool suit coat, bloated books. There was a spindly umbrella; collapsed, its spokes and leathery cloth reminded Alma of the shiny wings of a bat. She picked up the gray coat, thick and damp, and walked to the dog. She covered her arms with the coat, formed a deep pocket in the back, and quickly lunged to cover the dog's sharp teeth, its bony head, and folded ears. She held it by its strong neck, grabbed it around its shifting ribs. Now she popped the latch, and what was a taut metal spring suddenly went limp. The bar clanged loosely against the cement. The dog's leg had three bloody punctures from the trap's teeth, but they weren't too deep. As soon as its leg was free, it began to kick. She still had the dog locked in her arms. She didn't want to let it go. She didn't want to watch this moment on the dock anymore. She wanted to feel something, and the dog was real, its body vibrating with its low growling. She hugged its bony twisting head to her chest until it wrestled itself free and ran from her, startling more gulls, one scattering and then another, and then a spree of them.

She got up off her knees, draped the coat over her arm, and walked to the car and Henry. She said, "Well, let's go, I guess. Let's go on home." She passed him, shoulder to shoulder.

"I'm not going back," he said.

"What? Of course you are!" She snapped, like she was talking to one of the children. The gulls screeched overhead. Their wings stopped flapping. They stalled midair to glide.

"I came here to get rich, and I'm not going back until I'm rich. You can have the trunk."

It flashed over her that he was leaving. It was a trickle of information that swelled quickly to a broad flood. He was leaving her. She saw her father in his brimmed hat, his shadowed face. "I don't want the goddamn trunk."

Henry picked up the trunk, angrily, tipped it into the backseat, shoving it in the rest of the way.

Alma stood there. She was a woman with her hands on her hips. Her voice not as loud as it should be, because of the wind that seemed to lift her words from her, casting them up into the air, like something for the gulls to feed on. Henry scuffed his shoes in the dirt. He looked out at the water, his shirt flapping like a flag. "Who do you think you are? You can't quit me like this. You can't. You have dragged me through this much. It is your job to take me home."

"Take the trunk, Alma. Take the car."

She was shaking her head. What would she tell the children, coming home without him? They'd blame her. Hadn't she blamed her own mother all of these years for running her father off? They'd think she lost him. They'd mistrust her even more than they already did. She was a terrible mother. One son on his own, the other children in an orphanage. What more proof did anyone need? And now her husband was quitting her. "No. You're coming back with me."

"I'm not."

She couldn't believe him. "We are going to drive home the way we came here—together." Now she started screaming, her voice high and hoarse in her throat. "This isn't right. Can't you see what it could lead to? Didn't you know that the trunk was going to be worthless?"

"How can you say that? You believed it, too."

She had chirped all the way down. She had heard herself saying the most outlandish wishes, and for a long time she didn't know why. Certainly, she didn't believe that she was about to become rich. At first, she was playing make-believe. She was being romantic for her husband, and it was romantic. But then she saw that Henry had cast himself away from her, that while he drove, his eyes took on a glassiness. His hair bustled all over his head in the shifting wind, but his eyes were steady, fixed, and she knew that he believed that the trunk was going to change his life, was already changing his life. So her voice took on a dreamy singsong, because she wanted Henry to be the levelheaded one. She wanted him to take on the adult role, so that he could hear himself saying, "Don't get your hopes up too high." Certainly, she couldn't have been the one to tell him that it wasn't going to amount to anything. She remembered squealing, "We'll be rich as pigs, can you believe it?" her eyes brimming with tears, her hands clapping wildly, and he had tethered her, and it was a comfort. But she could always see the narrowing end, things coming to a dark, tightening tip. But she hadn't expected him to leave her. "No," she says. "I never believed it would hold a damn thing."

He looked away from her.

"You can't quit me! You cannot, Henry." Her voice softened on his name. Her throat closed around it. Her father had walked out the door while she slept.

"Alma," he said, and then nothing else.

Her hand rose up, a fury in it. She slapped him. His face registered the blow, returned to her slowly. His eyes teared. His cheek already flared red. Her hand stung and then dulled. That was the end of it. She walked around to the driver's seat. She could no longer feel her own body. Her legs had gone numb. She sat and slammed the door. The keys were in the ignition. She couldn't feel her hands. She pinched them, then held the key, twisted her wrist, pushing the button to start it up. The engine caught. She would be alone in the world. She thought of the girls lashing her with sticks. She remembered what it was like to bash a rabbit's head with a rock, to cut into it with a knife and peel back the taut, furred skin. She felt like she'd been struck senseless, a ringing in her ears.

Henry's face appeared in the open window, his full, flushed face, his ruffled hair, his teeth and lips. His face was too bright, garish with color and pricked with detail. The air was too clear. Alma missed the graying dust, the way it hushed, dismissing brightness, a muffling. She wanted Henry to disappear into a cloud of black coal. She didn't belong here. "I'll come back for you in a gold car one day, a gold car with slick runners and shiny tires. I promise." His voice was noisy in the box of the car, cut off from the wind. He knew better than a gold car. He was leaving her, and yet he could believe that he wasn't. He was lying, and yet he could pretend it was the truth, and she felt the tidal pull of the lie. She knew that because he had offered it, she would take it in and harbor it in some young, trusting part of herself, the dirt within her that he'd first sowed.

She put the car into gear. Her hand fit around the shift's knob. The car jumped forward and then lurched away. And she was in it. She was behind the wheel.

Alma pulls up her underwear. She gets back in the car, but then it chugs, heaves a few sputtering coughs, and gives out. The door that she has her elbow cocked against goes still, no longer jiggles with the car's motor. She turns the key, pushing the button. Nothing. Turns it again and again, pushing. Nothing. She rests her head on the wheel. She wonders when she last ate or drank. She's tired all of the sudden, deeply tired. She stays that way, arms slung over the wheel, her head resting on its hard center, for a long time. She doesn't want to leave the car and go for help. The last time she strayed it was to look for the dog. She glanced up and down warehouse alleyways until she saw the dog's mangy head, its dark body darting between boxes. She stopped the car, slipped out, and clipped down a narrow walk, holding her arms close to her body. She clicked her tongue, whistled. "Here, baby! Here, baby girl!" Suddenly she recalled her own baby born dead and then the eight-legged calf, the thin stick tapping its giant glass jar; the Mule-Faced Woman, her long legs, her oily peanut sack, distorted face, and broad, flared nostrils. It has become an incantation. There was a risen clot in her throat. She jogged around a few men who were smoking with their backs leaned up against a truck. She wanted to help the dog, scrub out the wounds and wrap the leg in a proper dressing. Who knew how long it had been trapped? It might need some water, a bit of something to eat. She called out, "Here, baby. Here, baby," but softer now. She could hear rustling behind empty boxes, one stacked inside the next, four or five deep. The sunlight had slipped now. It was getting dark. She pulled out the stacked boxes. A cat glanced up, a rat in its mouth, held like it would its own kitten, but it was not a kitten. The rat was limp with skinny pink clawed feet and a body so fat it bounced, dead weight, against the cat's chin and chest. The cat darted off. It had been eating from a nest the rat had chewed into the boxes and filled with newspaper. And there was something still squirming, alive, more than one wriggling body, small, sleek tails. Alma didn't want to see the pale, blind infants, so she pushed the boxes back into place.

Now, in the dead car, she allows her mind to go slack, lets all of the images come at her—she has no more energy to keep them away. And they do, a bleak parade of ugliness, until a mule and a woman are locked in sex, the woman bent beneath its heaving girth, but they do not make the Mule-Faced Woman—she pours out a nest of rats, and the hawker with the eight-legged calf drowns them in a jar of his formaldehyde that widens to fit Henry's dead body, too, soaked till bloated, then folded into the terrible trunk. And the tsking nun shakes her head with its heavy wimple.

Alma is rattled by a knock, a tap on the windshield. She doesn't know exactly how much time has passed. Her throat is dry, her stomach turning, empty. Hunger always gives her a surge of panic. She feels dizzy, gutted. The sun blinds her. There's a sore indentation of the wheel on her forehead. She rubs at the spot, squinting up toward the tap.

There's a woman, enormous, the bulwark of a muscled arm pinched by a dress sleeve, a face, stony and abnormal, as long as Lincoln's, bony, stretched. "You in need of some help?" Alma is surprised by the high register of her voice. She'd expected something deeper, a man's voice. Once a year in Marrowtown, the Rotary Club holds a womanless wedding, and the men dress up as women to sashay around on stage. Sometimes you'll find an errant member pumping gas wearing lipstick and his mother-in-law's outdated Sunday dress. But this is a woman—distorted, elongated, but a real woman, young, maybe twenty. Alma catches herself glancing up and down the street, looking for more of them, as if this one has wandered from a herd, but the road is empty. Alma looks up into the woman's face. She says, "It won't start up. It died on me."

"I see." Her jaw is oversize and heavy because of it. She ambles to the front of the car. She's wearing a handmade dress with a sloping hemline and work boots. Alma supposes it's hard to find women's shoes big enough. The woman has the leanness of a twelve-year-old boy, the awkward body that's being stretched tall and newly grown into. There's a loose lankiness to the way she walks, as if all her joints aren't completely stitched together. She fiddles with the hood and pops it open a few inches. "I'll take a look, if it's okay by you. I have six brothers, and so I've learned these things."

Alma nods. "That'd be just fine with me, as I am in trouble if it's gone for good." The woman disappears behind the hood. A few seconds pass. Alma imagines her brothers as buffalo. "My name's Alma."

"And I'm Roxy." Her voice is a muffled echo as she leans into the engine.

"I've been traveling on my own for a bit. My husband has decided to stay behind in Florida, just to take advantage of a possibility down there." She tries it on to hear how it might sound when she says it to the nun, but it's not quite right.

"Start her up now."

Alma turns the key, pressing the button, and the car catches and purrs.

"And give her some gas."

She does, and the engine revs.

Roxy walks around to the window. "I'm hitching north. I saw the stalled car and then you at the wheel. It gave me a start. I thought you'd fallen ill or dead. My mother just died, you see. Not in a car—in her bed. A slow death, but now I find myself on guard for it."

Alma understands her watchfulness. "Oh, no," she says. "I'm fine, really. Where are you headed?"

"I'm looking for work or something. I'm hoping I'll know it when I see it."

"I can drop you as far north, and a bit westerly, in Marrowtown, West Virginia. It's where I'm headed." Even in saying the name of her town, she feels the air collect a stenchy thickness, smoke and char.

"I'll take it."

Roxy jogs around the car, heavily weighted by her thick bones, and climbs into the passenger seat, her knees suddenly high, popping up below her hem, her back rounded so she can fit, and just barely at that. She folds her hands—huge-knuckled, the way you'd imagine God's to be—in her lap, a dainty leftover habit from having once been taught to be a lady, but her knees don't fit, even if tilted to one side, so she's pulled them up, pressed against the dashboard. Alma puts the car in gear, bumps onto the road.

It's as if she's put Roxy in gear, too. She starts to talk. "When my mother called me to her deathbed, I thought she was going to tell me to take her place, to take care of my daddy and all the boys. But she pulled me in close, and I could see the shine of her scalp because her hair was so thin, and she handed me an envelope of money. She told me to leave or I'd be slave to them for the rest of my life, and it would put me in my grave as surely as it did her. And so here I am. She is now dead, and I am out in the world."

Alma can see the dying woman, tall in her own right—she'd have to have been—but weak, her stark head. She doesn't know what to say.

"It's beautiful here," Roxy goes on. "I don't think I've ever seen anything as green as that field with them flowers dotting it, just purple and yellow, sprung out like some kind of beautiful rash. You'd cry if you looked at it too long." Roxy seems pure. Alma sees something of herself in her, a longing. She feels like taking care of her, perhaps because she's just heard that she's motherless and Alma is without her own children, hollow.

Alma looks at the field. It's the same one that she'd searched for the farmer who might see her pissing by the roadside, but it isn't the same, either. She hadn't seen the flowers or the green so bright as all that. She's seen too much, though, too much. She wants to close her eyes to the glowing field and Roxy's dying mother and all she's seen, good and bad. She's tired. It's wearied her.

Alma remembers that her heart was an engine, just a week or so ago. But she's had no time to think like that since. There's been too much to keep track of in her mind. She wonders whether she'd point out the field of flowers to her children if they were here. If she would let them get out of the car and pick some. She imagines them coming at her with beautiful ragged bouquets.

8

*I*rving remembers the twisting ride, Sir Lee's car grinding uphill, a monstrous huff and growl through the rain, like a wild boar rooting through mud. The front tire rammed the lip of a pothole, pitching Irving from his seat. He was dimly aware of the second car, a man named Fox—appropriately reddish and wiry—who was following for a card game, the flood and fade of his headlights through the car, crisscrossing Sir Lee's hair, slick as a wet beaver, his wide face each time he looked back over his shoulder. Sir Lee passed Smitty and Irving the glinting flask. He called it monkey rum straight from the row. It scorched Irving's mouth and throat, burned in his stomach like a hissing coal. The chicken he'd eaten began to churn, steeped in liquor. The spare front room of Sir Lee's cabin was stuffy with the windows shut against the rain, the chain-pulled bulb swaying, the hulking, slippery shadows. Sir Lee drank his liquor with a pinch of powder that he swirled with his thick finger till the ginger drink clouded. Then he sucked his finger, or Delphine did it for him.

But now Irving is in Sir Lee's closet, listening to the thump and tussle of bodies in the front room. Delphine's occasional screech. He knows there are knives. He saw them glint, and a rifle, too, perched on top of a wardrobe. Beside him, Smitty rocks, his body contracting so that his skull knocks the plastered wall, Sir Lee's hung pant hems brushing his shorn head. Sir Lee's shoes, four pairs lined against the closet wall, each heel a measured fat thumb-distance apart, are gaping holes, black yawning mouths. Irving imagines Sir Lee's giant, fat-padded feet fitting into the shoes, the cinch of laces. Irving squats to one side, afraid to disturb them. Smitty doesn't touch the shoes either. The closet smells of shoe polish, starch, Maccassar—this simpering, unctuous version of Sir Lee—and too, the dogs, smoke, liquor, a kind of angry bile. It's nothing like Irving's father's closet, where things are barely hung, one dark suit, a row of overalls slung loosely by their straps. Irving misses his father, his nonconvo-luted scent, his straightforward manner. Although his moods confound Irving—the sourness that can take hold of him for days at a time and then, just as miraculously, lift, as if his father has been under a table and emerges pretending the tablecloth is a maiden's kerchief—he has never been fright-ened by them. Sir Lee is a different sort. Irving would like

Smitty to show him how to act. He misses Smitty's cool bravado, the way he ushered him into the car and invited him along, without even a word to Sir Lee, like he made his own decisions. He misses Willard and Lettie, too, because if they were here, he'd tell them—like he always did—that everything was going to be okay, which often convinced him, too. Irving feels dazed now, trying not to think of the fight—the heaving, the boot-scraping. The front room was spare and humorless, but this closet scares Irving, its pants hung so that the pleats stay perfect, each hem the same length from the floor, folded just so over the hanger, as if everything were measured, even the dark thicket of hung belts. It's the closet of a crazy man, Irving thinks, and he feels a little crazed himself. The floor is soft, movable, watery, like one time when he remembers sitting in the foot well of the car because his father was picking up an old bedframe, and he couldn't see what was coming. The car had rattled and shifted beneath him.

Sir Lee isn't the same smiling man who'd stride up with his boy carrying in the box of liquor, but ugly and dark, and he could beat you for anything, even touching his shoes. The man in the other room, Fox, said the wrong thing—who knows what. Sir Lee stood up so fast at Fox's words that he stumbled, gawkishly, and when he caught himself, he had something to prove. So Sir Lee lunged at him. Smitty pulled Irving down the hall to the closet. He felt dull, numb, his arms and legs heavy as if he were taking on Sir Lee's weight.

Now Smitty has gone blank with fear and there's still shouting and cursing, low and guttural, the shuffling of bodies. It surges up above the rain rattling against the roof. It occurs to Irving that if Sir Lee wins this fight, he might just come after the two of them. The sores on Smitty's arms are cigarette burns, just as clear as day, and not by accident, not the way they're lined up, measured as this closet. And Smitty'll let Sir Lee know just where they are with his head banging against the wall. Irving is scared, can feel his heart beating away in his chest. He decides he might be able to make it out, what with all of the action in the other room. He can slip out and nobody'll even notice him. And then he'll be in the cool night.

Irving gently kicks the closet door. It swings open wide. He crawls out of the closet and through the bedroom door. He walks down the hall with his back sliding against the wall. When he gets to the end of it, he scoots down again. He can see everything now—Sir Lee on the floor, the lard bulk of his back, his thin white shirt with its whiter T-shirt beneath. Fox is small, but his face is large, angular, shining with sweat. He's up above, kicking Sir Lee, who's curled up as best he can with his girth. And Irving finds himself rooting for Fox, hoping that he does Sir Lee in enough to knock him out. Delphine comes at Fox now, and just a minute ago she was calling him sugar, saying, "Can I get you anything, doll?" He hits her, his flat arm across her chest. He sends her to the floor. But this gives Sir Lee some time. Hunkered as he is, he pulls a knife out of his boot, half stands, and jabs. It's slow, this part. He stabs Fox in the side. All the rushing stops. Everyone is quiet. Fox folds in on himself like a chair, drops to his knees. He holds his wound and checks his hand for blood. It's wet with it.

Sir Lee wipes off the blade with a handkerchief. He walks to Delphine. She smiles lightly, relieved. But then he grabs her by her frail wrist. He pushes her hand against the table, the knife blade poised over it. Irving can't see the knife, Sir Lee blocking with his wide back. But he can tell by the motion of his arm and the pinched whiteness of Delphine's face that she's being cut. He doesn't say a word, just slices deeply across her four fingers.

Sir Lee says, "Next time, I take off all your fingers. You hear me?" Irving doesn't know why he's saying this. Next time she does what? And maybe, Irving figures, Delphine doesn't really know either. Blood drips on Sir Lee's boots. He takes the handkerchief, puts his boot on a chair, and wipes off the shiny leather, actually polishes in tiny circles till it looks like it could squeak. "Clean this shit up!" He throws his stubby arms out to his sides, walks around the man on the floor, and punches open the screen door, his fist on the wood. The car starts up. Only now can Irving hear Smitty's head against the wall. It's gotten louder, and Irving wonders if it isn't so loud that he's actually calling for Sir Lee to find him, calling out in his own way.

Irving watches Delphine in the light from the bare bulb

hung over the square table. The bright reflection glitters with rain on the window. She shuffles to the kitchen. Fox moans. He says something like *sugarbaby*.

Delphine saunters in, says, "You ripped my dress." She wraps her hand in a rag, stands in front of Fox, showing him her long leg and the tear a couple of inches up one seam. She walks behind him, bends, grabs him under his arms, tries to lift and drag him. He pushes a bit with his feet.

Irving can hear himself breathing loud. He doesn't want to be found out from his own panting. He wants to be a man, to be of use. He stands up and stumbles into the room's light.

Delphine pauses. They stare at each other a moment. "You gonna stand there all big-eyed or are you gonna help?"

Irving runs over to her, and together, they drag Fox out of the house, down two steps into the cluttered yard. The rain has dulled to a soft ticking. The wet dogs come at them, and Delphine pushes the dogs' ribs with her leg, slaps a few on their wet noses. She pops open the door to his car and counts, "One, two, three." Together they heave his body up. Fox cries out, like a crow, but once up, he helps to push himself across the seat.

"Go get Smitty," Delphine says. "Drag him out if you have to. Son of a bitch'll beat him to death."

Irving starts to run inside, but there's Smitty, standing in the doorway, dry and pale. "I'm not going," he says.

"Get in," Delphine says. She's in the driver's seat now.

"He loves us, Delphine. He could have done worse to you.

He was a Dellslow prize boxer when he was young. But he loves us, you know that. He's like my daddy. And one day he's going to go to California, and if you're not here when he goes, then you'll be left behind. You heard him say that, didn't you, Delphine? Stay here with me. He'll come back and he'll be fine by then. And if we go to California, well, you won't get to. I want us to all go, Delphine. All of us together."

Delphine softens. She looks tired, worn down. She says to Irving, "Get in the car. In back with Fox. Hit him in the face if he starts to close his eyes. I don't want him to die on me." Irving goes around and gets in, lifting up Fox's head and shoulder to sit beneath him and keep him a little propped up. Fox stares at him, almost blankly, then he winks. Irving can feel the wetness of blood seep into his pants.

Delphine looks up at the front door once more, and Smitty is still standing there, his skinny, sunken chest and pale, red-pocked arms. Rain beads on the windshield. Delphine starts the engine. It catches and growls. With one hand on the wheel, wincing, the rag on her other hand now blood-soaked, she pulls the wheel, hand over hand, like someone pulling a slack rope waiting for it to go taut. She punches the gas, and the car heaves forward. Irving looks back over his shoulder. Smitty is gone.

Delphine parks the car as close to the doctor's house as she can get it. There's a little hung shingle that reads DR. SEVRAS. By now, Fox has lost a lot of blood. Irving's pants are soaked through and sticking to his skin. Delphine is too weak to help and so, alone in the dark, Irving has to carry Fox up to the doctor's front lawn. That is as far as he can get him, because Fox can barely help out with his legs now. Irving leans down to the man's ruddy, broad face and tells him he's going to be all right, that he's going to be fine.

But Fox shakes his head. "That Sugarbaby is going to steal my car."

"Is that your car?" He'd forgotten.

"I want what's mine, at least that."

"It'll be okay, Mr. Fox. I'm sure it will all come out good in the end." Irving runs through the slick grass, up to the house, knocks hard on the door, darts across the yard, jumping a hedge to the car, fast, just like Delphine has told him. But when he gets to the car, Delphine is in his seat, slouched down with her skirt still hitched from having climbed. Her head rests in the open window, tilted up to see the night sky. She lets the soft rain dot her face.

"Can you drive, kiddo?"

"I can try it."

"I don't even know where to go to. I'm in need of a Chinaman."

"A Chinaman? There aren't any Chinamen around here, unless you want a steamed shirt." Irving thinks of the yellow-skinned, slant-eyed man and woman who run the laundry on High Street. There is always an old relative out front, sitting on a bench in silky wide-legged pants under a paper umbrella. The relative is so old Irving can never tell if it's a man or a woman.

"You take over, okay?"

Irving has to sit at the edge of the seat, with his back as tall as he can stretch it. The windshield wipers pulse, wobbling and jerking. He concentrates on smoothing out his jumpy exchange of clutch and gas. He doesn't want to jostle Delphine, who seems to be almost sleeping.

"Darling, where are you taking me?"

"I don't know. I suppose I'm just trying to drive good. Is this Fox's car? He said it was."

"Oh, is it? I suppose it is. But it probably isn't. I mean Fox probably took it from some old lady who was in a bad way for a little shot."

"A shot?"

"Morphine for her aches and pains. We should go to New York City and find a Chinaman. I could become a philosopher if I got the right amount of pills."

"How about we go to my grandmother's house? She'll have something to eat." And he realizes that this is where he's been headed all along, out to the country. He's ready to swallow his pride and let the old woman glare at him with suspicion and disgust. Anyway, he's a hero now. He has a woman in need. He's just being gentlemanly because of her desperate state.

"I must look a fright. I need some makeup for my face. Sir Lee just got me a Lionel compact with a Golliwogg de Vigny perfume puff and some Tangee lipstick. Looking pretty is part of the job. I hate jobs! Don't ever hold down a job!"

"I think you look just fine. And my grandmother doesn't care about all that. She'll help you wash out that cut."

"Nobody can wash me. I go wild like a mule if somebody tries to take good care of me." She starts laughing. Her hair kicks around in the wind.

"Why do you stay with him?" Irving asks. It just comes out, just like that, because of the wind in her hair and how beautiful her mouth looks wide open like that, and he is driving a car like a man. He can ask these kinds of questions.

"I ain't the queen of England, kiddo. But I'm expensive, and he can afford me."

"There's plenty of men with money. Good men. I think Dr. Sevras could afford you."

"Oh, yes, the good doctor. Would his wife abide that? Certainly, he would if he could. Certainly. They all have it in them, darling. Each and every one."

Irving doesn't know what she means. He thinks she's talking crazy, from the loss of blood. He's tired now, wipes his face.

"Keep your hand up at your heart." He's heard that keeping something raised will help you not lose so much blood. But she's asleep now. He reaches over and tries to prop her hand up on her chest. His knuckles brush her breast, and heat rushes through his body. The hand falls to her lap. It's heavy, the rag now a dark red. He hits a pothole in the road, a deep one, and the car jumps. He grips the wheel with both hands. He turns a corner in the road and the headlights pass over a field. In it, he sees what seems like a hundred pairs of eyes. Deer, a herd of them, standing still and ghostly, the stern, solid gaze that a parent should have, that steadfast attention. And with all of those eyes on him, he wonders what his parents would think of him, driving a stranger's car, a stranger he left perhaps bleeding to death on a doctor's lawn, Delphine at his side, asleep, hopefully not still seeping blood. He wants them to be proud of him. He wishes they were here. He lets himself think that they've sent this mindful herd of deer, with their coats and eyes shining. And although he knows it's not true—his mind is talking like in a dream— it's the first time in a long time that he's felt like someone is watching over him, that he is being cared for.

9

The ride has been fine. Only at night did she think of all those horrible things, those dark, awful pictures that flash up in her mind. She remembers her notion that memories are constantly falling away, droplets from a leaky faucet, and she hopes that Henry will disappear quickly, tapping away into a silver drain.

Alma and Roxy slept in a motor cabin, because Roxy had her mother's money and insisted. The room was tidy, with two narrow beds, a nightstand with a thin drawer to hold a Gideon Bible, and a bathroom down the hall that they shared with the other guests, an old couple who called each other Mother and Father, and a family with squalling infant twins. But even there at night, it wasn't so bad, because there was much else to take in—the tall mirror; the writing desk; the tightly made bed; Roxy, too long for it, her feet like two white bass sticking out over the edge; and the smell that seeps into dreams of Bon Ami cleanser and body after body, a series of engravings on the motel's persistent memory. It makes her dream of the hosiery factory, not Henry at all, but the thousands of hose she turned over the flexed wooden pedestal foot.

During the day, she seemed to have energy only for telling made-up stories to Roxy of a happy farm-girl childhood, her joyous clean children, the kindly nuns, and the lively show people. She didn't mention the factory, but she wondered only for as long as she would let herself, only for a brief second, if she would have to go back to Mrs. Bass's steamy office, the shocking white part of her hair, her snapping teeth, to ask for her job back. When she was talking to Roxy, there was no need to think of the factory, because Henry was going to come home after the possibility in Florida paid off and they'd be plenty rich. In fact, it's Alma's idea that Roxy stay on at the boardinghouse if she wants to. Mr. Bucci can move in with Wall-Eye. Now that the bear is dead, he doesn't need his own room, and then Roxy can settle in and look for a job.

Roxy says, "Yes, that sounds good to me."

And it's decided.

It's night when they drive through Marrowtown and climb up the valley's other side toward Alma's road lined with tall hedges. At one point in a turn, Alma looks down on the city collected in the dark pit, the domed church, its spindly steeple, factories belching smoke, the outlines of buildings, homes; they look like tawdry hummels, dimpled with light, ugly, shoddy gimcrackery, gathering black dust, too loveless to be wiped clean. It is dark, but she can feel the dressing of ash, the murky photographic gray that leeches color, the drained fading. The sun will rise, lazing through the filtered air, grainy, piqued. The air's familiar soot blows in the windows. The wheel accepts its tackiness.

She's been gone only a week and a half, but the hedges appear, taller, overgrown, and then the house, stricken, tilted. There are no cars in the yard. The house is too quiet and dark. Alma knows right away that something is wrong. She kills the engine. The headlights cut off. The yard pools in darkness. She jumps out of the car, leaving Roxy, and runs up to the door, which has been left open. The house gapes before her, a rib case, and it seems to breathe like a laboring lung. She runs from room to room, calling, "Irving? Irving? Mr. Bucci?" No one answers. When she walks into her own bedroom, a blackbird lifts off the bed and starts circling wildly. It rushes at her, its dark body hoisted by the sudden hysteria of wings beating against the ceiling. She freezes. The bird panics her, a deep childhood panic, keen and real. She remembers collecting coal that had fallen off the train cars. An aching hunger, cold, birds riding winds overhead. One winter morning, she stared up at them and fainted, awoke to snow lighting down on her face. She'd wondered if she'd died of hunger and come back to life. The bird flaps wildly out of the room. Alma runs down the stairs, out the front door, to Roxy, her tall, hulking frame standing alone in the yard.

Alma doesn't know where she is. She doesn't recognize anything here. Over her shoulder, the house is lit up. She'd turned on lights as she went through, and now it looks as if each room is burning.

Roxy looks at her earnestly. "What's gone wrong? Something's gone wrong. Where's everybody?"

And Alma feels again like she's been let go in the world. Like a zookeeper in some ultimate act of pity has snuck in to let her loose. She thinks that it never was her house, her life, but another woman's, a woman who might have looked the same, who wanted something desperately, and maybe this was the thing she wanted after all. Not anything more, just less, just freedom. It is painful; her chest feels like a struck gong, shivering. *And yet,* she thinks, *when someone dies, isn't there something ecstatic about it?* She feels, for a moment, that she can drive off with Roxy and tell a new story, become someone else, and it will be equally true.

Roxy looks up at the house. She says, "Where's the little children, the ones you said would be just stepping out of their bath?"

Alma looks at her. At the car. The tilted steps that lead to the porch. Where are they? "The nuns," she says. "This was where Irving was to be, and the show people. The other two are with the nuns. Remember?"

"And Irving and the show people?"

"I don't know," she says. "I don't know what's happened. I feel all turned about." Alma stares at her feet, the buckles too tight, her flesh on the tops of her feet squeezing up from the cutouts. She starts walking, but not toward the car, not toward the house—out in the direction of a thin line of trees and what lies beyond it, the neighbor's field. But she stumbles, catches herself with the fat palm of her hand. Roxy coughs, rubs her arms to keep warm, maybe a sign of nervousness. Alma rubs the dirt from the palm of her hand. Her hand. It is her own hand. She would recognize it anywhere.

It's the middle of the night—clear, starry, the moon as bright as a lamp—but when Alma rings the bell, she hears the immediate shuffling of feet. It isn't the young spry nun who'd met her before, but an old woman, so bent over from her hardened bones that she has to look straight up—her eyes like something surface-bobbed, and eyebrows raised—to see Alma's face. The door isn't so heavy for her. She is oddly strong, toughened, wizened to this tight angle of calcification. It's still unsettling to Alma that they're so well prepared to welcome her. She wonders what else they're prepared to find at this hour of the night. Suddenly Alma sees the convent as a place that welcomes disasters, the small disasters of lust, and she sees herself as one of their emergency cases. She wonders what she must look like to the nun who's so tidy in her black habit, just floating hands and face. Alma must seem a mess of hair and flesh, and the pale dizzy print of her dress, the design of her shoes, her bare legs—still bare. How can that be? She wonders what it must be like for the nun each time she opens the door to a blustering, colorful stranger, slightly breathless with panic. Alma rubs the palm of her hand to get off the dirt stain.

"Please, come in," the old nun says. "Are you expected?"

She wonders how many people come in the middle of the night for scheduled appointments. "I'm here to pick up my children. Lettie and Willard."

"There will be paperwork. Follow me."

And so she takes Alma down the darkened tile hallway to Sister Margaret's office. This time the hall is empty. There are no boxes or piled cans, but there's still the stink of old clothes and used things, and, more strongly, ammonia, its high stink constant. Alma wonders what contagion they're dousing with it; perhaps every kind. Germs shed from all the worn shoes that shuffle anxiously to the office door, the scabby, lice-ridden children left with only a knock at the door. Alma wonders if her children will be returned, sickly, dull, with red-crusty eyes, a deep contamination of some unruly disease usually reserved for the motherless.

The nun turns on the light, opens the door for her, shows her the seat. Alma remembers that she'd refused the chair, and then needed it, and, too, that it was soft, comforting. She won't sit this time, however. She would like to do this as quickly as possible.

The old nun nods, says, "I'll go wake and ready the children."

Sister Margaret walks into the room. She looks like she's

dressed quickly in the dark. Her habit is slightly askew, and her fine orange hair, curly wisps of it, stick out around the wimple's frame. But she retains her stiff primness, her awkward cordiality.

"I've been expecting you," she tells Alma. "I'm happy to see you back."

Alma says, "Well, here I am." But it seems that the nun is saying two things, that yes, she expected her, but at the same time didn't really, not absolutely. There's relief that she's made it, "happiness," in fact. She remembers now how it was the last time, the nun saying one thing but meaning something else, and how she intimidated Alma with her measured comments.

Sister Margaret motions for her to sit. She feels, again, that she doesn't want to, but, also, doesn't want to appear odd about refusing the seat twice, so she sits. Again, it's too yielding. Alma scoots to the chair's hard front edge, which gives her a sense of mooring. Sister Margaret waits until she's settled, then begins. "We would like to keep Willard. He's doing well. I think he likes the regimen. He's learning a great deal."

"Excuse me?"

"He's stopped going to the bathroom in his pants. He's learned to write his name and to pray. He likes structure. He's thriving."

Alma stiffens, doesn't know what to say. She glances around the room, distracts herself for a moment, wondering how Roxy is faring in the car, if the old nun is preparing both

children. She had said *children,* not *child,* right? She looks up
at Jesus, still there, suffering eternally. "I want to see my children," Alma says. She stands up and walks over to the window. She pulls the curtain back with her hand, and Roxy is
there standing by the car.

"Of course. They're on their way. If you want to take
Willard home with you, there's no problem with that. But he
wants to stay."

"Did you put that in his head? He's dim-witted. He'll
believe what you tell him."

"You can ask him yourself," Sister Margaret offers.

"And Lettie? Have you turned her against me, too?"

"We haven't turned anyone against you. Willard loves
you, but he needs this environment. He's a boy with poten-
tial, more than you think, I suspect. And Lettie, well, she
needs *you.* She's a desperate child with desperate needs. It's in
her best interest to be by your side."

"You know these aren't wild children that you have here.
They haven't been raised by the hair on their head. I'm a good
mother. And they have a good father." She wants to go on and
say that she's a proper married woman. But is she still?

The nun begins again. "Let me ask you plainly: Where is
the father of the children? Why did you need us in the first
place?"

"He's seeking out a possibility in Florida. He stayed on."

"I've heard many stories of need. Many. Please accept
what is being offered. It's a gift."

"I don't need your gifts."

Sister Margaret stands. "Let us take care of Willard. You will always be his mother. We cannot offer him that. But what more can you do for him? *You* may not need our gifts, but *he* does."

Just then, the door opens. Willard and Lettie are ushered in by the bent nun. Both of the children are clean, the way Alma had been picturing them. Willard's hair is slicked back, neatly combed, and Lettie has just washed her face, her cheeks pink. The old nun must have awakened them, dressed them, and tidied them up. Lettie stands there shyly for a moment and then runs at Alma, wrapping her arms around the broadest part of her hips. "Where's Daddy?" she asks.

"He's stayed on in Florida to finish up business. But he sent me on home because I was so homesick for my babies." But this isn't true. She's guilty of not being homesick for her babies, of thinking mostly of herself, the sweet air, her own fancifulness.

Willard says, "Mama, look at this!" He holds up a paper of a drawing of flowers and the sun with his name scrawled on it. His fleshy face beams, exuberant. It warms Alma's heart to see his fine letters, his bright yellow sun, so yellow it's as if he doesn't know he lives in a cloud of ash. He's proud. When was the last time she saw him so full of himself? She wishes she could be that happy. For the first time in her life, she thinks of Willard as limitless, of Lettie as her fragile one. And Alma, what does she feel? She's envious of the nuns, their orderly lives, their uniforms, rituals, the impeccable order they've gathered around themselves. She thinks of the baby born dead, the sheet it was wrapped in, and how empty her body felt. There is that familiar ache inside of her. Is it hunger, or only the memory of hunger, the fear of it? It has been a long trip. She's weary. She wants to be a child, to be taken care of. She wants her own mother. After they took the baby away, after Henry took it out, her mother was there. Her mother put a cold rag on her face and wiped her forehead, her hair. She asked her mother if it was a boy or a girl, and she said, "It doesn't matter now, does it?" Alma asked where Henry was taking it. And her mother said, "Hush now. Everything's going to be all right." Willard is there holding the picture up like he's selling a Sunday paper. Does she even deserve him?

"It's beautiful," she whispers. "It's beautiful."

Alma drives to her mother's house in silence. Coolness seeps into the car as they pass trees in the dark. She imagines the witch-hobble shrubs, the delicate white petals, clinging to the forest's kept shade. Lettie knows to be quiet. Yet there's something about her that is so relieved—in a heartbroken way—that she doesn't have to say anything, and Alma can feel her sighing presence. Lettie's adoration is almost a consolation for having left Willard behind, but not truly. Irving is missing. Her husband gone. Her house empty, but for an angry, hawking black bird. There's little money left rolled up in her liver-pill bottles. Without Henry and the boarders, it won't last, and there'll be nothing to replace it.

Roxy stares out the window. Her body with its long, thick bones doesn't seem to fit in the car, much less in Alma's life, a teetering thing, nothing like the stories she told on the trip north. She wishes Roxy weren't here to see these ugly truths, one after the other. She reminds Alma, just by sitting there quietly, that Alma never was a happy farm girl or the perfect mother of her children. Alma rides on, a new steeliness rising up in her. And somehow she would like to blame Roxy for it, but she can't. Not quite. Poor girl, she has nothing. She belongs in this car, hunched and silent, lovesick for her dead mother.

Alma doesn't recognize the car in her mother's yard. She's alarmed, but this time she doesn't run. She marches solemnly to the house, Roxy and Lettie behind her. She isn't eager to know what's gone wrong here. She opens the door and finds Irving and Sir Lee's girlfriend, the pretty, pouty thing he rides around with, Delphine, one of her hands wrapped in a bloody rag. She's reclining on the old sofa, looking gaunt and shaken. Her eyes sag darkly; her thin brow is pinched. She runs the fingers of her good hand over her dry lips. Irving has found an old apple and has bitten into it jaggedly. He looks up, astonished, caught. He seems ashamed. His pants are stained dark. They look stiff with dried blood.

"What happened?" Alma says, looking around the room and then walking past them to her mother's bed in the back of the house.

The Madam

Irving calls out, "Momma, don't go on back there."

But she's already in the room. Her mother's shoes are sitting neatly beside the nightstand, her whittled body hidden by the puff of her wool coat, two of the buttons buttoned. Alma barely recognizes her mother's soul-sifted body. Her face is white, drawn, her mouth blue. There's no hint of the stitched pain she'd worn for years, the hard lines around her mouth, the grooves in her forehead. Her hand is clamped down on a piece of paper; a frame and its family photograph sit on the covers beside her. Alma doesn't have to pry the paper from her mother's hand. She knows that the picture is a pencil drawing of the Prophet. Alma's heart feels swollen. It aches in her chest, which is suddenly too small to contain it, that familiar ache grown large. Her cheeks heat, an angry blush. Didn't Alma know her mother was sick, dying? Shouldn't Alma have insisted on taking her in? The stubborn old woman would have said no. Part of Alma hates her mother, this rootedness. But Alma lifts her head, stares at the ceiling. Her throat is tight, puffed. She sobs, letting her head fall to her chest. Her mother is gone, and she takes so much with her. They didn't speak of the past, but there were things that only they knew about each other. She touches her mother's soft hair, strokes it. She recalls how, by the roadside squatting to take a pee, she suddenly felt free of her childhood, that she was no longer the nigger-lover's daughter. And she imagines now that this was the moment her mother died, Alma with her skirt hoisted, piss spraying onto her shoes, her bare skin. And now she may never know about the baby. She never did ask Henry about it. They never spoke of it. If she tried to, he'd say, "We'll have more. We'll have so many one day we won't be able to keep count." She would like her mother to wrap her in her arms and tell her that everything is going to be all right. But it seems now that her mother is the dead baby, her baby. Her mother is the dead baby to be wrapped and taken away. Alma staggers, suddenly dizzy. She kneels beside the bed, folds her hands in prayer, but instead of praying, she looks around the room. Everything is dusted in dog hair, but the dogs have run off. Their scent rises up alongside the smells of bowels, decay, like under-earth, like the death-rot stench of wet leaves. She wipes her eyes and pinches her nose. She won't cry anymore. Her mother wouldn't approve of it, anyway. Strength, that's what her mother would expect of her. Alma says to herself, *My mother is dead. My mother is dead.* But it doesn't seem true. She stands up and walks unsteadily back into the parlor.

Roxy and Delphine are sitting at the dining-room table. Alma stares at Irving. He's too thin. He's just a child. "You're skin and bones." It makes her stomach lurch. She feels like she might get sick. She despises the gaunt look of his cheeks, the hollowness to his eyes. He's sunken. There's a smudge on his cheek, mud or blood. "What happened to Mr. Bucci and the rest?"

"The show closed, and they went on to the next town." He puts his hands on his hips, puffs his chest, the way his father might upon interrogation. He looks around the room distract-edly.

"Have you used up the money?"

"I can take care of myself. I just wanted Delphine's hand washed out."

She looks at Delphine. "Sir Lee do that?"

Delphine nods. "He's some son of a bitch."

Now Alma looks at Roxy and says, "My mother is dead. You can go if you want to. You don't have to stay on. You didn't sign anything."

Roxy shakes her head. "I'll stay, thank you. If it's all right by you. I'm not surprised by death anymore. It doesn't shock me."

Alma nods. Roxy's got nowhere to go, and that's sad enough. She has been aching for a mother, and Alma for her children. They've made a good match. There's an unspoken tenderness between them, hidden in all of this straight talk.

Lettie says, "Is it true?"

Alma turns to Lettie, who stands there holding her skinny arms, sniffling and wide-eyed. "It's true that she's dead. Yes. Don't cry on it."

Alma's flush of anger returns. She looks at Delphine and Roxy. She thinks, *This is what I have. These two women and me, my babies to look after—Irving and Lettie are just babies, after all, just babies; my mother's a dead baby—and we are all lost in the world.* Except, perhaps, Willard, who seems now pinned down safely, protected by the convent's long drive, heavy doors, and stone halls. And she remembers that a woman cast out with her children cannot make it in the world. Her husband has left her. She is of no use. If she had crops, they would surely dry up and die. The children will kill animals they trap in the yard, collect coal toppled from train cars. Her mother's house and land will sell for enough to cover her debts, if she's lucky, but even if Alma's hands were the fastest of all hands, she couldn't make enough at the hosiery mill to keep the roof over their heads, to keep food on the table. She feels the inching of panic, her childhood a palpable feeling in her stomach. It's all too familiar, this old house, the wind coming through the windows, the dark collecting in the rooms, the emptiness.

She goes to the sink, fills a bowl with water, rubbing a thin bar of soap into it, a fizzing lather. She puts the bowl in front of Delphine, then reaches up into the dip in the overhead lamp where her mother hid a small bottle of liquor. It swings afterward, setting the shadows to shift against the walls. She puts down three glasses and fills them up. She feels forceful, pumping, her heart a growling apparatus. She says, "We are alone in the world, can you feel it? And we need to get a plan."

Alma sits at the table. Lettie climbs onto her lap. Irving pulls up a chair, too. Delphine looks around. She edges toward the bowl but doesn't let her hand dip into the water.

"Where's that husband of yours?" Delphine asks.

"He isn't here, is he? Let it soak."

Delphine raises her eyebrows, shifts in her seat, but stays

quiet. She inches her hand into the bowl. The water wobbles, flushes pink. The table is gritty. A stingy breeze pushes through the room. This is what there is left, a boiled essence.

"What have we got?" Alma asks. "We have got to have something, some sort of something to help us make it through. We are in dire straits. Don't you see it?" She stares at the two other women.

Delphine asks, "You mean some sort of talent? Some sort of ability?"

"I suppose."

"I know what I do best," she laughs. "This little trick on my back." She pulls her shaky hand from the bowl, letting the bloody water drip down her arm a second. She stares at the gash. Two pincurls are now slack at her cheeks. Alma watches her, the idle cock of her head and the tremulous hand. She's desperate, too. They all are. The room is cloying with desperation, a furtive pungence as common and rich as the smell of dirt. The walls breathe with lichen, the bread with mold. She can smell the respiring breadbox, her mother decaying in the bedroom, turning back into ash. Delphine laughs, a gruff snort. She says, "You should run a whorehouse, Alma. Everybody needs a whore. We never go out of fashion."

It's a lark, meant to shock, but Alma is beyond shock. She says, "Well, I suppose it's a business like anything else. And I've got business sense." She looks at Delphine squarely.

Delphine says, "Sex is a wonderful business." She leans in.

"Why would you do it for free?" She covers her mouth in mock embarrassment and glances at Lettie, who sits there wide-eyed on her mother's lap. "Little pitchers have big ears."

Alma shakes her head. "There's two ways to grow up, knowing and not knowing. It's better to know." And that's the truth. Her children need to grow up knowing about love and loss, sex and betrayal. She doesn't want them to be caught off guard. What would they learn among whores? Practicality. She thinks of falling in love with Henry, of following him to Florida for a lousy trunk, how ignorant she was. She glances at Irving, silent and stiff, and down at Lettie, who's taking it all in. *It's better for them,* she thinks. *The world is sinful. Passions run to ugliness. They should know. Their mother and father have suffered from it—incurables, maybe—and their grandmother is dead in the other room with her lover's picture in her grip.*

Roxy looks up at the lamp. She folds her long fingers together and puts them on the table, head bowed like someone about to start grace. Then she looks at Alma and says, "I have the ability to beat any man down."

Delphine says, "I bet you do, girlie."

Alma nods. "It'll come in handy."

Delphine talks about the girls around courthouse square, some of them married, fallen on hard times, with children at home. She thinks she can round up four or five nice ones, good girls, who would like a clean place—not to stay, just to do their business, out of the weather, out of dark cars on lonesome shoulders of country roads. "I myself am looking for a room to rent, having worn out a welcome with Sir Lee, but they just need a mattress when it starts to get dark. They're good workers, never fall asleep on the job."

Roxy talks about her brothers, her angry father, and how a house of women, of gentleness is where she would most want to be. "I'd be better in a house of women. I'm too tall, too ugly, too much a man to be around men," she says.

The soapy water deepens to a rusty red. Alma rinses and refills the bowl. They throw back their shots and pass the bottle. It eases Delphine some. Her face loosens. Irving pokes around in the kitchen, opens the ice box, and the room is filled with the sourness of old milk. He finds a few pieces of bread and another bin of fruit, cuts out the bad spots with a knife, and makes a little plate for everyone to pick from. Lettie falls asleep, her moist cheek against Alma's chest. The evening is like this, the stifled breeze, the lilting curtains, the wizened food and searing liquor. And it starts to come clear to Alma that she doesn't have to go back to Mrs. Bass, the factory's thunderous clatter. She is a different kind of woman, not just bare-legged and without a man. She is capable of living outside of things. She will never be a typical woman in a housedress, or even a good factory worker. And she will never be poor. Her children will never know to fear the rise of hunger, the feeling of being dazed like smoke-drunk bees to be taken from a dead tree. Her children will be plump on meat because she's more like the Mule-Faced Woman, more like the nun, living apart from the world, just enough—not like her stubborn mother. She realizes she may no longer be the nigger-lover's daughter, now that her mother is dead, but that it was a gift to be that girl, now grown into this ripe body, and her mother did give her that, an angry defiance. She was a strong woman, and Alma will be even stronger. She hears herself thinking, *What would Henry think?* And she likes it. A spitefulness. He may think that he's going to become rich and return in a gold car, but she will not need him. She will raise her children alone, fiercely.

Alma lets Roxy drive Delphine into town. It's nearly morning, but Delphine is antsy for something to help her sleep. She's a fiend of some sort, and Alma thinks it's a shame, her being so young. Alma doesn't know where you'd get something like opium or heroine or morphine, but she's sure there are places, and she allows the two of them to go off to find it. Lettie is asleep on the sofa and Irving is stretched out on the rag rug. Alma stands in her mother's bedroom. When the sun from the window slips in, she watches it light her mother's dead body, the brass buttons of her wool coat aglow. A whorehouse, is it so different from the hosiery mill? The on and off and on and off of stockings? Is it so different from running a boardinghouse of show people and their old bear? Is it so different from growing a crop? Except that its harvest relies on something more dependable than sun and rain: lust, weakness. The world has a generous, unending supply.

Part Two

1

*L*ettie still sleeps with her mother, who's grown bigger but not softer or more rounded. Her hip, in fact, juts up in the bed when she lies on her side, like a giant, squared, fleshy box. This was once the room her parents shared, and she can always feel that past in it even though Lettie can hardly remember her father, just his large swaying presence. She remembers him the same way she remembers Realdo, Mr. Bucci's bear, this large, furry, giant-toothed creature, something she was equally in love with and afraid of. In fact her father and the bear are more strongly linked in her memory than her father and mother. Most likely because the bear died just before her father left, and so they seemed to share death—in the way that it equals disappearance, at least. Now her mother sits at her small desk, counting money, a solitary figure, always bent like this to her coins and bills, this constant sorting and stacking. But even with her back turned, Lettie feels the heat of her mother's attention. Cloying, damp, Lettie feels soaked in it.

She is fifteen. She sits up in bed, wanting to tell her mother that she should have her own room. But it's a tired discussion. She knows full well what the answer will be, a matter of cost. From behind each of the bedroom doors at night, she can hear the *ching, ching, ching* of bedsprings. Her mother hears money in it, and if it weren't fat her mother's body was holding onto, Lettie is sure that she would weigh herself down with coins and bills. Lettie wouldn't be surprised if her mother kept money strapped to her body in some hidden spot. She knows her mother is afraid without it, that she gets skittish when the rooms are empty because the girls have headed to Sugar Hill in Wheeling at convention time. The Italians who've crowded the valley just down the road, and the miners, and a few men from town—a stray banker, an odd widower—she treats them all like old friends when they're here, when she's in the mood to go downstairs and shake hands and smile. She needs to make sure they're all happy. If one of them complains in winter that the house is drafty, she'll crank open the register with a yank on the pulley to open the damper and flood the house with heat—something she'd never do for Lettie or for any of the girls. *Put on a sweater,* she'd say. Lettie isn't allowed to go downstairs once it's dusk and the men straggle in. She has to stay in her room. But she can hear her mother's voice, false with camaraderie, ebullient, punctuated by loud *ha-ha-ha*'s, as if she thought any of it was the least bit funny.

No, Lettie has to stay away, held by the stern eye of her mother's love. It wasn't always this way. She remembers her mother before her parents left for Florida, her mother's love hazy, a thinly stretched blanket. But afterward, without their father, her love tightened. It bore down on Lettie and Irving; even Willard, living at the orphanage, was fixed in her intense attention, as if their father had been siphoning off more love than was his share and without him, there was finally enough for her children, or, perhaps, she was making up for the lack of a father. Lettie knew that her mother barely remembered her own father. And yet her love was the kind that a stranger might not recognize right off. There was a curtness to Alma, but the children could feel it, the fixedness underneath, and to anyone who knew them, it was plain, a festering kind of love that ripens sickly from a deep, infuriate sore.

Lettie doesn't despise the men who come to her mother's house. In fact, sometimes she pretends her father is among them. She listens to the hoot and clomp, the deep bass voices, and chooses one to latch on to and follow. Fathers have become strange to her. She's seen them in town, Sunday-dressed, leading stiff processions into churchyards, their furred necks shaven to a bright pink. But she sees them here, too, where they come to crow and fuck. They're big, loud. They wipe their wet hands on their backsides and rattle up spit from deep in their chests, bearlike; they moan sometimes in such a way from the bedrooms that she thinks it is Mr. Bucci's bear, revived. Sometimes she pretends that the men downstairs are a houseful of fathers just for her, joyful, rowdy, all clamoring to see their little girl—how could they have strayed and stayed away so long? She turns their desire, the real palpable lust that rises darkly in the house, a lusty ulcer, feverish and inflamed, into some kind of paternal love. She has created the notion that her mother doesn't run a whorehouse but an orphanage for wayward fathers. This is when she hates her mother for not letting her downstairs to claim her father from the abundant choices.

It isn't as if she doesn't know the workings of the house— two dollars for straight sex, five dollars for oral sex, and for the Mr. Pansies, the old men who want to French-kiss and sample the girls by taste, it's six dollars, because the girls hate it. They say it ruins them for their dates with their boyfriends later on. She's heard of the man who paid extra to have tomatoes thrown at his bare rump. Her mother takes half of all of it, but the girls make double here what they do on the streets, so it isn't terribly unfair. Delphine costs more—she knows that, too—because she's the queen. She doesn't go downstairs to circulate among the men, looking for a date. They come to her. Lettie knows by now the workings of the girls' vinegar-and-water douches, tinged red from droplets of iodine, that Dr. Sevras says will ward off the cancers. She knows when a girl drinks water clouded with baking soda that she's got a problem with having to pee all the time, and that a thin cloth doused with witch hazel can take the sting out if a girl is raw from sex. Once one of the men had a boil in a sensitive spot, and a girl told Lettie how she fixed it up with a rubbing of Snake Oil and pressing of a salt meat square.

Lettie knows about the liquor, too. She goes to the drugstore and buys fifteen cents' worth of Dr Pepper syrup in a cup, so that her mother can taint the cheap white whiskey to make it look charred, charging twenty-five cents instead of fifteen. Lettie knows how to shake a jar of moonshine and count how long the beads float to test its quality. There's no way to keep it all from her.

Just earlier today, for example, two of the younger girls peeked in on her. They'd just gotten in from a trip to the pictures with a man named Kirby Dent, whom they both are crazy for. "Which one does he like best?" Lettie asked them. And one of the girls piped up quick, "This one," she said, cupping her left titty, and they all laughed, Lettie, too. It made her feel a part of things. Her mother would have shushed and shooed them if she'd been nearby.

Sometimes Lettie thinks her mother would prefer her to live forever in this room, to turn into a woman like Roxy and Delphine who love other women and never have a normal life. But Lettie is aware of that other normal world. On her way to the drugstore for syrup, for example, she passes the Kit Cat Hat Shop on High Street, and she pauses at the glass front to watch the women bustle. She's aware of the door you can push open that jangles a little bell, and when you leave, you're swinging a hatbox on your arm. It is a world that goes on right alongside this one without ever touching it. She would like that, a hatbox swinging on her arm. She would like to meet a man who's never heard of whores and thinks of love as starched linens and clockwork, pure and clean, that love is a wedding day and a house to move into. But she doesn't live in that world. She doesn't even know people who do. When everyone finally goes home at night—the drunken men and her mother's girls toting their satchels, the house is quiet, just the four of them—Roxy, Delphine, Lettie, and her mother. Lettie pretends that it's a normal house, quiet by the side of the road. Who would look twice at it? She finds herself wishing for a simple mother, detached and happy. One who takes her to town to buy hats, for example, who would gasp at the mention of prostitution, the kind who wears tight fixed buns and belongs to some sort of gardening club.

Lettie also hesitates to ask her mother about her own room, because she wonders if she would truly want to sleep by herself. She remembers clearly the night her mother came home alone from Florida, the night they found her grandmother dead, how Lettie fell asleep on her mother's lap, and she didn't dream of the awful hand, the body drowning beneath it, but only of the smell of sheet cake, a picnic spread out in the grass. At the convent, she'd dreamed of the hand every night. She remembers that she'd never seen the dock before, but she must have. She must have seen the dock and then tailored the dream to it. Now and then, especially when her mother stays up late—helping one of the girls after a fight with their boyfriend, their lousy husband, or after a drunk spell or, as with Delphine, worse than drunk—Lettie goes to sleep alone and the dream returns. Even though her mother's body is a heavy magnet in the dream, Lettie is drawn away from her dense calves and rump, the cake, away, to the dock. Sometimes she bends over the guardrail and the hand is there, pleading with its outstretched fingers, begging her to stay, just to stay and be with it. It is needy, after all, desperate, and Lettie understands that.

The house is full tonight. Her mother doesn't like there to be too many girls. It just runs into trouble. Lettie figures there are four or so girls downstairs who take turns hustling men up, and Delphine stays in her own room. And there may be ten men, now. Not all of them come for sex. There are a few regulars who come to drink around the kitchen table and just have the girls sit on their laps while they play cards. Lettie can hear the men downstairs where Roxy serves them drinks, sometimes enough so that they can't really have a date upstairs. They can't even find their way to one of the rooms. Roxy does this best, goading them into drinking, twenty-five cents for one charred shot. It's her way of protecting Delphine, though everyone knows Delphine doesn't want to be taken care of.

Below, someone is pumping the player piano, "Mistress Mumbo Jumbo Jijjiboo J. O'Shea." She misses the show people who could play what you asked them to. Not the same rote songs again and again. "In My Sweet Little Alice Blue Gown" makes Pearly, one of the girls, cry every time. And how many times can you sing along to "K-K-K-Katy" and "Blues My Naughty Sweetie Gives to Me"? High heels clatter down the hall. A door slams. A headboard is banging against a wall. It's noisy, the low chatter, the stark rising giggle, all darkly lit. The house smells of perfume—Gardenia and Evening in Paris—the men's bay rum aftershave, alcohol, of some deep earthiness. The women, their bare arms, languid, or jittery, their full bodies shift under their thin dresses. It's sensuous, full, wet, bluish, shrill, and humming—that's what Lettie thinks of it all. If she could eat the house, it would taste too sweet, a fruit loose in its skin, fat and soft with bruises.

She says to her mother, "Irving had his own room before he left. It was hot as a box, but it was his own! Why can't I have my own?" Irving has been on his own for two years, running a laundry truck, diapers and damp wash. When he lived in the house, he was allowed to come and go as he pleased, usually opting to bang out the front door before the first john showed up. None of the children have been able to escape the tense interior that they've inherited from their mother. Irving can be somber, shy, but has an intensity, as if there's a hive within him, a soul as complexly drilled as a honeycomb, sweet and deeply buzzing. Even Willard, who is supposed to be too childlike to have concerns, grows edgy with nerves, picks at his scalp when the clouds hunker, doomed to rain. And Lettie is the most nervous. But the boys have been lucky—both have been allowed to step out of this house as easily as a man shrugging off a wet overcoat. Lettie is a scared girl in a fetid, bawdy house, who is sent upstairs at night to cower and fume in her dark room.

"Irving was the man of the house," her mother says.

"I thought Roxy was the man of the house." Roxy stopped, a long time ago, trying to pattern her own dresses and now wears the clothes that she can buy in her size, overalls, work shirts.

Her mother doesn't look up, doesn't say a word. She doesn't talk about Roxy's business, her heated relationship with Delphine, or anyone's, for that matter.

Lettie keeps on. "Or is it you? Are you the man of the house now?" She once caught her mother wearing her father's clothes, the ones she'd packed away in the dank trunk and shoved under the bed. Lettie woke in the middle of the night and watched her step inside of his pants, his shirt. It was a weakness, she could tell. It was a softness, the way she held herself in the shirt, the sway and rock of her body. It was years ago, maybe around the time they'd heard about the hurricane, but before they got the postcard, the only one they've ever gotten. It said simply, "I'm still alive in Miami. I hope you are alive, too." And an *H* for his name.

That was the only thing about it he wrote himself, Alma told her children, because she knows his handwriting, not this frilly, curly lettering. He'd gotten someone else to write it for him, and who could that have been? The *H* was his.

"Say your prayers and go to sleep."

Lettie flops back into bed with a huff. But she doesn't have time to drift off. There's a sharp knock at the front door, such a rap of knuckles that it rings through the house. It sends a sick pang to her stomach.

Her mother stands up heavily, mustering her strength, and then clips out of the room to head the police off at the front door, where she'll try to hold them by carrying on. Lettie hates the law, the riotous energy they create, the way they stir up the house into a tight, boiling frenzy. She can hear the johns scattering, the back screen door slamming, urgent voices racing off into the field behind the house, the jingle of a belt buckle, like someone's lost calf. The women are clamoring in the bathroom, pouring liquor down sink drains, out open windows.

Lettie is supposed to help, but she never does. She crawls beneath the bed, as usual, and stays there, her elbows propped against the hard wood, and breathes lightly. The trunk is there, too, under her mother's side of the bed. It smells old and musty, the scent she's come to associate with Miami.

Tonight the bedroom door opens, as it often does, and the small clots of dust shift from the abrupt gust of air. She watches the shiny black shoes, their heels, as the officer rummages through drawers. Usually, it's only for show. They don't intend to find anything. Most of the officers like her mother, are customers here from time to time themselves. Twice they returned the liquor to her the next day. They are generally an idle, pompous group who find it too much effort and too demeaning to check under the bed. But this officer is nervous. His narrow shoes clip across the floor. They are tightly laced, new and polished. He rushes around the room, moves the desk, the dresser out from the wall. Suddenly he's back at the bed, the two tips of his shoes. He kneels down, and his face appears inches from Lettie's, which causes her to gasp, sharply. He jumps back.

"Get out from under there," he says.

She shuffles to the side of the bed, rolling out from under the dust ruffle. She stands, brushing dust from her nightgown.

"What the hell were you doing under there?" he asks. "Are you a prostitute? Have you reason to hide like that? Are you a drunkard?"

She looks up then and she recognizes the face, the slight jaw-jutted underbite, the scrabble of hair, sticking up despite being combed and pasted down with some tonic. "I know you," she says.

"No, you don't."

She looks at his bare arms and makes out small scars, white and raised. "You're Sir Lee's boy." The last time she saw him, it was raining. Sir Lee had come to find Delphine and take her back. He pulled up wildly onto the front yard, blew his horn, and started yelling that Delphine was a dirty bitch, a whore, and that Alma owed him money. Lettie watched from an open upstairs window with some of the girls. Delphine yelled that she wasn't going to come. And all the while, Smitty was there in the rain-streaked car, his narrow shoulders hunched up, his eyes wide with fear. Irving walked up from work with his apron over his head to keep the rain off. He heard what Sir Lee was yelling. Irving charged him, his head down and fists wheeling. Sir Lee laid him out with a hard slap, his ring cutting open Irving's lip. Roxy cursed him from the porch. And Sir Lee said, "Call off your dog, Delphine. Call off your ugly dog!" And that sent Roxy out, and they fought, mud-soaked and bleeding. Lettie remembers her mother shooting the shotgun off into the sky. Her mother was wearing only her nightgown, clinging, wet, her gun now poised on Sir Lee. And he got in his car and disappeared. And her mother covered her mouth, a stretched intake of breath, and then she started to laugh. She cradled the gun in her arms, and tilted back her head, with the rain coming down on her.

Irving said Sir Lee probably went to California, maybe with Smitty, but a year later Irving said he saw Smitty, downtown, shoving around in a crowd of boys. And now here he is again. Grown into a man, an officer, no less, with a belt of bullets and a gun in a leather case, and his shiny new shoes.

"I'm not Sir Lee's boy. Do I look like a boy to you?"

"No," Lettie says. And now she realizes that she's wearing only her nightgown. She's aware of the rise of her breasts beneath it. And she doesn't wear underpants to bed. All the girls believe in letting your parts air in the night. They've taught Lettie many things about the body. She crosses her arms, smooths her hair. She usually rats it on top to give her height, but now it's flat. Her hair is mousy and thin, a pale brown. She touches the ends and then batts them back over her shoulders. "But don't you remember? Sir Lee and his car in the rain that night?"

Smitty pulls out his billy club, turns, and cracks it down on her mother's desk. The coins jangle from their piles; some fall down to the floor. He keeps an eye on Lettie as he does it. She jumps at the loud noise. He smiles. "Let's not talk about things such as that." He's soft now. "What do you say? Huh? What do you say, doll?"

He isn't like anyone she knows. It's like the bear, when he'd show his giant teeth, and she'd shudder and draw back and then realize it was only putting on a show, was about to put on his top hat and start dancing for her. He is a wayward boy who has made his way back to this reversed orphanage, fatherless, like she is. She feels heat across her chest, a blush rising in her cheeks. "Okay," she says. "All right."

The captain takes Alma out for a drive. Once, in the beginning of it all, she let him lie on top of her, rub up against her, in the back of the police car. He grunted, hefting his big body, thrusting his belly with the muscles in his shrunken buttocks until he came, lurching, breathless, on the folds of her hitched-up dress. And then he was embarrassed by the way she lay there, regarding him listlessly. He tucked in his penis, snaillike, a little slick and shrunken, a soft nub of okra, and tightened his belt.

But she was younger then, just a slip of a thing. Now she has extra padding, a certain toughness. If he were on top of her again, she figures she wouldn't quite feel it somehow. Hopes, at least, that that would be true. But honestly, it would never happen again. It's clear. He wouldn't dare try anything beyond his coarse come-ons, all talk. He still likes to make a show, and so every now and then there is this ritual. The road twisting in the headlights, his hand resting on his hard belly, then spread on the seat between them. And there's always the foul flirtation at the end of it all. She knows to wait for it.

Tonight he begins this way, neighborly: "I like you, Alma. I always have. And I know about your past, of course I do. I'm in charge around here. Your husband is most likely just another bindle stiff by now, riding blind baggage. And I knew your daddy before he left. Hell, I even knew the nigger." He has a sweaty chin, and he scratches at it. "And I'm here to tell you, Alma, it doesn't need to be like this. I'm here to tell you that you can track down that husband, divorce him, and marry an upstanding citizen of this good state of ours. You are still an attractive woman. You don't want to become an old worn-out bawd. Do you hear what I'm saying?"

She doesn't respond. She knows she'd be no good at wifery anymore. She likes to think she's outgrown it, but really she'd be forever suspicious, always keeping an eye out for the beginning of the end, questioning the full tank of gas, the reason why he came home from the opposite direction. She has imagined Henry settled down with the woman who wrote the postcard for him to sign with his turdy little *H*, a stiff-legged letter, narrow as a rickety house. An educated woman who perhaps takes care of him, who knows vaguely about Alma and the kids. Maybe she is the one who insisted he send the card, who whispered, *I can't imagine wondering if you were alive or dead.* Alma pictures, too, how he might arrive in the yard one night, call up to her bedroom window. She would pull the trunk from under the bed, push it out the open window, and watch it shatter into splintered boards nearly missing his head, and then, after almost killing him, she would take him in. And how she would make him pay and pay until the very air between them was cluttered with promissory notes, too much for him to ever be able to afford. Still, truthfully, she expects him back. It is this ugly, hated hope, this unshakable conviction that he will appear in the yard, call to her window. And no matter how much attention and work her life requires, each moment that slips without him is a small disappointment, a water-worn hollow inside of her that the Monongahela swells into, shrinks from, and then immediately refills with hope. His absence has a force, this constant river of hope and disappointment in her heart, ignorant of her levees, locks, and dams. She is always attempting navigation. Sometimes, for example, she'll wake up and expect his hand to curve over the soft dip of her stomach. She wonders if his body forgets where it is while he sleeps, and if his muscles and bones don't hold a deeper memory and are shocked not to rise up next to her warm backside. But she tries not to think these thoughts. She veers from them, sets her mind to the task before her. In winter, she puts her two feet on the cold floorboards and strides to the basement, opens the furnace's heavy latched door, to stir the dull glowing coals, to shovel new lumps into the smoldering fire, to open the damper to let the house warm. In summer, she dresses to tend the garden before the sun kicks in. An oversize hat, thick cloth gardening gloves, and then back to start breakfast, a pan slick with grease, the eggs whitening, firming, snapping at their edges. And always she is consumed by her children. Once she'd imagined them circling, hands held, like an open mouth, but now she has stepped into it. In fact—how could she have ever imagined this?—she dove. She has let her children consume her, and she is forever falling, headfirst, down their collective gullet.

The captain says, "I don't abide that indolence! I expect you to say *yes, sir* when I'm talking to you. I could put you in jail, and you know that. You know that!" He's getting worked up, spitting as he talks. Digs at his wet chin. "I know what you all do. And I know there's a need, and you are filling that need. Taking a burden off the good women of these parts sometimes, the way I see it. Keeping them from getting too worn out by these pruny men, always rollicky with lust. They come out shouting, 'I'm a curly-tailed wolf with a pink ass and this is my night to howl!' I've seen enough of them. One of these days, you and your girls are going to get into trouble. It's just a fact. And I am not going to help you out of it! I will sit back, mark my words, and I will say that I told you to get out while you could. I told you that, Alma. Do you hear me now?"

She wants to tell him there are families starving out on the farms, ghosts stalking their own dusty land, mines closing down, to leave their scarred, blackened men to skitter, and here he is getting after her, and the few men who can still afford to pinch one of her girls. Her house is a good one. If the men want something dirty, they can head out to Sugar Hill. She keeps things in line. She's often thought that if her father knocked at the door one day, older, a little oiled from the bottle, battered by some long other life, she would pretend not to recognize him, and she would be happy to send him upstairs with Pearly—sweet, sappy, chatterbox Pearly—and he would be taken care of, gently, lovingly, his deformed tongue politely ignored. She profits from men's weaknesses. It seems better than the other options: simply enduring, or ignoring, or falling prey to them. "Yes, sir," Alma says, flatly. "Yes, sir, I do, sir."

He pretends not to notice her tone, taking the words for what they are. "Well, now that we have it straight." He turns the car around to circle back now that he has won her agreement.

Alma has no patience for him—or for any man, really. There's only one kind, the itchy kind, even her own Irving—so sweet and good, he's still a man, and there's nothing she can do about it; he's taken up with that hussy, Lucy, gone—and Willard . . . well, he will remain a boy. That's his blessing and curse. Captain can say what he wants, but she isn't interested in marrying a good citizen of this state of ours. She prefers to be called a housemaid and proprietor. She scrubs out the sheets, the bloodstains drinting under the press of cold water. She wipes boot-tracked dirt off the floors on her hands and knees. She beats the rugs, Vaseline smeared on her nostrils to keep the billowed dust from clogging her nose. She keeps her books, tidy rows of numbers and dates. Yes, she's a whisper sister, and a good one, who always checks the liquor's beading, who isn't above slipping in a dash of cola syrup to make it look charred, selling it for more. And she's a bawd. She's taken two girls, knocked up, to Dr. Sevras's back room in the middle of the night to get scraped. *Slinking,* the girls call it, too soft a word, Alma thinks. The nurse, too smiley, dauncy in her little cap, saying, "Keep your dobbers up. It'll be over soon." Alma's life is ugly sometimes, but simple and consuming. She has learned to despise men and their urgent needs. She has always remembered the Mule-Faced

Woman, has often thought of the Mule-Faced Woman's mother, who—according to the tiny woman who took her nickel for the show—was forced to have sex with a mule. Then, it was shocking, but not now. She believes it to be absolutely true, easily true. She's heard of worse. And she would no sooner give her body to a man now than to a mule.

The captain pulls the car up in the driveway. He nods instead of saying good night to her, hisses, "You must get lonesome up there. Or do you take in a man now and then yourself?" His face is purplish in the dark, his cheeks high up, shining like two bulbs.

"I have no interest in this grunt work called sex. I'm no punch-hole to be punched." She opens the door, gets out, slams it.

The captain's men are lined up, waiting for him, some chatting up the girls who look down from the porch. He calls to her, "It's a shame, there, Alma, to let all that go to waste!"

She stomps up the steps, aware of the swish of her backside, unable and unwilling to try to contain it. She tells the girls to get inside. She says over her shoulder, "Show's over." She shuts the door.

The girls, five or so, bustle around her. "Are you okay?" "What did he make you do?" "That fat old son of a bitch." She hates the close-knit circle. She can feel the heat off their bodies, their breath in her face. She turns away and spots Charlie Holman sitting on the love seat. His drunk, dull eyes rove slowly around the room, one strap of his overalls unhitched, a frayed hat in his lap. He's one of Delphine's regulars. An old miner who suffered a stroke, he's usually carried in on somebody's back and set down like a sack. Roxy is often the one who carries him upstairs to Delphine's room when he's had enough to drink, although it's clear Roxy despises him. One side of the old man's face is still alive with nerves, puckering, tightening and untightening, as he works at a wad of chewing wax, while the other is slack, soft, a silent gentleman, a jowly banker, perhaps, who should be wearing a boutonniere on the lapel of a dark suit. His face reminds Alma of the half-man–half-woman at the carnival. The outfit a suit and dress sewn together, one set of eyelashes, one half of a thin mustache. Her mind is a wheel that churns without her say. And it's worse when the old man talks. Just now, he says, "I don't see how I'm going to make it home this evening." Half of his mouth moves with a cinched tightness, hard-working lips, stitching that draws them up and loosens them into words, and the effort always makes Alma think of her father with his clipped tongue. She tries to avoid Charlie Holman because he flares the recollection of her missing father.

"Hopefully one of the boys will come back for you. Or you could pay to stay on," she offers.

"Do you have any more horse liniment, Miss Alma?"

"I don't think you need another drop. You're lit up like a store window. You're nearly burning with a blue flame."

He hiccups, gives a small belch. His eyes water. She hopes

he doesn't throw up or start to cry. The men do that sometimes, get drunk and dissolve into a fit of tears.

She turns to the girls. "The night's over. You can go on home now." She thinks quickly of the farmer who used to call in his cows at the end of the day. The farmer has since sold off all but one, and it's skinny with sores, a dry coat, sunken eyes. It pains her to see it in the field, stark and lonesome, a frail ghost of the buttery herd that once was. Alma sees something of herself in it still. Once she'd been fit to spill over, she was so full of something, and now there's this single sickly cow. The girls have started to shift, gather things up. Some head upstairs to collect their things. Others shamble toward the door. "Where's Delphine?"

One of the girls, an ugly one whom the men seem to favor, points upstairs. "She went to her bedroom and shut her door."

Alma knows this means she's taken out her bamboo pipe and is setting to smoke as many pills as she needs. Alma has imagined how Delphine got hooked on hop, lounging in Chinatown's opium dens, a young starlet whore. Sometimes Delphine talks about the sweet smoke, how she was taught to burn each pill, the gob hardening, and how she was smart then. She could see the intimate clicking of each tiny creature bustling to create the entire world. She could hold onto that one thought even while she was having sex with some gangster. Alma likes to listen to Delphine talk. She doesn't want to smoke, but she understands weakness. She knows what it is to want to give in, and she lives her life in some small resistance. To what, exactly, she isn't sure. Part of it is Henry's dogged presence. She isn't sure how someone can be more present because of their absence, and yet she finds Henry everywhere, a cupboard he nailed shut as a quick fix, the laggardly squeak of his closet door, the closet now filled with Lettie's drop-waist dresses and swishy crinoline, the dip in the yard where he buried the bear, a mound that has collapsed, and their bed, the dull singular clank of the metal headboard as she lowers herself, a podgy weight, onto it. Mostly, when the house is quiet, she imagines his loping through another room, on the other side of a wall, just having slipped past a doorjamb. But Henry is only a painful symptom of something deeper that she fights moment to moment.

Alma sets to make sure that Lettie is nowhere near Delphine now that she knows she's smoking. She doesn't mind the way Roxy and Delphine have taken up like husband and wife. There's no need to protect Lettie from something as pure as love and devotion, even if it isn't the standard fare. Alma's Aunt Faye, who was so frail, had fallen in love with her teacher, an older woman, or so Alma's mother said. Faye became bookish because of her. The teacher then moved away and left Faye, with her sickly heart, one that Alma's mother thought to be corrupted by the romantic notions in books. Aunt Faye never married and died young, shortly after Alma's mother took the two of them to the beach, and Aunt Faye was so unnerved by the screeching gulls. It never bothered Alma that a woman could love a woman or two men, for that matter, one white and one black. (Had her mother ever really loved her father?) It seemed so miraculous that people could fall in love and stay together, so mysterious, why bother with the details once it's happened? But Alma doesn't like Lettie to see Delphine high. And she hated it when Irving was still living in the house, because he admired Delphine so, was in love with her, she guesses. And now he's got his own whore in that little Lucy. It's Alma's fault. How could it not be? He grew up in this house long enough to wear a soft spot for these loose, tireless hustlers, with their weak eyes and thick-muscled hearts. His picture sits on the mantel, so cocky one foot's on the laundry truck's runner, wearing his delivery suit, chalked white whenever it was smudged. He has missed Sunday dinner. She wonders when she'll hear from him with his well-practiced excuse. He always has a good one, often Lucy with her headaches. Even if it's not true, she appreciates the attempt. Willard is gone, for the better, certainly. And Irving has left her, too. Sometimes Alma knows it was not purely her desire to keep food on her children's plates that urged her to be a madam. It was something closer to spite. She likes to think it was only for them, a sacrifice, but her heart knows better; it kicks up, sputters like a gasoline engine.

Alma hopes that Roxy is there in the room with Delphine. "You seen Roxy?" she asks Pearly, the sentimental one with the mean husband who takes her money and then slaps her for being a whore.

"She's up with Delphine." Alma can tell Pearly is hoping there will be a story—she's a blatherskite who loves to pass things around—she should know she won't get a tale from Alma.

Alma heads upstairs, knowing that Lettie is probably still under the bed. Fifteen and she hasn't yet outgrown her girlhood nervousness. Alma shouldn't have ever gone off and left her as a child. She shouldn't have ever agreed to go to Miami after a trunk, in the first place. But for all the good that the orphanage did for Willard—who now tends an entire garden that stretches the length of the building—it did as much damage to Lettie. As Alma walks up the stairs, she can hear the bustle below her, the hush above, and she can feel herself bleeding into the house. She becomes a division of rooms, some raucous, some solemn. The toilet's gushes of water, the tug of light-switch chains, the faucet's drip wearing away at the sink's rust spot. Mottled walls, dust, clatter, moths tinking bulbs. She can locate the parlor in her chest, the sun passing through it on an afternoon when no one is there to see it. She closes her eyes a minute, trying to blink the notion from her mind. She has no idea where her notions come from and why they are so stubborn. She thinks deliberately of the predicament of Charlie Holman on her love seat. She wonders how much she will charge him to spend the night there. She wonders if Roxy would be willing to haul him out to the car and drive him home and how much she might charge for that. She thinks of her stacked money, the sorting of how much she needs to live on and then the extra that she divides three ways for her children so they will always have enough even if she catches consumption and dies. She often thinks of her death, afraid of how it would set her children loose in the world. She left them once, and she never wants to do it again. Her love for her children is so sharp, a constant pang of worry. She attempts to cast it off casually, but it must be apparent. She feels afire.

When Alma nears her bedroom door, she thinks she hears Lettie's voice, a hushed whisper. She opens the door and Lettie ducks in the window so fast she knocks the back of her head. Lettie rubs the sore spot. The money piles are a mess, Alma's coins scattered all over the desk and floor.

"What happened here?"

"I got nervous," Lettie said. "I knocked it with my hip and it fell to pieces like that."

"It did, did it? Were you talking to someone?"

"No."

Alma doesn't want to think her daughter is lying to her. She doesn't want to think that there may have been a boy below her window. She refuses to think of her adoration of Henry at Lettie's age, having sex between rows of her mother's corn. But everything changes. Time trudges. Her mother's corn, for example, no longer ends in rows next to an old wooden derrick. There's a tank field now, newly built, shaped like silos, but giant, wrapped in stairways, squatting in a field that once was barley. It all becomes too complicated if she entertains the notion that her daughter is turning into a woman in a house like this. Alma can feel her life rising up for new consideration, but she prefers the way she has been for years now: A morning goes by and then an afternoon. Eventually there's evening. She sleeps. She is within it all, desperately so, and she doesn't have to think beyond it. Sometimes at night, falling asleep, she's aware of the trunk beneath her bed, still filled with junk, woolens, and swollen, faded books, and she has added the clothes Henry left behind. It is a heavy, dense relic of loss, but even then she has learned to sleep above it. She is proud of how close it is and how she has learned to ignore it. She is strong. Each moment demands her attention, and she gives it more than it deserves, so she doesn't have to step back, outside, and watch. She was a woman on a dock in Miami, a woman who was aware of everything, and it did her no good. Now she is a woman surviving. She prefers to work in the details of that survival, never to enlarge, never to see something like the passage of time. Lettie is just a child still, Alma thinks, just a foolish girl who gets scared when the police come to the door, so scared and foolish she can knock into a desk. Alma doesn't want to look at her standing there. She's too tall, her breasts filling out, becoming plump on her chest. Her face is thinning, lengthening into a woman's face.

"Well, help me gather them up." And the two of them kneel, plucking coins from the floor.

*   *   *

Delphine is preparing her ceramic bowl, her bamboo stem, her lamp, needle, and knife. She feels good and thinks that if she could always have days like this, where the men come and go and she doesn't seem to feel too much, holding onto the warm-chestedness of opium, then she could be generous. She could love each one of them, in a way, the men and the other girls here, too, everyone, even Herbert C. Hoover, for God's sake. But there are other days, dark, her soul clustered with meanness, and even when she feels good, almost kind, almost clean, she knows it won't last. Sometimes there are voices. Sometimes she feels ghostly, as if her clothes are no more than things hung on a line, wind-kicked, and the voices are more real than she is.

Roxy, on the other hand, is very real, her body a solid mass, as thick, in parts, as a tree. She sits on the edge of the bed, her elbows on her high-up knees, and when she's in that pose, it makes Delphine think of her daddy, head hung low, worrying. He used to have rituals, too, before preaching, almost like this. Delphine lights the lamp, starts to sing "Nearer My God to Thee," which always recalls a certain gangster she loved, who could make a horn sing. Once when he was in jail, a Salvation Army band came along to play its lurching hymns, the women in those ghastly black bonnets and the men in their military caps, "soldiers for Christ." He said, "I been saved. I feel I can play that horn. I feel God inside me." And the Christian gave it to him, and he blew the ass off of "Nearer My God to Thee." Last she heard, he'd made friends with the paid prison cook so that he could get his hands on the juice runoff from the canned fruit to ferment and get a liquor ring going. She misses him. It starts up. It's enough to churn her stomach, to cause her mind to race. It's summer now, and everything should be bursting forth, the whole world, flowering toward some colossal outpouring of— what? Love, almost, something like it. But these days, since the droughts, the crash, there's an odor of death always hanging in the air. It was there before, a hint, but now it's grown with the conviction of documented disaster. The gangster is probably dead by now, but she aches for the old dens in Chinatown, a bustle of wrongheadedness, bad decisions, glorious lies. Sharpers, pool-hall hustlers, gamblers, failing actors, young gangsters as sweet of face as he was, wires, yeggs, and women, like her. Not immoral or bereft, not just these whores here in this house with their douches who hope nothing slips by their Dutch caps, whores because there's nothing else for them to be. No, she misses those who see life swelling right in front of them and who can't be orderly and polite about living. Those in need of something more than the deliberate world with its truth, with its workaday tedium. She's always despised the gainfully employed, with their pride and their contented lunch breaks—her father, for example, tidying the pews Sunday afternoons, and her sister, Eloise, a schoolteacher, grading papers late into the night. Without it, they jump out of windows, just like last fall, droves of them! As if the world weren't enough, just to be in it.

Her mother, well, her mother is more like her, although she won't admit it. Her mother calls it nerves, but really it's her aching soul that seems to contain her knowledge that the earth is more important than heaven, if there is such a thing at all as heaven, and here her mother sits just wasting time when she could be—what? Fucking and singing, pulling fruit from trees. And her mother must act just so. She must wear her gloves and hat, her girdle, but there's nothing to contain her soul, except her medications, so precious. Delphine understands that. She and her mother are just alike. If her mother could allow just one transgression, then her life would unravel, and she knows it. They both do. And couldn't her mother easily find herself a grateful whore in this odd house in love with this gargantuan woman, this oversize saint?

Sometimes her mind prattles on like this, a tumble of words. Has she been talking out loud? There's the memory of a whisper in her throat, but she isn't sure what she's said or whether she's just been singing softly. Roxy is quiet, thoughtful. She's a tender soul who will sometimes put fresh flower petals in Delphine's pillowcase to make it smell sweet. She doesn't smoke. She tried it once—threw up and swore off it. "You lack the necessary determination to be a good hop addict," Delphine told her.

Roxy lets her go on and on, lets her give her little speech to the men who come to her. "I'm the Grand Arms Hotel. Always open. Always a vacancy." She lets her smoke as many pills as she wants. "It's the sweetest birth control in the whole wide world, Roxy. I haven't bled in years!" Delphine would love company, but she knows Alma would throw her out if she so much as offered some to one of the girls. Delphine doesn't like to do it alone, and so she asks Roxy just to sit with her, to watch and talk. She knows she'd be better off if she switched to morphine, like so many fiends. Shut herself up in a room. There'd be no need for all of this preparation. Only a delivery boy from the drugstore on a bike. Her needles, $1.25 a box, shipped to the doorstep by Sears and Roebuck. But she prefers the old Chinaman's wife, nodding and shuffling. Broken English and an exchange. She likes all of the things she must care for in the process, a tenderness for the act, a sacredness. Nothing so barren, so sterile as a pinch in the arm.

Delphine dips the needle into the bottle, then tries to steady the glob over the lamp. Her hands are shaky. They've been shaky for as long as she can remember. As the opium bubbles, swells, doubling and tripling in size, she recalls dropping her mother's butcher-wrapped meat off a trestle bridge over the coal-clouded Monongahela. It was iced over. The meat skidded, leaving a pink trail of blood. Her mother made her climb down through the iced reeds to retrieve it. Her mother, her scarf wrapped around her throat to hide the goiter, nearly as large as a baseball, at the side of her throat. The ice cracked, splintered. The river's jaws opened and set to swallow her whole. Her dress and coat ballooned for a moment. Her legs froze, instantly, the water inching up her coat. She clawed at the ice, and then saw her mother, who'd been so angry before, now terrified, coming at her on her belly like a seal. She grabbed her hand and pulled her back, the toes of her boots digging in behind her. Was Eloise there? She must have been, looking down on it, perhaps from the end of the bridge, thinking, even then, that it's unfair how the careless ones get more desperate love.

"I'm as devout as a Turk, as well-practiced as a Chinaman. It's been a long day. Don't you think? Are you happy, Roxy? Are you mad with me again? Don't be. Don't be always mad with me. I don't like the way you look at me sometimes."

Roxy shakes her head. "I don't have to say it again."

"Nope, you don't." Delphine doesn't want to hear that she can change her life, that she and Roxy can pack up and go somewhere else and start all over again. Or she could even clean up right here, just stop taking in men, stop smoking. See if they can work out a deal with Alma. Delphine anticipates the high. She can already taste a sweetness, feel the tightening of her lungs and a certain warmth spreading out from her chest. Delphine rolls the opium, now cooked, in the bowl until it becomes a small pill. "It's a loud world, too bright, too colorful. Don't you think? Sometimes these men come in, and I wash them down. I squeeze their tips to see if anything comes out, if they're sick, and their meat is so pink and thick a thing, with its blue veins, ticking away from their hearts above. It's too much. They're too alive, if you know what I'm saying. We're all just too goddamn alive."

"I don't like to hear about it," Roxy says. "You know I understand you. You don't have to talk about them men's bodies."

Delphine looks over at Roxy, her wide eyes, her long face heavy with big bones. "I wasn't saying it to make you feel bad. You know it's just the way I am. I say what is there in my mind. I couldn't do that before with the men I was with. But I can with you, Roxy. It's like being with another part of myself." And this is the truth. When they are in bed together, it isn't like being with a man at all. It's like doubling herself—more than doubling, because Roxy is so large. When they are wrapped together, Delphine recalls all of the stories of Roxy's youth—you'd think it was sorrow that made her grow so tall if you'd heard all Delphine has heard—and Delphine feels that by taking Roxy in her arms, she's making her whole again and, in so doing, saving herself a little, too, because there's finally something worth saving, goodness, redemption. Isn't that a kind of love? She's known too many to count. So far, this is the best. Making love to Roxy is nothing like having sex with men, which always seems, even in its best moments to be more about struggle. She walked in on one of the girls with a man, just a few weeks back, and she had to stop herself from calling out. She can no longer recognize the difference between passion and a fight. Delphine knows that she hurts Roxy, but whenever she begins to feel guilt, it's always consumed by anger. Delphine can hear herself thinking, *Roxy*

signed on to this wreck. She knows what I am: a whore, a fiend.
She can't be angry about it now. She says, "I'd prefer to be
called a piece of calico. I like that expression, but I'm a
clapped-out hole. That's the truth of it. And I'm having a
good day." There's a catch in Delphine's voice. She despises
it. Her father always talked about Jezebel, thrown from her
window for being whorish, her body trampled by horse
hooves, torn up by wild dogs till there was nothing to bury.
But Delphine imagines that she would have buried what
she found if she'd come across Jezebel, even if it were the
body parts of a stranger—the dead are all strangers. A hand
pressed to dirt, a fine rib, an arch, an ankle, a tilted pelvis
tipping light like milk. Delphine clears her throat. Begins
again. "I'm having a good day. And you know they're rare.
Let me enjoy it."

She forces the pill into the hole in the bowl's center. As
it heats, she remembers how her mother made her walk
home, her dress and coat frozen over, her stockings stiff.
Her mother cuffed her on the head once. Cuffed her good in
front of her father and sent her to the tub. And Delphine
sunk down its rounded sides, let her knees, red and bony as
doorknobs, rise out of the water. She held her breath and
imagined an imbricate skin of ice, the catfish cruising the
river bottom, their whiskers as thick as piano wire, and how
it would be to die, let the water take you in, as the ice above
her head healed over.

She sticks the needle through the hole, withdraws it, then

tilts the pipe until the pill hits the flame. She puts her mouth
to the pipe's long tip, draws the fumes into her throat, her
lungs, holds onto it until there's a giving in, like the first
small gestures one makes before getting undressed, the world
relaxes, steps out of its slip. It's like this. She steps out of her
slip. Roxy puts her head in Delphine's lap. Delphine drinks
the smoke, gulp after gulp, thickly down like honey. She
looks out the window and sees herself reflected and beyond
that, a girl in a dress walking quickly across the yard. A boy
appears, stands out from the bushes. The girl is wearing a
white dress—or is it a nightgown—and Delphine wonders if
it is her own soul she sees, drifting out across the yard.

2

*L*ucy wakes Irving up with a few sharp nudges of her bony fingers on the beef of his bare shoulder. She is a small woman with a narrow waist and tiny hands. Her hair, so dark and shiny it looks greased, is cropped, sharply meeting her jawline. She's wearing a white dress, see-through in its gauziness. With the sun from the window at her back, Irving can make out the dark outline of her body, each thin leg. He puts his hand over his eyes and lies back on the bed. He's angry about the sun. He hates the way she wakes up and opens all of the shutters until the room glows dizzy with light. And then she'll complain about the thick heat, ask him to take her to Cheva's to cool off under their slow fans. She has no sense. Cheva's is still dank and hot, humid with bodies, and stuffy, as if the yeasty beer were constantly rising like bread dough all around them.

It's no wonder he'd been dreaming of heat, the shiny backs of elephants. His mother rarely talked about the trip to Miami. Once, however, he remembers she mentioned an elephant on the docks. He'd heard of circus elephants all the way from Africa where darkies ride them like horses, but he'd never seen one, still hasn't, and, although it's childish, he would like to go to Miami and have a giant gray elephant with wide ribs and a short hairy tail, enormous, to greet him. He'd actually thought of telling Lucy that they should steal the laundry truck—not forever, just for the trip—and go to Miami to see the ocean. Not to find his father. Lucy never knew where his father had gone to, never had asked. The trip would be a way to hold on to Lucy, to delight her, because she needed much delighting. And in the beginning he had delighted her just by swooping her up in his arms and cradling her like an oversize baby. (It reminded him sometimes of Willard, his charge, taken away. He misses the babyish bloat of his face, can't stand to go for visits, to see his brother so walled in and contented. It makes him exhausted by failure.) But Lucy grew sullen and testy, pacing the room, dim when he could persuade her to keep the heat out. He could tell that she was antsy, but he never mentioned Miami. He could never quit his job. He could never steal the truck. He could never disappear on his landlady, Mrs. Trimski, who needed his money each week. He could never tell his mother that on a whim, he took Lucy to Miami. It would be a betrayal, against family rules to even mention Florida.

Lucy wipes her nose, as if she's been crying, but there are no tears, no puffed eyes, only this little display of drama. She says, "I was going to write you a note, but there's no use. I'm off." She picks up her suitcase. It's actually an old empty accordion case. He's never seen the accordion. He asked about it once, but she said it was none of his business. "You'd like it if I said I was heading back to make confections and live at my mother's house where you found me, but I'm not. I'm going to Wheeling, because it's my nature, to turn my hand to the work you hate. Didn't you always expect me to? Didn't you take me in knowing I was on my way somewhere else?" She has one hand on her hip. "This is just like me. Isn't it? And it serves you right. You can tell your mother that she was right about me, too. She never liked me, and I am not so sure that you ever liked me either. Not really."

It doesn't surprise him. He's learned that even in the middle of summer when he feels like he's struggling against the sun, not just to block it out but to try to hoard darkness, even now on a blistering day like today when heat seems as tricky as a leak, the way water can begin in one spot then run along the unseen pipes and beams and pool in another, Irving is always anticipating winter. He knows that the heat will slip away, incrementally, and suddenly a cold will arise and the snow will fall white, like moths, and turn gray, then black as it collects soot from the air. He is always steeling himself for loss. She's right that his mother never liked her, and he decides she's probably right about his affections for her, too. He never really knows if he loves a girl. He doesn't know anything about love. It's a sickness, a malady, something we're doomed by. He wonders if his father loved his mother. It's a difficult thought, because sometimes he feels his father never really existed. He has become a myth, tall and glib, a bear-fighter (although the bear was dead), emphatic and exhausted, glossed to a brilliant shine by Irving's forcible memory. He'll never really know.

Once, though, he learned something new about his father. He saw Smitty on the street, Sir Lee's boy, in a thuggish pack loping down Court Street, not too many blocks from Cheva's Pool Hall. Irving walked right up to him. He said, "Smitty, Smitty. It's me, Irving."

The other boys circled around, but Smitty put up his hand. "Yeah, so what is it, boy? What do you want?"

He could tell Irving was after something. Irving asked him if he'd ever been to Florida when Sir Lee went down to get his trunk, the one that made him enough money to buy that car.

Smitty reared back with his pointy jaw, his sharp angles, laughing. "Sir Lee is a son of a bitch. And you all believed him." He paused. "You still do. He never got a goddamn trunk in Florida. He was running a scam in Biscayne Bay with a guy name of Jake who worked with an old man name of Charlie, who'd gotten a shipment of junk. Jake bought it up, and Charlie would sell it. And every time Sir Lee got some fool to go down there for a trunk, he got a kickback. We were fat on kickbacks all that summer. If you'd've had more money, he'd've sold you a swamp."

Irving was memorizing words—*Miami* and *Biscayne Bay,* *Charlie* and *Jake*—because he thought that once he was a man with his own money, he was going down to Miami and find his daddy. And tell him what? He didn't know. And bring him home? He wasn't sure that was the point of it all, either. Irving has tried not to envision his father, as that kind of imagining is a waste of time, or so his father told him time and again, a warning against sloth and laziness, but sometimes his father's face is almost clear, and he's got a white hat, a cigar in his teeth, a bear-fighter now in Miami, ludicrous. Whenever Irving conjures it up, he scoffs at himself for it.

Irving says to Lucy, "Well, now. There you have it."

She huffs a sigh. "Is that all you're going to say?"

He stands up. "I guess I'm late for work." He walks to his closet and fishes his shirt off its hanger. He gets dressed while Lucy glares at him.

"You look like an idiot in that bow tie! You shouldn't wear it. As if you need a bow tie to take people's dirty laundry! You're as skinny as a Western Union messenger pumping his wobbly bike in his choke rag and knickers." She turns and walks out the door, slamming it behind her. He listens to her feet on the stairs and for the front door to swing open, always hushed by the thick fur rug, and then shut, jingling a leather strap of sleigh bells so the old lady can keep track of who's coming and who's going from the kitchen sink where she smokes cigarettes.

He positions himself by the window, hidden by the line of straight hung curtains, edged with fringe by Lucy in a fit of domesticity, and watches her skitter down the street, her white skirt bouncing behind her like a swinging doggie door, her ass this little flurry of action.

Irving adjusts his bow tie, which now embarrasses him. He thinks of the day set in front of him. He'll pick up and deliver door to door, exchanging clean, folded laundry for dirty and sour. Clothes and linens bunched with sweat, piss, blood. Sheets stained by sex. And he'll hand the ragged homemakers—red-cheeked from working their gardens, entire yards taken over to produce enough to survive on—their damp wash to be ironed. Windblown and breathless, they'll say they can't afford the service. Sometimes they put their hands to their mouths and start to cry. He'll take what money they hand over, but it's hard for him. He wasn't raised to take money from women. He was raised to stay out of their way, to let them take care of themselves. He's afraid of them.

He walks out of his apartment—it still smells like Lucy, a sweet, choking perfume that she would daub everywhere, even on her shiny hair—down the stairs, and up the sidewalk toward High Street. It's morning, but already the day is gathering heat. He squints. Cars jog down the street. The streetcar winds its way around a corner. Two women jostle by, pushing prams with their large metal spoked wheels that squeak. They are maternal and happy, their stomachs bulging like sweet lower pouting lips. He wants to imagine Lettie being a mother one day, chatting idly with another mother about prices, rashes. It's possible. Lettie could rise out of the house. She's a skittish girl, but still good, still whole, a virgin, although he's known more than a couple of men to ask how much for her. Lettie could become a mother, in some other town maybe, like these women—perfect, sturdy, nearly happy. He wants to lie down with them in a large bed, sexless, content. Is there such a thing? He would like to be a father one day, to raise up a baby proudly, the way he'd been doing with Willard before his mother gave him up.

Irving glances into the prams as they pass. Inside one, there's a fat baby, nearly too big for it. In fact the baby is pulling up, both chubby hands on one side, so that the pram leans, tipping unevenly on its large springs. He wants to stop the woman and tell her to mind the baby before it falls out, but he thinks of her face turning on him angrily. He glances in the other pram, hoping to see a tight bundle, but instead there is a brown paper–wrapped ham, its bone sticking out of the top, headless. It makes him feel sick. There's a windy spot at the top of his stomach, an empty fatherlessness. It is repeated each time he is disappointed, even in some small way: a streetcar pulling away as he turns a corner to catch it; expecting a baby and finding instead a ham with an axed bone for a head; Lucy gone.

He wonders why he took her in. Because he's no better

than the men who come to his mother's house or the loud, gusty men at Cheva's or his own father? How could he be? It's all he's known. Perhaps because at first she reminded him of Delphine. He met Lucy at a party. She'd danced barefoot and stepped on a shard of glass. She was bleeding, needing him, and that brought Delphine back to him, the car's jerky gears, the field of deer he saw that night by the roadside. But Lucy turned out to be nothing like Delphine. Lucy is wide-eyed but conniving. She loved to have sex. Sometimes she'd wake him up in the middle of the night, her warm mouth on his dick. She was like that, and then she could fly into a rage because he called her mother a flour girl—which she was, working for Kincaid in one of those puffed white hats—and she would yank a lamp out of the wall, smash it, and fall limp on the bed in tears. He never knew why, and so it was in a way comfortable, because he was afraid of her and yet a little lovesick, and this is how he's always felt about women. Roxy, of course, could snap his neck, but also Delphine and the other whores, even his mother, they all make him nervous. They are ravenous, bitter, and then inexplicably affectionate. The girls will curse you for being too clomping and then kiss your cheeks and lavish you, wriggling on your lap, rapacious and needy. Now, Lucy is headed toward Wheeling, by train, perhaps, to become a whore. He thinks, *Thirst has no season.* It's a Coca-Cola advertisement pasted on drugstore walls all over town, but it seems to him dark and monstrous. It often pops into his mind.

The Madam

Irving walks down a side alley to the back of M and H Delivery. He'd like a pack of Chesterfields, passes a glass storefront with a giant advertisement, working girls with cropped hair . . . CHESTERFIELDS—MILDER, BETTER TASTE. ABSOLUTELY PURE. SMOKE AS MANY AS YOU LIKE. He hasn't gotten paid, lacks the fifteen cents. He feels the warm press of sun on his back. Sweat trickles down his legs. His pants are already damp, his shorts inching uncomfortably. No, he decides, the damage has been done. He'll never fall in love, or, if he does, he won't know it the way a man should, and Lettie will never be a normal woman pushing a pram down the street. They will never shake their childhoods—and not just their missing father, but also their mother with her ugly decisions. His mother will talk about poverty, skinning rabbits and collecting train coal, but, truth, she could have gotten by renting rooms to normal people and working in the mill. She could have refused the nuns' courtesy and brought Willard home, but she didn't. There was something in her that made her arch away from a decent, quiet life. Irving will never understand it, because that's all he wants.

Sammy stands in the dirt parking area. He owns two delivery trucks, stands feet wide, hands on his hips. He's bulbous, with a red nose pitted like a strawberry and scarred cheeks, always slightly grudging and flustered. He's talking to Art, who's already in a truck. Irving recognizes Art's tanned, sinewy arm, hanging out of the window; his other arm, pale, is out of sight.

Sammy yells out, "Irving, right there. It's full. You owe me a morning's loading." He points to a truck. "I left money on the seat. It needs gas. Go south first and then tank up, loop back. Your check's there, too, on the seat." He gives a wave to Art, then disappears into the back door, where he'll jaw at the workers, women in aprons pinned to their shirts and cinched at their bulky waists—none of them narrow like Lucy's.

Art glances over his shoulder to Irving. Art is old and struggles under the weight of each sack. He has a permanent expression that is most of all forlorn. At this very moment, Irving is certain that Art once loved a woman who left him to become a whore, and that Irving could become Art once his old bones washed away to near nothing like a bar of soap. Irving could simply wake up one morning, with his driver's-side arm tan and his other pale, looking saggy-eyed and washed out. He doesn't know much of anything about Art, whether or not he has a wife and children, if he lives in town, or out in Star City. The only thing Art has ever talked about is playing for the Star City baseball team, some glorious moment in a tedious life. And yet Art is always here with his tired salute, and it suddenly seems heroic to Irving. Art's ability to show up every day, year after year, to deliver laundry.

A gust of wind kicks up a spray of dust. Irving turns his back to it, rubs his eyes. He thinks about his father in Miami. It's the same sun. It could even be the same gust of wind that started out somewhere down there and wound its way up to him. Irving sets his jaw. He's been wronged. He despises his father, who could be rich, chewing a cigar tip, wearing a white hat, or worse, he could be a bum, having abandoned his family for nothing more than Miami's staggering heat, a wood-warped dock. All Irving knows is that there was an elephant hauling wagons like a workhorse, and a worthless trunk, and his father could have gotten back in the car on the dock and come home, but didn't. He made the wrong choice, and yet there are right choices laying there right next to the bad ones. His father is a weak man. Lucy is weak, too, sometimes lavish and other times mean. But it is her weakness that made her leave; it was his father's weakness that made him stay on a dock, sending Irving's mother home alone.

Irving is tired of these people. It takes inordinate strength not to take a train to Wheeling, not to leave your wife and children, but to do this: push the pram to the butcher's and home again, to iron the damp wash after tending the garden, to toil, to appear every day to work, toting laundry, to pat the outside of the truck door like it's a horse and pull out, as Art does now, to stay and stay and stay. *Thirst has no season.* Irving decides to live his life in defiance of his father, in opposition to Lucy's restless, aching soul.

He will do this: drive the southern part of this route, fill the truck with gas, and not keep on going to Wheeling, to Miami, but circle back to this dirt lot, park his truck, and go back to his apartment, the blinds shut tight against the sun. And he may swell with pride, he may just feel like he is a hero, returning to the land he's spent his life defending. It is something so simple, so pure an emotion of resistance and success, only he could understand how victorious, how heroic it is to come home and turn on a lamp, the same small, glass lamp, day after day.

3

Alma has a pair of shoes and a box of oranges. The oranges are tough-skinned, as leathery as the shoes, and she wonders if there will be much juice in them. She imagines the tough, stringy pulp, the sections that become unswallowable wads to be spit out. She has a toothache, a new rot. The idea of chewing something hard pains her.

"Maybe the orphans could use these oranges for baseballs," she says to Lettie, trying to be lighthearted. But Lettie is lingering behind.

"I don't think I'm going to go. Tell Willard to bring himself here to the car."

Alma wants Lettie to come with her. She wants the nun to take a look at her, to say something about virtue. She's become aware that her daughter is slipping out at night. Once Alma woke to an empty bed and waited for her until almost dawn. Grass stains on her dresses, a rise in her cheeks, a new way of cocking her head. Lettie should know better, having seen so many lovesick women. She should never want to fall for a man. Alma looks out to the garden. She sees Willard's face shaded by a wide hat. "He's awful serious about what he's doing. He may not want to stop. He's like that, you know. You should come with me and say hello to him."

"No," Lettie says. "Tell him to wave."

Alma nods. She won't disturb Willard just yet. He sometimes gets cross if he isn't allowed to finish what he's set out to do. She leaves the box of oranges and the shoes beside the stone entranceway and walks out to the chicken-wire fence. Sister Margaret is there in her black habit, standing in the chicken coop, hands clasped in front of her, patiently. The nun is always patient, even with this wild ruckus of hens at her feet. A young novitiate in a white habit is flapping, much like a giant bird herself, after the chickens, which squawk and flutter. The light is dusty with risen feathers.

"You must be confident," Sister Margaret shouts. "You must let the chickens know that you know what's best for them." The novitiate, rakish and pallid, looks up blankly. Sister Margaret reaches forward into a group of head-bobbing hens, picks one up by the neck, and, with a firm twist, the chicken's soft white body circles. The neck breaks. It was one swift motion, like someone cranking an old car. Sister Margaret holds up the twitching bird. She hands the bird to the novitiate, who looks ready to cry but takes it by the neck,

quickly supporting its body in the cradle of her elbow. "Next time, you'll come with me again. All you need is confidence by way of practice and experience."

Sister Margaret walks out of the pen, nods to Alma, brushing feathers from her habit. "Is it Tuesday already? Time has a way of going quickly. Sometimes I wonder what year it is."

Time doesn't work this way for Alma. Sometimes she feels herself willing a minute to fall away. She's learned, though, how to pass it as best she can, like an invalid, an inmate, by remaining within the bullish trudge from task to task. She wishes that life could be an accumulation of actions, but even in this thought, she finds herself guilty of stepping back. Her heart is afflicted, and she suffers these small relapses. Memory and her mind's inclination to dilate are to blame. She battles against them. Alma says, "You move in there like a farmer's wife."

"It's the other life I could have had. I was raised on a farm near a lake, and after working, we would swim. I was a fast swimmer. I liked to hide underwater. I thought that there I could feel the pressure of God's love. To become a nun, I gave up a husband easily enough. I never wanted one. And children, because, well, I'm still surrounded by them." She pauses and looks out toward the river with its clipping current. "But to give up the feel of my body underwater and then buoyant, that was a trying sacrifice. There is a swim teacher in Uffington to teach the children—Willard, too—to

swim in a pond. Sometimes I go and watch. We have to teach
them to swim, because of where we're situated. We'd lose too
many to the Monongahela." She turns quickly and looks at
Alma, a cursory glance. "We all have other lives we've lived
and ones that we gave up living along the way. I imagine you
do, too."

They walk together up toward the convent. Alma must
nearly jog to keep up with the nun's long stride. "I worked at
the hosiery mill. I could have kept that up and have died of
pneumonia by now." She imagines her lungs packed with wet
cotton.

"It is respectable work."

"It didn't suit me."

"A suitable path. I didn't choose the expected one, either.
You and I have much in common, more than anyone could
ever imagine."

This is the way they talk to each other, two bullheaded
women, but more than that, two leaders, two heads of state,
taking a promenade on the grounds. She feels like they are a
pair of bishops, so chummy they need not talk about business. They can talk about most anything. Alma enjoys it.
When she's with the nun, she realizes what it's like to be
around herself, for other people, the girls in the house, for
example, some of whom get giddy, others abrasive. She likes
the way Sister Margaret tells her things, confides in her.
There's a softness the nun has allowed by conjuring up the
picture of her as a young girl, a fast swimmer slapping across

a lake, dipping under to hide from the world. Alma is certain she doesn't tell everyone these things. They are secrets that for some reason, the nun shares with Alma.

"I brought you all some oranges and thought the children could use some shoes. And this." Alma pulls out a thick envelope, but Sister Margaret raises her hand, and Alma shoves it back into her purse.

They walk into the dim convent. A nun is leading two single-file lines of boys and girls down the hall, an echo of shuffling feet. The two nuns nod at each other. The children are silent in navy blue uniforms. There's a slowness, a melancholy in the children like a troupe of show people with no one to do tricks for. She recalls Mr. Eddie, Mr. Bucci, Nettie, Wall-Eye, his hoarse parrot, a pathetic troupe, old, garish, tatty with chipped gilt costuming. She's glad she wasn't there to see the show close. She wonders if they still have a show, their dour flouncing. The orphans are carrying small brass bells with black wooden handles, but each has them cupped underneath so the bells are quiet, except for a constant faint clicking, like a chorus of death beetles.

Sister Margaret opens the door to her office. And once the door is shut, she holds out her hand. Alma gives her the envelope.

"It's thick. Business must be booming. I suppose hard times don't stop men."

"Sometimes it causes more of a rush."

Sister Margaret puts the envelope in the desk drawer. Alma

doesn't like the office. She always remembers leaving the children, the feeling of having Lettie pried from her chest, a gaping emptiness, a moist dress front, instantly cold against her skin, and then later knowing that Willard would not be coming home, that he would stay here forever perhaps. She knows that the official business conducted here is desperate. She's never seen a lovely young barren couple, smiling, holding hands as they assess children at play. She wonders if those couples exist.

The nun always invites her in. Sometimes they have tea. This time Alma has come with questions, none of which are formed, but she's carried them in, an armful, and she's certain the nun can tell.

"What is it?" Sister Margaret asks.

"It's going to be fall, again, and an ugly fall. The ugliest."

"Yes, it's dreadful. Sin and disaster. And babies, always babies. They don't stop just because it seems like the end. In fact, I think when people are most frightened, they become like rabbits. Our businesses boom on similar clocks." She sighs. "But that's not it. You're not here to discuss the world, are you? Not today."

"No, but I am here to discuss children."

"Willard is fine. He's doing well. He's a great help. Our muscle, our reliable muscle."

"No, it's Lettie. She's gotten too old."

The nun looks up now, squints over her bifocals. Her face pinches itself, a purse cinched to a tight O. She nods solemnly. "How old is she now?"

"Fifteen."

She looks at the floor. "And have any of the men hurt her?"

It's been clear for some time that the nun knows what Alma does for a living, but this is the first time Sister Margaret has mentioned the men in the house directly. "No, no," Alma says. "Nothing like that. But I think that she is sneaking off with someone."

The nun stands up and begins to pace. "I know that you may think that I take your offerings for the orphanage while at the same time I'd call it all sinful, but there are many paths to sin in this world and very few choices for women. It's your duty to keep Lettie safe. I was raised by my grandmother. I had a solitary childhood. She protected me by isolation. Because my father was gone, working far off, and my mother was dead." Here she paused, just briefly, a hitch, but only that, and then she forged on. "No one ever told me, exactly, but this is what I've learned: My father killed my mother. He beat on her till there was nothing left to beat on. My grandmother couldn't have admitted this truth—not really—to herself, not to me. And by the time I was old enough to ask, she was an invalid." She looks at Alma now. "This is not something I would confess to the young novitiate who couldn't kill a chicken. I wish my mother had killed him. This wish was the beginning of how I came to understand the burning work of prayer. I believe he beat her more because she resisted more, after I was born."

The story doesn't surprise Alma. She's already glimpsed something of herself in Sister Margaret, and it must be this part, a shiny, dark reflection, the stilled center of grief. "Is that why you became a nun, to protect yourself?"

Sister Margaret lifts the curtain. "There she is. She's walking down to the dock. She *has* gotten too old. That's certain. I think that it may become dangerous."

"I suppose you want her to become a nun." Alma has never thought of Sister Margaret as evangelical, but all nuns want there to be more, and so it came out.

"That would be nice, but I don't think this life is for her."

"Then what, Sister?"

"I couldn't bring my mother back to life. But I have found that sometimes prayer helps in a situation like this. An answer will come."

Alma wants to tell the nun about her own mother and the Prophet, who was killed, about her father, the buried tip of his tongue. She can smell the upturned earth, see the exact spot in the yard. She would like her father to appear, or the Prophet, some close approximation. Her mother taught her that love can be found in unlikely places. She has no time for this nostalgia, this desirousness. She prepares to go, gathers her purse, stands up. "I should be off. I need to talk to Willard. He's expecting me, I figure."

The nun has moved from the window, the black bell of her skirt slightly lifted in the back as she looks out, one hand holding up the curtain. "She's a beauty now. I didn't notice it before. Be careful. And remember: If a child asks for a fish, the parent does not give it a snake. If a child asks for an egg, the parent does not give it a scorpion. Ask and you shall receive. Knock and the door will open."

Alma says, "I understand what you've said about your mother and your father."

The nun lets the curtain drop but doesn't turn to face her. "That's why I told you."

The sky has clouded over, dun colored, like the breast of a bird. The wind flips up the brim of Willard's hat. He's wearing knickers. In fact, he's never worn long pants. He's still a boy, a big boy with chubby knees, red from kneeling, holding up the pressure of his wide belly. Sometimes Alma finds him grotesque. His mouth never shuts all the way. He swallows loudly. The wet pink of his full inner lip always shines with spit. His eyes are slow. They blink too hard. He's awkward, lumbering, and excitable. Sometimes he claps his hands and it looks ridiculous, like a full-grown man acting like a bunny. Alma wonders if she'll find him grotesque today or if he will only soften her heart. He can do that, too.

She notices right away that his face is no longer covered in soft, downy fur. He's clean shaven, and she wonders who taught him this. She imagines one of the nuns going to town to buy him a razor. It should have been his daddy, Alma thinks. Oddly, it doesn't make him appear more grown-up. He looks like a chubby baby with his smooth, windblown cheeks. He's pulling up weeds poking up around cages of tomato plants. His hands are quick, although his eyes are closed, his face held up to the sky. Alma stands in his light. The shadow moves across him, and his eyes blink open as if he's just awakened from a lovely dream.

"What are you doing?" Alma asks.

"Pulling up the chokers."

"Why are your eyes shut like that?"

"Because I can do it with my eyes shut. Just because I can."

"Oh." She sits down awkwardly, drawing in her breath, which hurts her sore tooth. The grass pricks her legs.

"I can feel the furry stems of some of them. Others are wiry like grass. In the flowers, I can tell the color by touching them." He points down the wall to a bunch of dark purple and light pink cosmos, tall, bending over with their own weight. "But now I'm learning only about vegetables. Them children need the food." Willard always calls the orphans "them children." He isn't one of them, and he likes to make that clear. "Where's Lettie at?"

"She went down to the dock."

"She hates that old dock. But I'm not afraid of water. I have swim trunks and all."

"Do they teach you how to pray out here, Willard? All that kind of thing?"

"They do. I know my prayers. But I like to come out here when I've got troubles."

"What kind of troubles?"

"The same kind everybody's got. I don't know how many kinds there are."

Alma looks over her shoulder and sees Lettie walking quickly from the dock to the car parked on the dirt driveway. Her arms are crossed. She wipes her face like she's been crying. Alma wonders what draws that girl to water when she knows it will only upset her. Alma thinks about what the nun just told her: the snake, the spiny scorpion, and the glinting fish, the egg, whole and white, perfect. She wonders what her children have asked of her, and what she's delivered. She knows that Sister Margaret is talking about God, but Alma worries that she's given her children poisonous creatures. This has been her strategy, to show her children evil, at an arm's distance, so that they can spot it before it bites. She would have felt dishonest if she had only handed them fish and eggs. Willard is different. He can be sheltered. But Lettie and Irving live in the world. She has been preparing them with knowledge of sin, and is that so bad? She's done it the only way she's known how. "You should wave to Lettie," Alma says.

Willard jumps up and calls out to her. She picks up her head at the noise. He waves both arms in the air over his big head. She smiles, pulls her hair out of her face, and lifts her hand. But she doesn't come over. She strides to the car and shuts the door.

"I should go," Alma says.

"Wait, wait, now." Willard's knees are dirty and pocked from sharp pebbles. He kneels in front of the cosmos—it looks grief-bent to Alma suddenly—takes off his hat, letting it sit beside him on the grass. He closes his eyes. His fingers find a stem, shimmy up it, and lightly touch the petals. He leans forward and lets them brush against his cheek. He says, "This one is darker than the others." And he's right. It's a deep purple, like the sky before a downpour.

Alma leans over him, holds his massive head in her hands. She can feel the bones of his skull. She bends and kisses his thick matt of hair. And she imagines what would happen if he were to die before her. If his heart, lodged deep in his broad, fatty chest, were to give out on him, she would be the one thrown out of the church for wild, heartbroken, almost lustful, mourning. She would pound her chest and throw herself on his casket. She imagines the room of nuns, the air thick with the heavy scent of flowers. The orphans, and the crazy mother, blinded by this pain.

"You know how I know about the colors?" he asks, as if he's just performed a magic trick.

"I don't know."

"Well, it's a funny thing. I just know. I just do," he says. "I just do."

The brim of his hat catches in the wind, and he dives after it, flattening it with his hand, denting its curved top. Alma walks away, quickly, before she, too, is crying, and he watches her, holding his crushed hat to his heart.

*   *   *

Lettie sits in the parlor, kneeling on the love seat, elbows over its back. She sees a distant glowing globe, a dark hand underneath. It's Smitty. She knows his walk, the eager sideways glances, the readiness to duck. He sidles up to the window, holds the globe to the side of his face, now weirdly lit, green with shadows. He taps on the window with his nightstick. The globe is a Mason jar teeming with lightning bugs, the sides alive with black legs. He's smiling broadly, showing his underbitten teeth. She imagines him coming home, having caught an enormous fish that she'll bone and skin and fry up for dinner. It is something that one of the hatbox ladies' husbands might do.

Lettie creeps out of the house, careful with the screen door, because she's felt a certain tension with her mother. She's sure that the woman knows something is going on. Minute to minute, Lettie worries that she'll ask her about it, but the minutes pass and she doesn't.

Smitty says, "Hey, dollbaby." He grabs her hand, leads her, running around to the back of the house, through a line of trees. He climbs the farmer's fence. She climbs up one side and lets him hold her waist, lifting her over. The field is broad and dark velvety green. He's set out a blanket, more jars of lightning bugs, like lamps around the edges.

"It's a pretty sight," she says.

"I set it up just for us. The farmer's cow is milk-sick. I heard while on duty. His wife's a near wreck about it, as it's their last left. Milk won't foam. It's silver black. But this field is nice."

"It's nice." She thinks of the cow, moaning, and then of the bear in Mr. Bucci's bedroom before it died, and her father. A fleeting pang. Death. The way someone's absence can root, grow, tower. Sometimes she can see her father clearly, and she says, *Dance,* and he dances like a foal, knees buckling, puppetlike, until his face is red and pulsing like a giant heart. It's the same way Mr. Bucci used to command the bear—*Dance*— and the bear would begin to shuffle his paws, upright, in his bow tie and blue-band hat. But then the picture of her father fades. She can't hold the collection of features. What was the shape of his jaw? Was his nose straight or bent? Did his eyes sag just a bit? He breaks into pieces, becomes a red-faced blur, and the absence is there again, big as a tree, storm-swaying overhead, and she is tiny in its gusty shadow.

Smitty sits down on the blanket, legs out, feet crossed, hands flipped out to prop up in back. He lets his head tilt back and regards the sky. Lettie sits beside him, curling her legs to one side, under her skirt. She glances up to see what he's seeing.

"I don't like the idea of you ever leaving my side," Smitty says. "I don't like that one bit. People shouldn't go disappearing."

"Where did Sir Lee ever go to?"

"Sir Lee would be surprised to see me now, in this uniform. I'd arrest him if I saw him. I know enough rotten things he's done. But I hope he'd resist arrest, so I could shoot him in the back."

"But is he around here?"

"I don't know. I woke up one morning and heard his car in the driveway and then the motor pulling away from the house. I jumped up and ran after the car, but it was dark, and I tripped and skinned my knees, tore them up. He probably went to California to lie on a beach, but I hope he drowns in the ocean. He can't swim any more than I can. I don't know why he'd want to go to the beach. But he sure cleaned things out for good, the son of a bitch. It makes me sick to think about." He pauses. He looks down at his hands in his lap. They shake. There is always a small tremor; Lettie has noticed it. "Can I confess something to you, Lettie? Can I tell you something I've never told anybody?"

Lettie nods, but she's afraid. She isn't sure that she really wants to know, and she feels guilty about it, for holding back tenderness. Smitty needs tenderness. In fact, she believes that if all of her mother's customers were granted more tenderness—not sex, it wasn't always about sex—then they wouldn't need to come to her mother's house at all. She believes this.

He says, "He left one thing behind. An extra gun that he kept hidden under the sofa cushions where I'd been sleeping. He left the dogs behind, too. And after it was clear that he wasn't coming back . . . maybe days went by, me and the dogs pacing the yard, the house. And before I walked back down the mountain, I shot his dogs. Not out of hate, like you might think, Lettie. But because I knew what was going to come of them. Lonesome and starving. Set out into the wild. I shot them. I should have shot myself, too." His eyes are teary, a hysteria in them. "But I never would have been here with you tonight."

He cups Lettie's face in his hands. She is his savior. She is needed. He won't ever leave her. He closes his eyes. She kisses him softly.

"It's such a wide-open field," she says.

"I think we should have a house, then. Build one right here."

"That might be a nice thing."

"Sure it would be nice. I think we should get married."

"You do?"

"I do. What do you think?"

"Well, are you asking me to marry you?" Lettie thinks of being married to a policeman. She figures they could live in one of the little houses being built on Greenmont Avenue, that they could afford a new Hudson Essex each time the old one wore out, and have children who wear costumes that she's stitched for parades, clowns in pointy hats.

"I set this all up, just for you, just for tonight. So I'm asking you."

"Well, it is really very nice." She pauses. Her mind hushes, waiting for her to make a decision. There is a poised moment, her life teetering. She thinks of the hatboxes, her children in pointy homemade hats, Smitty riding up in their Hudson Essex, pulling out the big fish. She doesn't want to be like her mother, padded in her new layer of fat, hunched over her money, her one eye's constant gaze locked on her children, who shuffle within it. She doesn't want to live in a house of whores, dirty men, loveless, the heaving, grunting chorus of sex. She believes in something pure. Not every man leaves his wife on a dock in Miami. There are rows of houses on Greenmont Avenue, one after the other, with their tidy fences and gardens, who give their hard-won money to bankers behind grillwork counters. She wants to step into the picture. She cannot say no to it. "I think I will marry you. So yes. That's my answer."

At this, Smitty stands up and gives out a long hoot. Lettie shrieks and laughs. She's on her feet but teetering, holding onto her ribs, giddy. He tosses up one of the jars and hits it with his billy club. It shatters. Some of the lightning bugs drop, like pellets, but others find themselves midair and fly, their wings suddenly frantic. He yells out like a coyote. He howls, then picks up another jar.

Lettie pulls at his shirtsleeve. She says, "No, don't."

But he is too agitated now. He tosses it up and smashes it, and then another and another, until they're all shattered, the field littered with glass. The light scatters, dims. It's dark. Suddenly quiet. He's breathless. Lettie looks at a lightning bug that has fallen to her arm. Smitty moves to her and stares down at it, too. He unbuttons the top of his shirt, then yanks it up over his head. He plucks the bug from her arm and smears its green oils on his chest. She imagines the delicate casing of its brittle shell cracked.

"You ever done this when you were a kid?" he asks, pulling another bug from the blanket and pressing it onto his skin.

"No," she says. "We just cupped them in our hands so they looked match-lit." She can see both of her brothers' hands, light blinking from the spaces between their fingers. Even Willard, with his clumsiness, was always gentle, never so much as cracked a wing. Lettie thinks that there is little Smitty does just once, and she doesn't know what to do with him. He's so different from her. Loud and shirtless. He's wild. Partly she wants to save him from his wildness and partly she wants to become wild herself. Soon his chest and arms are spotted with glow marks. The whole night has made her feel unsteady—the crawling jars, the confession, the proposal, the broken glass—but love should be like that. It should make you feel off-kilter and wheeling.

Smitty opens his arms and encloses her, the billy club against her back. He pulls her in close. "Do you love me?" he asks.

"You're crazy," she says, squirming, her backbone pressed against the club.

"Don't say that," he says. "Don't say I'm crazy."

She can feel his hardened penis against her stomach. He is taller than she is, bigger. She is aware of her bare neck, how

The

simple it might be for someone as strong as he is to snap it. She's afraid of what might be coming next. She's fended him off so far. She doesn't want to get caught with a baby, but tonight he is wilder than ever before. The girls have told her often enough that the way to a man's heart isn't through his stomach like the old saying goes, but right up through this bulge. She thinks of all the things the girls in the house have taught her about washing a man down, checking him for disease, about using a sheepskin, a Dutch cap, douching, the ugly process based on distrust. She refuses it. And they're going to get married, so it should be okay. It's different from those girls turning tricks.

They kneel down, kissing. He rolls her to her back. She can feel the sharpness of a few bits of glass that scattered onto the blanket. He's breathing hard, sidling out of his pants. He pushes her underwear between her legs, to the side. Before she knows it, he is inside of her and she's twisting away from the sharp shards. She says, "Smitty, it hurts." Not just her back now, but a sharpness inside of her, too tight. He doesn't fit. "Smitty, no, no." But his face is in her chest. He's working at her hard. She says no, again and again. But his hand goes to her mouth, smothering her voice, making it hard to get air. She panics, thrashing her head back and forth. She wonders if she could die this way. She worries if the farmer's wife is dying, too, if she's panicked because she drank the poisoned milk. She feels Smitty jolt as he releases inside of her. She's heard a man's juices called thick milk sweets and worries if it could be poisoned, too, like the cow's milk. She confuses one for the other, herself for the farmer's wife, souring like the cow, teats engorged with blackened milk. Lettie feels sick, curdled. Smitty is done. He pulls away from her, sits, yanks up his pants.

"I said no to you. Didn't you hear me?"

"It's okay. This is how it is. You'll get used to it. You're gonna be my wife."

She stands up and knows that there's blood. Between her legs, splotches on the back of her dress. Her body is sore, shaking. The wind makes the blood cool and instantly sticky on her skin.

He stands up and walks toward her unsteadily, like his legs have fallen asleep. She's afraid of him, and he reads it on her face. He looks around as if seeing the mess for the first time, the bloody blanket and shattered glass, the billy club.

"You still love me?"

She says, "Yes, yes." But it is a reaction, said wide-eyed, her head still ringing, shaking no. A gush slips from her, more blood or deadly milk. She steps back. His skin is still marked with the lightning bugs' green oils, and he looks like a leper with horrible, glowing wounds.

Alma burns a sheet of notepaper in an ashtray, waves it, blowing, to kill the flame. She rubs the paper's waxy residue between her fingers, opens her mouth, staring into the vanity's warped mirror. She coats her sore tooth, filling the hole as best she can. It pains her to touch it, but when she shuts her mouth, sagging against the chair's back, she cannot stop tonguing the ache. She looks older now, even in this forgivingly blurred reflection. Her jawline is softening to a sag, and under her eyes the skin is skirted with two puffed lavender crescents. She wonders at what point Henry will no longer recognize her, how many years will it take before she is a different person. Even now, would he know her, Lettie, Irving? Only Willard, she suspects, because he is still the same, ageless.

Alma's thoughts snag on Lettie, the empty bed. She has let her daughter slip out into the night. She's turned her back, because there's a moment when you must let them go. Alma was once fifteen. She was in love with Henry, and it was pure and good. His genitals, she remembers thinking they looked like bits of thing from the garden, swollen radishes, a fleshy, unknown vegetable, grown rigid, tuberous, an edible root, colorful pink, red, a bluish tint, not as blue as a possum's cod, but tinged. The soft sprig of hair as fine as the finest spray of roots, and afterward, flushed, contented, his penis looked kindly, like the long supple teat of a cow. And it was sweet between them. It was like waking up and the morning is set in front of you, glorious with sun, and she would have liked to have stopped there. Two bodies of promise, so intact and whole, swimming with urgency, but they trudged on into blazing heat, the exhaustion of toil the day expects, and then a slow descent of light, a gathering of darkness, the animalness of night.

Alma closes her eyes. She should pray like Sister Margaret advised her. She knows that she is supposed to pray for her daughter's soul, her virginity, for her to fall in love with a gentleman. Alma can guarantee the hard march of life, but she can only hope that her daughter has that early joy, knows that pure swimming sun.

Alma realizes that she doesn't know how to speak to God. She moves to the bed. Her back flat on the bed, she lays her hands at her sides and says, "God, oh, God." She imagines Jesus on the cross, a serene pose like back-floating on a lake. She imagines Jesus flying off of the cross, pulling down armfuls of water, and Lettie gliding, fearless, on the surface. Her tongue works at the painful tooth, better now, a bit better. It is as close as she can come to asking for a miracle.

4

lma hears a car rattle to a bereft exhale in her driveway. She has been scrubbing the floor, and when she rises, her knees ache. She bends to rub them and watches through the window as a man makes his way slowly across the yard. He seems astonished to have found himself here, midday, alone. He has the nervous, faded look of a county man, someone official, from the census bureau, certainly not a customer. His eyes shift from the wildflowers, clots of color, to the lone cow—tattered, its ribs sticking out like banister rails, its milk-well sickly engorged. The cow watches him with one wide eye on the side of its head. It seems to startle him, and Alma is sympathetic, because she has felt eyed by that cow before. It can look so mournful, so filled with longing. Alma feels calm now, as if she's been expecting this stranger, as if her prayer, more an unraveling from her heart, an endless rope, has received some kind of tug.

As he walks up the sloped porch steps, Alma presses back her sweaty ringlets, but adamant, they spring forward. He knocks, and she rushes, opening it too quickly. The screen door claps the wood frame. He swipes his hat from his head.

"Can I help you?"

He glances behind himself, as if she's spoken to someone over his shoulder, but then he quickly returns to her. "I was supposed to ask for Alma."

"I'm Alma."

He seems taken aback. She wonders what he's heard, perhaps that she's a madam, and he expected red-painted lips, a feather boa, not a woman, slightly frumpy, in an outdated housedress, knees sorely red from scrubbing. She prides herself on not looking the part. "I'm the Reverend Line. I've come to see my daughter. I've heard through a good bit of passed-on information that she resides here. Delphine Line?"

Delphine has never said much about her family. Alma has never asked, never truly imagined Delphine as a little girl with a father, a mother, a family, much less that she was a reverend's daughter. She suddenly feels a surge of guilt. She's been shortsighted. She wonders what he knows. She hopes he knows all of it so she won't have to be the one to tell him his daughter's a whore and a hop addict. "Did you say you're a reverend?" Alma is thinking about her miracle. She prayed, and now there is this reverend, shuffling, stooped, ordinary, in dusty shoes, but perhaps miraculous nonetheless.

He seems resistant now to admitting it, as if he senses her urgency. But he says, "Yes, I am."

"And you're here for Delphine?"

"Yes. I'm a married man. I have a ministry just two towns away. Imagine her hiding here for so long." His face breaks into a momentary smile, but then regains its composure. "My other daughter isn't like this at all. She's a schoolteacher. She still lives with us, sleeping in the bedroom where she's always slept."

"That's nice," Alma says.

But he seems embarrassed, perhaps that he mentioned bedrooms, a hint that he knows what goes on here. He clears his throat. "Is she here?"

She glances over her shoulder. "I'm very respectful of her privacy. She may be resting. I can go ask her if she'd like to see you." Alma assumes that she won't want to see him. She's never mentioned him.

He must have guessed the same thing. He runs his fingers over his bald head. He shakes his head. He turns the brim of his hat in his hands, takes a few steps toward his car. He says, "I shouldn't be here. I'm uncomfortable. I thought you might think I've come for some other purpose."

"No, no."

"I'm not perfect. My wife," he says, "she's sensitive. Her skin is easily alarmed. And I was afraid of what I might," he pauses, "see here. I used to bury my head on the side of my wife's neck that was not swollen by the goiter and I whispered sweetly, not foul, nothing foul, but now I find myself alone with my lust. I don't like the faintness. I admit I have momentary lapses in an otherwise hardworking soul. I have a hardworking soul." He looks up at Alma now. "I suppose I'm confessing. The Catholics confess all the time—and just this way, through a screen."

"Do they?" She'd never seen the nuns at the orphanage confess. She isn't sure what to do with the reverend's outpouring. She feels sorry for him. She says, "Well, I'm not a professional, reverend, despite what you might have heard."

"I didn't hear anything, not bad. Honestly. I knew that I wouldn't see my girl. I knew that I'd go home empty."

Just then, at the end of the driveway, a car pulls in. A woman's wide, white face behind the wheel. The car comes to a stop, very close to the bottom porch step, so close there's a rise of dust. The reverend starts to cough. It's Mrs. Ming, Delphine's connection from the Chinese laundry. Alma wonders if Delphine will come down to greet her, if she'll find her father on the porch. She finds herself hoping that Delphine will show up.

Mrs. Ming gets out of the car, her hair tied back, black but shiny as a kettle. She's wearing a very American skirt and blouse, but she seems uncomfortable in the getup. She's pretty, with fine features, small, dark eyes, her face heavily powdered. She pulls out a small, tightly knit bag; it tinkles as if filled with bells. Alma wonders what the reverend thinks of all of this. He's wide-eyed, his face wet with sweat, a bead inching along the curve of his brow. He pulls a handkerchief from his back pocket and wipes his forehead.

Mrs. Ming shuffles to the steps, little bells, little bells. She climbs the steps, bows to the Reverend Line, who isn't sure how to respond—whether he should bow, too, or nod or tip his hat. He does a clumsy combination, nearly losing his balance, and then walks down the steps into the yard.

Mrs. Ming shuffles to the front door. She says to Alma, "I got what Miss Delphine want." She has a southernness to her accent that always surprises Alma. "She need to pay me. You know it, sweet lady?"

"I know. I know," Alma says.

The reverend stands by his car but doesn't get in. He's watching Alma, now a distance away. She wonders if he notices that she's wearing no stockings. It's the first time she's felt aware of her bare legs in years. It gives her a small jolt of arousal.

There's a screeching above. A window opening. "Mrs. Ming? Is that you? You're late. How long now? But all's forgiven. You're my savior."

It's Delphine's voice. The Reverend Line scrambles toward the house, gazing up. Alma steps off of the porch. The sky is blinding, her face just dark, at first, against it. "Delphine, I wanted to let you know—"

But the reverend cuts her off. "Delphine! Delphine! It's

you. You look like a dream to me. You look wonderful." But it isn't true. Her eyes dark and small, as if peering out of pits on her face. Her cheeks and lips are drawn. Delphine stares at him, blinking. "Where's Mrs. Ming?" There's a rise of panic in her voice. "I heard her. Just now. That's her car!"

"I'm here to take you home."

"I am at home."

"Don't you know who I am?"

"Do you think I've lost my mind? Do you think I cannot recognize my own daddy in the brightness of an afternoon?" But then she rubs her eyes, as if maybe she's not so sure herself. She looks backward, into the room, as if responding to someone who might be talking to her—Roxy. Her figure appears in another window. Her long face, full of bones, cheek, jaw, bridge of nose. Alma sees the reverend glance at her. She wonders if he thinks it is a woman's face, but too large to be a woman. Roxy disappears.

"Sorry to be late!" Mrs. Ming says. Now the Chinese woman is beside the reverend. She startles him. He flinches, instinctively covering his genitals with his hat. Alma wonders what jingles in her bag. She always sounds this way. Perhaps he doesn't hear little bells as much as the ting of knives. He's scared. She can see the terror on his face.

"Come up, Mrs. Ming. Join me! I'm looking for company. Come up now," Delphine insists.

"Sorry, I cannot stop. It is too much for me if I do each time."

"I'll join you, Delphine. We can talk," the Reverend Line offers, as if the Chinese woman has brought food. Delphine stares down at him. He looks small, like a child waiting for some word from her.

Delphine gazes at him desperately. "Where would I go if you were there with me? Where would I go? You see, I go places in this way. It's the wonder of it. What would I say to you? No, it wouldn't work. You need to stay in the place where I keep you."

The reverend looks at the Chinese woman now shuffling through the door, her plump arm pushing it open. He looks out at the cow. Alma follows him, surfacing beside him. The idea has come to her, so purely, so heaven-sent. She says, "I'll take care of her. We can work a trade. I have one that needs to live with a reverend and his wife and his schoolmarm daughter. And I'll watch over yours. I'll keep an eye on her. I'll keep her safe here."

The reverend looks up. He's confused, stares at her as if she's speaking in tongues. He blinks and then blinks again. He says, "Everywhere there's the sunspot image, a dark reflection of Delphine, her body leaning out the window, her face." He looks up at the house. "The house is tilted," he says, "it's leaning toward Jesus, as they say." He looks frazied, sick.

"Are you okay?" Alma asks.

"I had a bird when I was a little boy. A bird that no matter what the time of day, I could cover its cage with a sheet and it would fall asleep. It was so trustful. And I could play

God. I could make night and day. It is a mistake. A sin I commit again and again. I still have birds. A house of cages. I cover them at night and count myself lucky."

She knows that he can barely hear her. He's blanched, unsteady. She says, "You might not be able to save your own, not the way you want to, but maybe you can save one all the same. I was waiting for you. If you believe that kind of thing. You are the miracle sent to me, for my daughter."

"My daughter?"

"No, *my* daughter."

She hands him paper and pen. He writes down his name and address. He is agreeing, nodding, but she isn't sure that he is really understanding her.

He says, "I'm thirsty. But it isn't thirst. It only resembles thirst." He looks as if he's about to sob. He says, "Ma'am, can I have a drink of water?"

"Oh, yes," she says. She runs to the house, to the back, where she fills a glass with water. When she gets to the screen door, he is staring at the cow. It is grotesque. It eyes him horribly. She stalls. He pulls out his handkerchief and presses it, the ball of his hand and his fingers, to his eyes. His chest gives a small heave. He walks away from her, past the Chinese woman's car, to his own. He climbs in, waves his handkerchief, and she raises the glass of water as if she can still reach him.

Alma stands above the pan, which sits in the dirt in front of the porch step, holding the hot kettle of water. When she bought the chicken, it looked plain and fat. She was only shopping for size. But now, dead in the pan, it glows white, its beak orange and clawed feet red, as if painted by someone who had no sense of what he was doing. A chicken should be dull colored, not allowed such signs of brightness, but there it sits, looking almost glorious, and Lettie is there on the bottom step, one foot on either side of the pan. She looks like a queen with something delivered dead to her feet. Lettie is beautiful, her green eyes and dark lashes, her full bottom lip, now bitten by her pretty white teeth. But Alma knows she's being lavish again. She is stepping away from herself, being fanciful, a weakness she's practiced against. For five years, she's worked to dampen it so that now she walks around with a clean, spare mind and labor. But it's been harder since she met the reverend. He is Alma's miracle, after all. For the first time, perhaps in her whole life, she's doing the right thing. She nearly loves the reverend, his shyness, his tendency to tremble his head, ever so slightly, as he speaks. His lips puffed and soft, his bright blue eyes watery, his dark brows lifted with concern. He's a perfect father, as gentle as her own but not nagged by doubt and wrongheadedness. Her father was muddled, his core slack, sapped by punishment (his mother had tried to beat him out of the habit of seizing), stunted. And the reverend is nothing like Henry, who was so full of himself, boastful and robust, yet really, under it all, quite feeble. No, the reverend is more like the Prophet, appearing as salvation, someone Alma is not allowed to love. The reverend appears weak, scared you're going to slap him one minute to the next, unsure of everything—where to stand, how to hold his hands, whether to put his hat somewhere, and, if so, where. But under the weakness, there is some other-worldly strength or at least conviction, sent from God, she supposes. He reminds her of Wall-Eye. She should have married a man like those two, calm and measured. Wall-Eye, in his own little house of shelves and shelves of books. She could have learned to overlook the parrot always clamped to the shoulder of his jackets, so loose and long in the arms it seemed he'd recently shrunk, like wet wool in the hot sun. She could have gained a contentedness. She would have liked to have been a reader, sitting in a well-lit room, turning pages, becoming someone of knowledge. She wonders if the reverend has books, not just the Bible, but many books on animals and science. She wonders if his wife reads them, too, if they sit together and talk about the things that pass through their minds. It's an inkling, really, that something else exists, more than it is based on any fact.

Lettie is looking up at her from the bottom step, wait-ing for her to loosen the feathers with boiled water so she can pluck it. But when Alma's eyes catch hers, her daugh-ter becomes teary, her eyes rounded. She looks deeply sad, her voice whispery and confidential. "The neighbor's cow is milk-sick."

Alma wonders why her daughter is so moved and, too, who she's heard this from. Who's she been talking to? Alma has seen the farmer and his wife a number of times, but they don't speak. They are two quiet pillars that move somberly about their farm, silent, childless, and probably more solitary because of the lack. Childlessness raises too much suspicion and sympathy, too much to bear, Alma thinks. She has always let them alone. She always felt more akin to the cows and was sad to see fewer and fewer until they were down to this last one, a bony thing, soulful and lonesome. "I suppose this will kill it. Are they poisoned, too?" Alma can feel the small hand of panic, more people going hungry. It gives way to a certain grim anger. She despises a world that allows poverty, handing over death like teacakes.

Lettie shakes her head, bends over to wipe her nose on her dress hem. "I don't know."

Her daughter is so easily woebegone she wonders if she will ever toughen. Alma pours the scalding water over the chicken's plump body, and the feathers dull, the bird seems to shrink down. It suddenly looks frail, meatless, all bone. It's a disappointment. She's angry about how much she paid for it. She doesn't like the grocer, thinks he's a cheat. He eyes her not so much like she's a whore, but as if he is one. As if he's mocking her with his raised eyebrows and the pursing of his lips that he sometimes shows her when no one else is looking. She doesn't understand what he wants from her. She, on the other hand, is the normal one. She's come for a chicken, one as fat as she's paid for. Alma can feel her cheeks redden. She despises going to town. She doesn't like the way hate flares up in her, and even more the spontaneous rushes of love. Today a black girl, not but fifteen, looked her in the eyes. It was a brief moment. The girl, poor and thin with one mottled cheek, lifting her baby to her lap, covering its head with a worn blanket so it could nurse. She was searching Alma for reproach, but Alma had none. She wanted to say, *I'm the nigger-lover's daughter, the madam of a whorehouse. My husband has left me. I'm as alone in this world as you are, as each of us is, even if we pretend not to be.* She felt so much tenderness, she thought she might cry. Every time, she says it's the last trip to town, and yet she sometimes needs the throng of people, how she can get lost in them, at least for a while, until that hushed whisper at her back, an accusation of who she is, the pinprick of suspicion and hate. She's different. It's taken sometimes as a rebuke. As if her choice not to be like other people were a condemnation. And, well, sometimes it is.

Lettie hitches her skirt above her knees, getting ready to set to work as the steam rises and the bird cools. Alma doesn't like the bruised redness of her knees. She knows her daughter has been rolling on the ground with some boy or—worse—a man, but it won't be long now. She is here to tell her that she'll be living with the reverend and his wife and their daughter, Eloise. Alma just got word today. A letter in rolling script. They will pick up Lettie tomorrow. The rev-

erend will take Lettie away, whether she likes it or not, and
Lettie will not marry the first man who shows her some
attention. Alma will not allow it.

Alma arches her back, watches her daughter fan the
feathers a bit by quickly grabbing into them. "Be patient. Let
her cool," Alma says.

Lettie gives a short huff, taps her shoes, and then starts in.
She grabs handful after handful. Occasionally, she pulls her
hands back, pressing them against her dress to get the hot
sting out. She piles the slick feathers beside one shoe. They
stick to the dirt; some come unglued and are picked up by
the wind and trail off a bit through the dirt. A week from
now, even two, Alma will find a feather in her garden, dry
again and white, its quill sharp as a pin.

"You're getting too old to live here, Lettie," Alma says.

"I know that!"

"I've decided that you'll be living with the Reverend Line
and his wife, Delphine's mother and father, and their daughter, Miss Line, Eloise, who teaches school. They come tomorrow to pick you up."

Her daughter's hands don't stop pulling. "Delphine
should live with them if she's the daughter. Not me."

"Delphine will stay here with us. You know she can't go
back home. She's a grown woman now. And a certain kind."

"I'm a grown woman."

"No, you aren't."

"I'm going to get married. I'm almost a wife."

"No, you are not."

"To Smitty. I'm getting married to Smitty. He is a police officer now. He's upstanding."

It's the first time Alma has heard the boyfriend's name. She's surprised she recognizes it. Smitty was the boy with the liquor boxes, the runty slave of Sir Lee, and now he is the runty slave of the captain. She doesn't like his manner, his gruffness, his sharp teeth. She wants to convince Lettie of the quiet house, the reverend studying, the days that yawn into solitude and thoughtfulness. She would have been good at that life. She knows it, the way a musician knows that he can play a piano before he puts his fingers to it. She wants to tell her to marry someone like Wall-Eye, not Wall-Eye himself with the bird-stained shoulders and the skittering eye, not a show person, but the idea of him. She realizes that it's through Smitty somehow that Lettie has heard of the neighbor's milk-sick cow. Her daughter has secrets and shares them as it suits her. Alma says, "Well then, I've made it in time. Just in time."

Lettie is already crying. And Alma is relieved to see it. Because of it, she knows that Lettie has already conceded, that her daughter is crying over the idea that she'll have to do just what her mother has said. Despite the relief, Alma wishes her daughter would fight more. She shouldn't be so easily tearful and, in turn, obedient. Was this the way it had been for Alma and her own mother? She can't remember. There's only this sick longing. She doesn't recall her mother ever telling her not to marry Henry. Maybe her father would have, if he'd been capable of staying, enduring humiliation, for her sake if not the family's. She wishes now that her mother had, and wonders if there had been at least one small moment when her mother had thought to spare her by warning her, by maybe even begging her not to get married to a willful boy when she was so young. And although she knows she wouldn't have listened, she can feel the moment turning, her mother's mouth almost opening, but then not. A slow recession, an arm extended and then recoiled to rest in a lap.

Lettie's wet hands are covered in feathers. She holds them out at her sides, indignant, and then slowly her head gives a twitch. She looks almost stricken. She stands up, turns, her dress flaring at her red knees, and she runs into the house.

Alma sighs. She decides to go in after Lettie, although she has no idea what she'll say. She begins to walk up the porch steps. She feels heavy, as if she's hauling her body up. The cow, she thinks of the dying cow, and feels more of a burden because of it. As she reaches the top, there's a darting movement, out of the corner of her eye. She looks and sees a snake's pointed, triangular head, then its long body pouring out of a splintered hole in the porch boards, black and tan stripes. She holds perfectly still. It's a bell-tail, a rattler. Its end, crusted with horny, crisp gauze shakers, suddenly buzzes, whirs. There's a new button about to bloom into its own hollow segment. It isn't so young. For a moment Alma is dazed. Her eyes dart to the window, catching a pane of sky, the sun-struck hubcaps, a razor left on the porch rail where Pearly had given one of the johns a shave, the blinding brass pot of the steaming chicken. Her mouth forms the opening sounds to call Henry. It's been so long, and yet she still expects him to be there somewhere, ready when she needs him. Her mouth folds in on his name. Her face floods with a rush of blood, anger. Henry should be the one facing the pointed head of the snake, not her. She could have seen its head nudging from the hole, but then he should have appeared with a butcher knife pulled from the kitchen drawer. She despises Henry, his pride, his greed. He has abandoned his own, and how could he, that son of a bitch, let her die of a snake bite on her own porch? She wonders if the snake has a nest, shifting with leathery, yellowed eggs. How many others, she wonders, rattlers under the house? If the snake bites her and the poison sinks into her blood and she dies here, what would become of her fearful, sensitive daughter? Sister Margaret would take care of Willard perhaps forever, but Lettie wouldn't have it. She's too old now anyway. And Irving would marry that no-good, mean-hearted woman? Delphine and Roxy would be set out into the world. Where would they go, a hop fiend and her enormous lovesick lover? Even Pearly would be returned to walking Courthouse Square, turning tricks in cars on country roads where she could be gang-raped, get her throat slit.

Alma picks up the razor, then clicks the heel of her shoe on the boards. The snake turns, beats back to the hole, tucks its head in and begins to slide. She grabs its body above the rattles, the skin softer than she expected, more alive. She pulls it out just a bit and slices it cleanly in half, a thick, swift cut. The front of its body falls away through the hole. She assumes the eggs, if there are any, will shrivel, or will die, born motherless without coiled protection. She folds the razor safely and sets it back on the porch rail.

She walks out to the small stand of trees, the tall grass to one edge of the yard, and tosses half of the snake into the grass. She won't say anything about the snake. It would only upset everyone. By the time she trudges back to the pan, it already seems like a dream. She isn't sure if it happened now at all. She wonders if she did in fact pull out its scaled thick body from the hole and cut it in two with the shaving razor. She squeezes her hand, the one that she'd grabbed hold of the rattler with. The feel of its cool, scaled skin, the flexing thickness, lingers in her grip. Her hand remembers, just as her body recalls the dead baby passing through even though now there is no proof of that child, and even the work to conceive it, her thighs recall the way Henry moved between them. The world is slick with snakes. She looks down on the dead chicken. She will have to pluck the rest of it. She stares at its upturned eye, a black, shining bead.

Roxy is afraid Delphine will smoke herself to death. In the past, she's worried that a rot will start in her lungs and she'll one day wear a hole, just a small one at first, a thin spot, like in the sole of a shoe, but enough for her to leak air. Or she has worried that over time her throat will go too raw to swallow food, and she barely eats now, but will stop all together and die, like Roxy's mother did, being swallowed by a bed. A sliver of a woman in the end.

But this is the first time she's worried about the poison itself. Opium is surely poison. Like liquor, it eats away at your innards. But unlike Roxy's father, who got spitting, fighting mad because of drinking, the hop makes Delphine calm. Sometimes too calm. This Roxy knows.

Tonight the cicadas rise and fall so loudly she can't make out Delphine's ragged, shallow breaths, and so she has to keep her hand on Delphine's ribs. She's been counting breaths, quick panting and then the lull. If she keeps count, she's doing something. She's helping. If it gets worse and they get the doctor to make a visit, she can tell him how many breaths she's had, and the rhythm of them. She could beat the rhythm out on her knee.

Delphine's head is on the pillow, her mouth open. Roxy watches her lids flitting, like someone who's just walked up from a root cellar into blazing sun, but they never catch and fill with sight. Just flit and flit.

Roxy sings, "There's a hole in the bucket, dear Liza, dear Liza. There's a hole in the bucket, dear Liza, a hole." But her voice is low, raspy. It warbles terribly, so she stops.

Roxy didn't see her mother die, actually. She saw her

being handed over to death, but not the final exchange. Her mother made her leave the house before, just days before, to make sure she wouldn't be kept there. Her mother insisted on seeing, with her very own eyes, Roxy leave. She wanted to hear the rabble of her sons, her husband, the panic of them without her, without Roxy taking care of everything. Although it made her mother supremely happy to see her go, Roxy hadn't wanted to. She wanted to stay by the bed with a washcloth, ice chips to cool her mouth, to change her messed sheets and fit the pillows around her just so. Roxy supposes her mother died in soiled sheets, yellowed with piss, in her dank room, listening to the tumult of her riotous boys below her.

Roxy wishes she'd been there not only to comfort her mother but also to know if this is what it is like: a lull between ragged breaths and the lull lasts and lasts until it isn't a lull but a new truth. Roxy sits on the edge of the bed, wilts down, resting her head on her knees, squeezing her eyes shut. She wishes that Delphine's daddy had never shown up. She wishes that they weren't coming back to get Lettie, even though she knows it may be best for her. Hell, even Delphine said it might be the best thing for Lettie, but it didn't stop her from smoking pill after pill, and drinking, too. It's just the sight of family that threw all this on. It's just knowing that you've come so far from where you started out that can do it. Roxy has imagined her own father and her brothers showing up here, wanting to take her back. She imagines what they would do if they knew how she loved Delphine and how the two of them have learned to move against each other, with each other, more loving than the way Roxy was made to be put on this earth, she's sure of that. Roxy has wanted to take Delphine away from the house, the whoring old Mr. Holman, for example, half his body dead, but his dick still poised and trained on Delphine; the opium, its ugly ritual of smoke and talk and listlessness. She's confided in Delphine her dream of pretending to be old-maid sisters in a quiet town without her bamboo bowl and pipe, without a Chinese laundry and its handwritten invitations in the up-down scroll that only the fiends understand as opium. She's told Alma, too, that they may not stay forever, that one day they could have a garden with a birdhouse. A place of their own with new curtains and cut flowers in a vase. She has hoped for this ordinary life, has imagined a woman kneeling in a garden, wrenching weeds, a bland light, pouring equally, normally over a small house, a stoop, a bicycle leaning against a shed, a dull day, an ordinary moment within it. Roxy could be that woman, and Delphine could be calling from the front door, lined with stout, trimmed bushes, "Lunch is ready. Come in before it gets too cold."

But right now, Roxy cares nothing for any of it. She promises herself that if Delphine comes to, she'll never mention it again, because it does no good. It makes Delphine alternately sullen and nervous. And now all she wants is the life she has with Delphine in Alma's house, even with Mr. Holman's rigid dick and the whores and drunk men and the hop smoke. It is, in fact, the best life she's known. She has devoted herself to it, and sometimes it grows so large under the lamp of her devotion that Delphine rises up from the house, enormous, in Roxy's imagination. So large and ever present that Roxy feels small, tiny enough to curl in Delphine's broad lap, and more than anything Roxy wants to be that little and taken care of.

Roxy lifts Delphine's hand. It's cool and damp. She pets it like the hand is a small rabbit, ears flat to its body. She strokes it sweetly. She feels like she is going to start to cry. She says, "Wake up. Wake up, Delphine." She says, "Be my bride. Be my bride forever and ever." She says, "I am devoted to you. Devoted." She says all of this so many times she isn't sure if hours have passed. It becomes a prayer even though she doesn't know much of God. And then there's a little give in the hand, a small tightening, and Delphine's eyes catch. And Roxy feels like she has brought her back to life.

"You were almost dead," she tells Delphine. "You nearly killed yourself."

"And you are an angel from heaven."

Roxy cannot speak. Her throat is tight. She kneels down beside the bed and lays her head on Delphine's chest. She listens to the soft patter of her fragile heart.

5

*J*ust days later, he's back, Delphine's skittish father, with his hat slowly spinning round and round in his hands. He takes it off too fast. It catches on some hairs, flipping them up, and so he smooths the strays and smooths the hat, many more times than necessary.

"Come in, Reverend. Come on in," Alma says.

He ducks in as if too tall for the doorjamb, but he's a small man, and the ducking is actually a polite nod. The car, parked in the dirt driveway, is bulky and old. It looks like a hand-me-down junker, treated now with a tenderness, a homely pride. It's clean and polished; even its tires look like they've been scrubbed not too long ago. His wife, Mrs. Line, sits in the passenger's seat, a handkerchief raised to her mouth so from here she looks like she has a thin white beard; even so, there's the obvious bulge of a goiter. His daughter,

Eloise, plain-looking, stout, stands beside her, talking through the open window.

Delphine is upstairs and won't come down for Lettie's departure. Roxy is here, in her place. She's set out tea, but it doesn't seem like they'll be staying for long, in light of the fact that only Mr. Line has come to the door. And so she shifts by the tray, ready to offer, but too shy to bring it up. Roxy is a gem, sweet and awkward. She's not what she appears to be, big and strapping; she's actually the gentlest person Alma knows. Who else would put up with Delphine and her moods?

Reverend Line nods at Roxy, and Alma introduces them. Roxy sticks out her hand and shakes his like a man would. He's obviously frightened by her.

"Is your daughter ready?" he asks.

"She's just getting a few things." Alma turns and calls for her. "Lettie! It's time now, darling. Lettie!"

The reverend is looking back toward his wife, his daughter, his car, protectively. Suddenly, Alma hears a growl in the driveway, another car. Her stomach turns. She's immediately wary. She wonders if it could be an angry husband, a love-struck john here off hours, or the captain, to take her for a ride, the sweaty chin, the speech on trouble on its way, the wide hand on the seat between them, filled with innuendo, but, no, it's broad daylight. The reverend walks closer to the parlor window. His hat circles faster, a twitch, twitch, twitch, sliding through his fingers.

Pearly hops out and jogs up the porch steps. Her chuffy hips jostle and her full breasts sway loosely. She stumbles in, smiles and gives a giggly wave to the reverend who coughs. Alma is relieved, but why is Pearly here? Alma doesn't want the reverend to see her at work. Alma stares at Pearly gravely, grabs her by the wrist, and pulls her away from the reverend, to a space under the stairs.

"What is it?" she asks in a hushed whisper.

"Well, I need my room. I have a date and he was a good old customer, but must've got himself a girlfriend, 'cause I haven't seen hide nor hair of him in ages. Some said he'd adopted the pox, but he looks healthy. I'll check him good first. I'd like to keep him. Can we come in and use a room? I need the money, Alma. You know my husband is out of a job."

Alma doesn't like even the rumor of syphilis. The gossip of a man with the pox coming around can kill business. But that's beside the point, as is the fact that Pearly's husband is unemployed. She's never known him to have a job. It's not a good time, and this is her house, after all. But before she has a chance to say no, the door creaks open and there stands Mr. Bass. He's still wearing the same old getup, the white shirt with its stiff collar. There is the sharp knot of his Adam's apple, the slick black flap of his hair, small fingers. She wonders if he's got the pox or not. She looks at his hands to see if they're mottled, perhaps his chest hides a rash, or, for now, perhaps there's only a seared burning, a painful, unending itch. She despises him, recalling Mrs. Bass, his narrow-boned, ugly wife, her poor jabbing broom trying to conquer the swirling dust, how she spoke to Alma in her stifling office, told her that her husband had no children, only the idea of them. And Alma hasn't thought of it for years, but Mrs. Bass was right after all. Henry has no children. He never really did.

Mr. Bass looks over at the reverend. "Your first time in a place like this? You look nervous as a cat!" Mr. Bass still talks too loudly, his ears scarred by the factory's din.

Alma remembers some of Mrs. Bass's speech. It comes back to her clearly. She walks up to Mr. Bass, she says, "You are full of ideas, Mr. Bass. Only that. And this is not a good one."

He's taken aback. "Where did you hear that talk?"

"Go home, Mr. Bass," she says, now shuffling him out while Pearly huffs loudly behind her, an audible pout.

The two of them clamber down the steps. Pearly is talking in her sweet singsong, trying not to lose the date. Mr. Bass's car engine revs, wheels churn on the gravel. Alma is sure that everything has gone wrong. She's the madam of a whorehouse; what does she know of miracles? That's the nun's business, and what does she know of it, even? Wasn't the nun once just a farm girl swimming a lake? Couldn't she simply be a farmer's wife striding through a coop, swooping up chickens and breaking their weak necks? Would she take advice on miracles from a girl in a lake, a farmer's wife? Alma looks around the room, a little lost. She remembers leaving the kitchen that last time before sifting through the sugar can for her liver-pill bottles stuffed with money, Irving waving, just a long-armed boy, from the porch. She was hopeful then, too, wasn't she?

Reverend Line turns to Roxy. "You have bees." They're standing together like two men in a barbershop waiting their turn.

"What do I have?" Roxy asks.

"Bees."

Alma has overheard them, but she's not sure if she's understood. "What did you say?"

"You have carpenter bees boring into your shingles. I can hear them from here."

There is always the constant zip of flies, but above it, thicker, deeper there's a low hum outside above the window, more electric, a tapping buzz as bees bump up against the house. It's a strange, lurching moment. The three of them stand quietly, breaths held. Alma looks at the reverend. She wonders if it's a warning. Is he saying that if bees bore holes until her house is nothing but chewed wood, it's best that it not fall on her daughter's head?

"When they are asleep, you can seal the holes with tar," he offers.

Alma thinks of her tooth, plastered over with creosote. She'll add more tonight. "Are you a handyman? Or did you read it in a book?"

"No," the reverend admits, shrugging. "I've heard others say it will work. I'm making conversation." He blushes, and again he is a miracle in his suit, his placid tie. He is the perfect choice.

Lettie appears on the stairs. She is lugging a suitcase, one shoulder hunched up to carry the weight. Still it knocks against her knee and thigh. When she gets to the last step, the reverend is there to take it. He hoists it up with a bit of muscle and totes it out to the car.

Roxy says, "Sometimes life isn't the way you want it. It's not just like you expect, but it can still turn out good. Sometimes it's better."

Alma nods. "It's the right thing. It's the best thing. I know that to be the truth."

Lettie says nothing. Her eyes are puffed, red-rimmed. She smooths the bodice of her dress, a small gesture of resignation, and walks out the door. Alma follows her across the porch.

Reverend Line is behind the wheel. Eloise waves her plump, pale hand, moves to the back door of the car, opens it for Lettie, who climbs in. It is at this moment—Roxy and Alma now side by side on the porch, the house calm except for the thrum of drilling bees overhead—that the passenger's door opens and Mrs. Line nearly tumbles out. She still has the handkerchief in her hand, but now waves it wildly like a flag of surrender over her head. She calls out, "Delphine! My baby girl! Delphine! I know you hear me!"

plays. In her house, there is only her mother's sternness, and the girls, who are actresses. Sometimes they get upset and carry on, but Lettie has seen them flaunt and whoop and shimmy with this exhausted showmanship, a glib professionalism, that she has trouble knowing when they're telling the truth. She doesn't know what to do with Mrs. Line's small outbursts. She wonders if they're real or for show, and then if she is the audience.

When they arrive at the Lines' house, tall and narrow with black shutters, it's nearly time to eat dinner. The Reverend Line opens the door for her, then returns to the car to get her suitcase. Eloise is helping Mrs. Line, who seems to be resisting coming home. She stands in the yard, shaking her head, sharp jerks that loosen a spray of fine hairs fanning around her head. She turns back to the car, and Lettie notices her wide, flat backside, the dress clinging to it in bunches.

Lettie walks into the house alone. She thinks of the orphanage, cold and empty, the nuns in their stiff skirts, their stone faces, the shushing like a hiss pushed up and spit out through the narrow gaps of their teeth. The mattress there had been flat and hard, and she'd never slept by herself before then. There'd always been her brothers' restless bodies on either side. So she felt loose in the orphanage bed and was afraid she was going to fall out onto the hard floor. But she rarely slept. She listened to the other girls, their deep rattling coughs, their murmuring sleep talk. When she did drift off, her dreams were so horrible she would wake up screaming.

Once an older girl stormed over and put a pillow over her face. Lettie kicked and kicked, clawing at bare arms, but the girl was thick and strong. She held her there so long that Lettie stopped being able to breathe. She came up gasping as if she'd been drowned. There was one time she followed a mouse out of the chambers into a small chapel, but she isn't sure if it was real or a dream. She remembers it clearly, the statue of Mary, her angelic, lamentable face, and being carried by a stiff-chested nun. But her dreams are so vivid, she can't tell them from memory. This is only the second time she's ever been away from home. She has already made plans not to stay.

The entranceway opens into a parlor. It smells of wood polish, liniment, wet newspaper print. Small, dark, tidy, the antimacassars glow white draped over the backs of two stiff armchairs. It's quiet, and seems empty, but for a deep restlessness, a shuffling. And then she notices that she isn't alone. Her eyes adjust and she sees the bird cages, one in every corner. Yellow and blue canaries. The birds' little feet clutch swings. Some perch cockeyed from the cage bars. They are intently interested in Lettie. Their little feathered heads fluff at her intrusion.

Mrs. Line dashes past Lettie to the kitchen, where she starts rattling pans. The Reverend Line puts the suitcase down. He looks disheveled by the windy car, exhausted. He sinks into a wooden chair next to a small table with a Bible on it and on the wall, a picture of an old man with a white beard praying over a loaf of bread.

Eloise says, "Father will study here." She points to her father, and then motions for Lettie to follow her. She walks Lettie past the kitchen. "Mother will prepare dinner." She walks her up a narrow staircase, steep as a ladder. At the top of the stairs there are three doors. "My parents' bedroom. The lavatory. And our room. I shared it with Delphine before she departed."

Lettie wonders if this is the way she usually says it, as if Delphine died tragically. The room is tight. Two narrow beds with matching dark mahogany headboards take up most of the room. Against one wall, there is a small desk of papers and books. Lettie hefts the suitcase onto the bed.

"Not that one," Eloise instructs. And so Lettie hefts it again to the farthest bed. She walks to the window that faces out to the road. She's relieved that she has a clear view. She'll be able to see Smitty in the car from her window when he comes for her.

"Why don't you unpack? I'll be grading at my desk. I'm teaching summer classes to some of my most intelligent students."

Lettie doesn't inquire about Miss Eloise's smart students, although it's obviously been offered as a subject for discussion. Lettie isn't interested. Her mother would take her to school each year, but then she would start to cry and then to flail and cling. The teacher would tell her mother to leave. Once the teacher said, "I'll hang her on a coat hook until she calms herself." For years, they would trudge home together,

Lettie's fingers clamped around her mother's hand. Finally, by age nine or so, before her father left, she wanted to go, but by then she was far behind. She lost hope quickly, couldn't ever see the point, and when she returned after her mother started her business up, the other girls snubbed her. They hushed as she approached and snickered at her. The last teacher she remembers was softer than Miss Eloise, but young. She lavished Lettie with pity, often coupled her up for classroom projects with a crippled girl, and she would gaze at the two of them, her head tilted, so proud of her own bigheartedness. It made Lettie sick. "I prefer just to rest my eyes," she says. If she unpacks, she'll just have to fill the suitcase again once everyone falls asleep.

Eloise nods as if she were asked permission. It's obvious that she's a schoolmarm, used to being asked for allowances. Lettie doesn't like it. Eloise goes to her desk and begins to mark papers. Lettie closes her eyes. She can feel Smitty on top of her, the biting glass. She presses her knees together, to force away the image, and there's a tenderness between them. She's still puffed and sore.

Eloise never looks at Lettie. She never looks up from her papers. She just begins to talk. "Mother has nerves because her brother died when she was little. It was a fire. And she's been nervous ever since. My father married her because he thought he could calm her, that, through the Lord's power, he could help her. But he never could. And Delphine was difficult for her. And she'd have to lock her up, the girl was so

wild, so full of, you know, the fire." She pauses, twists in her
chair to face Lettie, who is thinking about fire, house fires
and the ones that are in a wild girl like Delphine, like herself,
too, she figures. Eloise says, "What about Delphine? Is she
okay?"

"I suppose she's okay." But really Lettie isn't so sure. She
knows about the opium. Its deep scent has bored its way into
Delphine's clothes, her hair, the drapes, the wood, the mattress of her bed. It clings to her. And she's seen her drunk on
it. Roxy has tried to hide it, but Lettie knows about her wil-
lowy arms, her red eyes, the too-tranquil smile. She's seen her
wobble to the bathroom. And, of course, there's the fact that
Delphine and Roxy are lovers. She doesn't think that Eloise
would approve of that. She wonders if she doesn't marry
Smitty, what might become of her. She's scared that she's got
the fire like Delphine and that if Smitty forgets her tonight,
she could become a fiend, a whore. Or, maybe, she would fall
in love with a woman.

"What about you?" Eloise says.

Lettie props herself on her elbows. "I'm getting married,"
she says, although she thinks she could have just as easily told
her she was poisoned, that she let Smitty inside her and she
might die, milk-sick, rotting, even though it isn't clear-
headed.

"Are you?"

"Yes. We're going to buy a house on Greenmont Avenue.
Do you know where that is?" Her mother would like her to

stay here forever, would be happiest if she had a daughter like Eloise who could grade papers while she counted her money.

"Yes, they're new houses, small and pretty."

"I'd prefer to live in a house that's never been lived in before. I like the idea of it being fresh. I won't be staying here long."

"I will always stay," Eloise says. "Delphine left, and so I have to stay. It's a kind of agreement. It has broken their hearts to lose Delphine. I will never leave them. I'm a small consolation, really. I do what I can, and yet she has the power to kill them. She does so every day. Slowly. They will die with her name on their tongues. Not Jesus'. That's the truth."

It's quiet for a while, and then a little bell rings from downstairs. Eloise straightens her papers and stands, pushing in her chair. "Dinner is ready."

Lettie follows her down the stairs through the kitchen, a pale yellow, so pale it looks drained, faded, like Mrs. Line's blouse and her face, too, for that matter. She has a sagged expression, her eyelids heavy, the pouches beneath them drooped. Mrs. Line looks at her wearily, her face moist from a pot at the stove, her goiter like an enormous cockeyed lump in her throat. She stares at her with this awful love, a sickening sadness.

The table is already set, the plates identically allotted with exact portions: four small carrots, a heap of peas, a crust of bread, and some kind of dark brown fatty soup. In the other room, Lettie can hear the birds rustling, chirping. Reverend

Line sits at the head of the table, his wife at the opposite. He motions with his head where Lettie should sit. The chair is hard. The plain, thin wooden cross on the wall reminds Lettie of the orphanage, except their Jesus was always on it, bleeding, permanently dying, and they were told that he was dying for them, their sins, their hearts darkened with evil thoughts and deeds. She wonders if Jesus is dying now more than ever on the orphanage crosses, knowing what she let Smitty do to her. But it seems that no matter what they did, they were killing him, and he took it. Lettie wants him to step down off the crosses, to give up on her. The nuns seemed to think the orphans were lost causes anyway, their soiled souls. Why go on? Why persist? She wonders if Jesus doesn't find some pleasure in dying. Why else would he do it so gorgeously with the thorned crowns and the ladder of ribs? She prefers the empty cross, simple, austere, but honest. He died and then rose. It's more hopeful. She can become clean and white again. No one says that a wife is impure. A wife is a wife.

The reverend bows his head, and everyone else follows. He says, "Thank you, Lord, for this gracious plenty. Thank you for all of your gifts of life. Thank you for bringing Lettie to our table."

Lettie lifts her eyes. Eloise's head is bowed deeply. But Mrs. Line is gazing at Lettie again, her body leaning forward toward her. She wonders if Mrs. Line is waiting for Delphine to emerge, if Mrs. Line thinks that if she looks at Lettie with enough pitiful love, she'll turn into her lost daughter.

"And watch over our wayward sheep," the reverend concludes.

Mrs. Line puts her hands to her lips now and prays fervently, her mouth moving quickly. Everyone says amen, except Mrs. Line, who is lost in her own set of prayers, her chin to her chest, her eyes screwed tightly. They wait for her to finish, and finally she reappears, like someone who's been underwater, like someone who prefers it to all of this light and air.

Eloise says, "You'll get used to things here, Lettie, so that you'll like it, I'll wager."

Lettie imagines her own house. Her mother would be giving over the downstairs by now, the parlor filling with men, Lettie retreating to their bedroom. "It's very different from what I'm used to," Lettie says.

Eloise asks, "And how is that?"

Reverend Line, too. "Yes, dear, how are things different?"

But Lettie doesn't have a chance to answer. Mrs. Line is irritated. "How can you ask that, knowing where she comes from? Knowing what she was raised with? Filth. All that terrible filth." She turns to Lettie. Their eyes lock now, but Mrs. Line has lost her gaze of deep adoration. "Don't look at me like that," she says bitterly. "I didn't make her that way, you know. I was a good mother." She turns to the reverend. "Did you see that? The way she looked at me like I did something wrong?"

Lettie has no idea what Mrs. Line is referring to, but she

quickly looks down at her plate of carrots, peas, bread. She sips at a spoonful of the soup. It's beef stock without any signs of beef. Reverend Line and Eloise don't say anything. They continue eating. Mrs. Line is glaring around the table, awaiting a challenge. But no one offers her one. Lettie glances at her. She sees a thin line of blood drip from her nose. Mrs. Line picks up her napkin and wipes it away, but the napkin is red now and the nose is dripping quickly. Four red splotches plop to her dress front. She gasps lightly. The reverend and Eloise look at her. They are not startled. She stands up. "Excuse me." And rushes to the kitchen with her head tilted back and the napkin pressed to her nose.

Reverend Line says, "Don't mind her, darling. She's got a bad case of nerves."

Eloise agrees. "Yes, she does. It's an awful shame. She's always had nerves like this as long as I can remember."

The reverend says, "Thank goodness the good doctor has managed to help her."

"Yes, yes," Eloise chimes, "thank the good doctor."

"And the Lord," the reverend reminds her.

"Yes, and the Lord."

Lettie looks up from her plate, glances into the kitchen to see Mrs. Line sipping from a bottle of medicine. The napkin is bright red. Clutched in her hand, it looks like a corsage. Her hands are so shaky that it's difficult for her to put the cap back on. Lettie wonders what kind of life this is. She dislikes the quiet, thick with nervousness. The clicking, the cap against the bottle's glass, birds chirping, the scrape of the Reverend Line's spoon against his bowl. She and Smitty won't be like this. For his faults, and she can admit that she's afraid of Smitty—the way he becomes unreachable with anger or passion—he will not be this quiet, this passive. He will not see her bleeding, sobbing, screaming in a stranger's yard, and not do anything about it. And she will not behave like Mrs. Line. She will not be hysterical and then skittish. She'll have beef in her soups. She'll sigh at the end of prayers like her heart has just been aired.

The headlights tour the yard. Lettie watches them streak the walls, a bright momentary flare. She sits at Eloise's small vanity. She quickly lights a match from a box she stole from Pearly's dresser top. She blows it out and rubs the char on her pinky tip, then presses a fine line of its ash on her eyelid, close to her lashes, to outline her eyes, a trick she learned from watching the girls in her mother's house primp in front of mirrors. She listened all night, pretending to sleep, while keeping up with the whereabouts of each of the Lines. Mrs. Line clattered up the stairs first, all grunts and sighs. She scrubbed in the bathroom and then fell heavily into bed. Eloise was more dainty and quiet, only making ruffling noises until she fell asleep, at which point she gave out a puff-and-hiss snore. Lettie waited for the Reverend Line. Once he walked upstairs to use the toilet, but then he headed back downstairs and never returned to bed. Now Smitty is here in the yard, his car door ajar. He's standing waiting for her.

Her suitcase is heavy. She tiptoes while hefting it with both hands, one on top of the other, grasping the handle. As she makes her way down the stairs, she can sense someone in the living room. A breathing presence. She tells herself that it's just the birds, their accumulated breaths, but she knows that it is the Reverend Line. She braces herself for a word from him, but the room is quiet. She stares into the room, her eyes running over the dark lumps of furniture. Her heart races. Smitty is in the yard, shifting, pacing, but she feels frozen, panicked. Her eyes rest on the floor, a dim square of light from the clouded moon. There are two dark objects— the reverend's shoes? Her eyes move up the chair. Is he seated there? The white blur, is it his hands folded in his lap? She doesn't know why she has stopped here. She doesn't under-stand why she wants him to say something, but she does. She wants him to blurt out her name, to wrestle her, tearfully, to the sofa and beg her to stay, to be his little girl. When she was little, she could walk on her hands, a fleeting thought, disconnected. It made her father proud.

Perhaps the reverend will come to help her with her suit-case, if nothing else, offer a final blessing. She says, "Reverend Line?" And there is a commotion of wings. The birds dart suddenly through the room, uncaged. The air becomes a brisk stir of their small, skittish bodies. The white spot on the chair, his hands part, each one spread on a knee as if he might rise, but then the birds settle. The reverend doesn't stand. She can feel the manacle of her mother's hope, and remotely, Irving's hopes for her, Roxy's and Delphine's, even the Lines'—Eloise and her crazed mother and the reverend, silent—but she doesn't know how to fulfill them.

She opens the door, her suitcase bruising her leg, out into the night. Smitty smiles, waves, his hand a flurry over his head, suddenly boyish. He is her husband-to-be, and her future is as clean as a fresh white bed linen.

It is midday but dark. The air is thick with ash, as if the sky has capped the rising smoke and trapped it. Alma opens the front door, holding the squeaky handle of a bucket of potatoes curled in three fingers, and a knife, its sharp tip pointing out, pinched by the same hand's pointer and thumb. And there suddenly, poised to knock, is the reverend. His eyes widen at the glinting knife, and she comes to a quick stop so as not to stab him in the stomach. He flattens his tie with his palm. She points with the knife up into the sky, pulls a handkerchief from a pocket, and covers her nose and mouth. "What's this weather? The air is soupy with char, isn't it?"

"It's a change," he says. "It happens. The farmers say the temperature shifts and it forms a lockup in the clouds. It'll break."

"How do you know?"

"I'm in the business of discussing the weather."

"I thought you were in the business of discussing God."

"When people are dying, they prefer to talk about the weather."

"Has anyone died?"

"No, no."

"Then what?"

"Alma," he says, tilting his head, his eyes downcast. It's dim, his features nearly lost in the gray air. He pauses, looks back behind himself, to the empty car, the field where the cow usually stands but today is not. She doesn't see it, doesn't hear its hollow tocking bell. Perhaps it's dying in its stall. When his eyes return to look at her, they are teary. She already knows what he's come to say. The car is empty. He's nervous. He hasn't made the hazardous switchback across the mountain to retrieve a bracelet, a hair comb. She looks at his mouth, the softness of his lips. She wants to kiss him. The notion announces itself in her mind. She hasn't wanted to kiss anyone for years, not since Henry, and here is the frail reverend, nearly trembling. He seems afraid of her.

Alma says, "She's gone." It comes as no surprise to her. She is almost proud of Lettie. She has been a tractable child, too often eager to please. *And what about me,* Alma wonders. Isn't she tractable, too? She is a madam of a whorehouse, and yet she's a pristine woman who peels potatoes on her front porch, metal bucket, peeling knife, her old pinching shoes, a thin sweater, a simple life, in her own way, one that's grown worn and comfortable as a stuffed chair. "I'm not shocked," she says.

A mosquito rises up around the reverend's face, dangling its thin legs, and lands delicately, its pronged feet on his cheek. She says, "Reverend," and points to the spot. He must have felt it, because he smacks it squarely. There is a spot of blood, too much to be the mosquito's alone. Alma hands him the handkerchief that she's been breathing through.

The reverend seems surprised by her full face, as if he'd grown quickly accustomed to seeing only her narrowed eyes. He looks away, into the yard, and dabs the bite with the handkerchief, red-splotched, until it no longer bleeds. He says, "I'm sorry."

"For what?" She isn't sure if he's sorry about having bloodied her handkerchief, having killed the mosquito, or having let her daughter run off.

"I wanted to do a good deed," he says, "to save her. I've failed."

Suddenly, he reminds Alma of the elephant. She hasn't thought of it for years. Once she saw a cow in the fields, pregnant with twin calves, and she told the children about the elephant working on the Miami dock. It was the cows' widened ribs that had recalled it, and the memory had caused a sharp pang. The children could sense it. Irving was especially wide-eyed, and she knew what it was like, the hushed silence that fell on her as a child whenever her mother told a story about her father. They asked no questions. But it isn't anything physical this time. It's that the reverend seems so out of place, as wondrous as the elephant, as grand a thing as that, but not made use of. Put to work like an ordinary mill horse.

Alma takes a step closer to him. She wants to see him more clearly, and it's dark, the sun a dusky spot in the sky. She puts her hand on his cheek, the small swell of the bite. The thought is gone. She won't kiss him. She's touching his cheek, a gentle benediction. It's soft, shaven, warm. He puts his hand on hers. He leans forward and kisses her on the mouth. It is momentary. Fleeting, but her eyes close. Her body remembers this gentleness. Then he withdraws. Her eyes flit open. He backs away, fumbling in his pocket for keys.

She calls out, "Reverend." But he is already down the steps. She worries now that he thinks she's a whore, like the others. She runs out toward the car. She's angry at herself for having given in to memory, having for a moment forgotten her place—she was going to peel potatoes: the bucket, the peeling knife—and then the reverend came to discuss her daughter. She returns to this simplicity. He has already shut the door, but she puts her hand on the open window. "You came here to tell me about my daughter. Where did she go?"

"She left in the night. A car came. And she snuck out to it."

She wants to tell him that she's not a whore. And that if she were, it would have been different with him there on the porch. The reverend looks at her hand, lets his eyes wander up her arm, her neck, to her eyes. It is a gentle gesture. She touches her mouth where his lips had been. He looks down. He says, "I'm weak. I am a weak man. If I weren't a minister, if I weren't married to my wife, the father of my two daughters, and devoted to Jesus, I would be different. But I'm not. And I tell you, I know about loss. I know how it takes up company and doesn't ever leave you. Do what it calls of you to save your daughter."

She lifts her hand from the window, lets it fall to her side, and he drives away. Alma stands in the yard, and she feels like a stranger, new to the darkened yard, the hedgerow, the field, her lilting house. When did her lot become a field of bluets, their white petals cupping pinches of coal? It seems small to her. Everything, not just the flowers, dulled by layers of coal dust. She senses a familiar tension, a tightening of expectation. She remembers the loud, riotous machines in the hosiery mill, and how she likened them to her own restless heart. She would eat the yard if she could. She is wanting. She would open her mouth and swallow it whole.

6

*I*rving has finished eating his lunch, meats from a warm tin, in his room. His white laundry truck is parked out front, and he jogs down the stairs to get back to work. It's afternoon, but lit like dusk. It's been dark and ashy all day. In fact, the globed row of lights on High Street are lit like it's night, and Irving has driven with his headlights cutting the thick air. All morning the women in the houses on his route talked to him about the darkening sky, and how they will all perish, suffocate under a blanket of soot if it doesn't break. Irving buried his nose and mouth in the crook of his arm and kept to work. "I'm sure it'll break," he consoled them. "Just keep the babies inside today, and tomorrow the sun will come through." They smiled at him weakly, as if they thought his optimism were a sign of stupidity. One woman even said, "If this doesn't kill us, sure enough something else will come along. The end is nigh. Don't be a fool."

Irving opens the heavy door. The bells jangle, alarming Mrs. Trimski. She pipes up from her spot at the sink. "I have a letter for you." He has never been invited into the parlor that stands between the doorway and the kitchen where the hefty old woman bends to her cigarette tip pinched between her thumb and fingertip. It seems clear that Mrs. Trimski isn't budging, so Irving lopes carefully, nearly on tiptoe, through the dim parlor filled with glass-front desks that tinkle with trinkets. One of Mrs. Trimski's cats sits curled in the corner of a stiff love seat, its head tucked away out of view.

The kitchen is also dark but for a dim, watery light seeping in from the window. Mrs. Trimski hands him the butter-stained envelope without taking her eyes from the greasy panes. "She come in here in a hurry, all bustle and flurry, said to give this to you. It's from your mother."

Irving wonders if Lettie delivered the note. "Was she young?"

"No, plumpish with a wiry man in the car who hollered that she should hurry. Snappish man."

"Oh." Irving imagines it was Pearly, then, and her ungrateful, laggardly husband with the stained teeth. "Why didn't you call me down?"

"I don't know who's in and out." She waves the smoke around with her plump hand dismissively. But Irving knows that she is always aware of her tenants' comings and goings.

In fact, his white laundry truck partially blocks her view. Often if Mrs. Trimski meets him in the hall peeking around a stack of folded towels, she'll say, "Mr. Weathers is going for a stint in the country. And the redhead is sickly." She updates Irving randomly. He's certain that she purposely didn't call him down because she wanted to have a chance to read the letter first, alone, with her buttery toast. The crescents of crusts, dented by a crushed cigarette butt, sit on a small plate on the counter. She looks at him blankly. "Are you going to open it?"

"Later," he tells her. "I'm late." He isn't late, and she knows it. He hasn't been late since Lucy left him and he made a decision to live a stable life that relies on things like punctuality. But he doesn't want to give Mrs. Trimski the satisfaction of seeing his reaction. His mother rarely writes. It's usually only a rebuke, in the guise of a reminder, for having missed a Sunday dinner, but sometimes she drops in bits of news, which could include someone getting knocked up or a drunken client who needed to be tossed out. His mother doesn't want Irving to miss out on her lessons on the risks of passion, what it could lead to. She doesn't want him to become romantic while away from the homestead. And these little extra tidbits would vindicate Mrs. Trimski, who, from her perch, has a hunch that she's better than everyone else, and likes to have those hunches confirmed.

The old woman stubs out a second cigarette into the plate. She says, "Well, go on, then. It's like night out there.

Be careful. The new boarder in room two twisted her ankle on a curb."

She turns to her window, and Irving creeps back through the parlor. He spots the cat again, but it isn't a cat. It's a fur hat. The curved back is really the hat's domed top. He pauses, wondering if he should tell Mrs. Trimski that someone has left their hat behind, but who would wear a fur hat this time of year? Perhaps it's a decoration, a relic from the days of old Mr. Trimski, although he can't imagine a Mr. Trimski, a bookend male version of the sour landlady. Really, he just wants to touch it, and so he reaches out, two fingers brushing the hat's soft fur, but then the cat's head appears. A great yawning hiss. Ears flat. A quick paw swipes at Irving's hand. He stumbles backward, grasping his hand, but he realizes that the cat has no claws, only stubbly padding. He lifts his hand and there isn't even a scratch. The trinkets rattle, and he lurches out of the parlor. Mrs. Trimski peers into the dark room, but Irving is already in the hall now, opening the door.

Two blocks down, he pulls the truck into an empty spot under a streetlight, a dusty glowing bowl. He unfolds the letter, see-through where it was stained.

Dear Irving,

Lettie has run off with Smitty. Do you recall him? Certinly you do. I would like you to keep an eye out for them, as we would preffer Lettie to be at home with us than out in the world with Smitty. I find him trubled. Please, if

*you see ether of them, tell them that Lettie is too young a girl
and must come home—her mother has said so.*

*Please come to Sunday dinner. Bring Lucy, if she would
like to come.*

Love,

Your mother

Irving lets the letter sag in his lap. His sister has run off
with Smitty. It seems unlikely, pieces from two different puz-
zles linking. Smitty belongs to him. He was the one who'd
run off with Smitty. It was his story, not Lettie's. Not that
anything good had come of it, but nonetheless Irving felt
suddenly protective of the memory, the boxed chicken, the
winding drive in Sir Lee's grunting car, the closet where
Smitty banged his head against the plastered walls, dusty,
paint-chipped. He'd always felt guilty about leaving Smitty
behind. Undoubtedly, Sir Lee came home and beat him, but
also Irving had felt manly about it, too. He'd been drunk,
after all, and each man needs to fend for himself. He'd saved
Delphine's life, possibly. In some way, he owed this heroism
to Smitty, who'd taken him in. Were they in love? Irving
wondered. Was it possible for Smitty to fall in love? He was
doubtful. He would have to tell his mother that Lucy had left
him, trying not to give any information about her professional calling in Wheeling. He would have to endure his
mother's smug I-told-you-so and little speeches on how he
will be better off without her.

He folded the letter and stuffed it into the envelope. His route was only half done, the laundry behind him divided evenly between clean and soiled sacks. His life was newly devoted to the simplicity of returning to the lot with his job done, and yet his mother never asked for his help. He couldn't remember her once asking him to come to her rescue. Roxy was the one who threw out the unruly men, not Irving. Roxy was the one to do the heavy work of hauling trash and burning bundles, and if not Roxy, then his mother would do it. She was burly now with the weight she'd taken on over the years. Irving ground the truck into gear. He would do a little looking around—Cheva's, for example, wasn't too far off his route. He'd go down High Street to get there, because Lettie liked the ladies' shops. And so he headed out.

The streets were nearly empty. Most people were staying indoors, windows shut to the sooty air. But Irving looked over each shadowy figure. Their bodies would begin as a distant smudge that emerged into shape, gender, hat, cane. He walked through Cheva's, even glancing for shoes under the men's bathroom stall. It was on High Street that he began to feel frantic. He popped his head into each dress shop, each hat shop. At first, he pretended to be shopping for ladies' gloves, *my wife's birthday,* but then he gave up on that. It took too much time. He soon barged in, lorded around, and then skulked out. He was needed. His mother needed him. He was looking for his lost family, Lettie, Smitty. He could protect his sister, her virginity. He had a second chance to save Smitty, from what? Not Sir Lee; that was long ago. He was looking with such urgency, he wondered if he might actually dig up his father. It was the first time he'd searched people's faces. Perhaps his father had been walking these streets for years, waiting only to be acknowledged. But the search dwindled. He didn't know where else to look. Even after he'd decided it was a lost cause, he was still looking, up and down side streets and alleyways. He saw a few couples, walking arm in arm, hurriedly to get out of the coal-thick air. Once he called out, "Lettie! Lettie!" But when the girl turned, she was piggish with a lazy eye.

So when he actually sees Smitty walking out of a drugstore with two bottles of pop, he doesn't register it immediately. He stays in his truck and watches Smitty cross the street, his eyes skittishly glancing around for traffic. He opens a police-car door and through the dim overhead street lamp, Irving sees their two silhouettes lean together. A long kiss. His sister's hair turned toward him, hanging like a veil. Irving reaches for the handle but doesn't move. The police car starts up. Headlights shine. They pull out and drive off, and Irving lets them. They are doomed. Although no one who met them would suspect it, they are both as fragile as blown glass. He knows this much, and yet he can't stop them. They have a force. They are being propelled, and Irving is a stalled man. He feels weak. Smitty is an accumulation of other people's bad decisions and selfishness, but so is Irving, and if he thought he himself had found some ounce of joy, if he thought he had the ability to fall in love, he would want to be free to go. Cursed, yes. He's been his mother's best student in the destructive powers of love. And his father is not a stranger strolling down High Street. He's gone, for good. Irving will never find him.

He's wasted his day on this chase. He should have stuck to his route, ignoring his mother. He should have been more loyal to his new life. He drives out into the country to get as much of his route done as possible before night. The gas gauge is low. He stops at a service station. The dirt is dry, cracked. A man dozes with his back resting against a small, green shuttered house. A lantern sits at his boots. His hat, which may have been used for fanning or covering his nose and mouth from the dust, now lays flat on his chest. He is waspish, a large tube of a body, with spindly legs hanging down by the stool's legs. Irving has been here before, although he doesn't know the man's name. Irving steps out and starts cranking to fill the glass tank above the pump with gasoline. The metal gears squeak, and he remembers the wheels of the prams, the headless ham, and he wonders if Lettie will try to make a life with Smitty. Will they get married and have children? Will their offspring come out deformed like a wrapped ham with a protruding bone?

"You gonna pay? You gonna pay for that?" It's a voice like a parrot. The sky is truly darkening to dusk, but he can make out a woman sitting in a chair, her hair plastered back, a glossy sheen to it. He steps closer. Her eyes are puffed, sealed, only a small flitting slit to each and short eyelashes that look almost purposefully trimmed. She's older than Irving, but not by much.

"Well, of course I'm going to pay."

"Come here," the woman purrs. "Come here to me."

Irving walks over. She has a large shiny leather Bible on her lap and, on top of it, something that looks like a type-writer, with paper in it. "I don't like mister," she says. "I don't like him. Take me with you."

"I can't take you with me," Irving says.

"I can't see. I'm a blind woman, but he is ugly, isn't he? Tell me. He's an ugly man, mister is."

Irving looks over at him, and he is pasty with a flushed redness to his cheeks. His shirtsleeves are rolled up, and Irving can tell he's a hairy man, nearly furred. "He isn't so bad," he tells her.

"He bought me this machine, brand-new, with all the right parts. It writes Braille. I'm educated. You should take me with you."

"I wouldn't steal you from your husband there." Irving tries to laugh.

"He isn't my husband. He just keeps me, and how do you think I got here?" she asks. "All men are thieves."

He wonders if that is true. If men don't fall in love, they only claim property, and then sometimes relinquish it, as his father did. Perhaps Lettie hasn't run off with Smitty as much as he has stolen her. Irving looks at the blind woman's face. It's pretty, actually, without the nervous eyes, that sometimes flash a pale, watery whitish blue. "I am trying to be a good man," he says. "I wouldn't steal you even if I fell in love with you." And now he feels like he could fall in love with the blind woman at the service station in the country. He wonders if this is how it happened for his father. Some odd moment barely lit, this time the sun's low yellow eye weakened, blurred by ash, and you make a decision. Your life takes a dogleg turn. "No," Irving says again. "I'm a good man."

"I like good men. Sweet men. Kind and gentle. A blind woman relies on it."

She reminds him of his mother, somehow, the way she just comes out with things. He wonders if it wouldn't take a good man to say yes, come with me. Maybe this is how one acquires responsibility—a momentary hesitation, and the right person is there to take advantage. "I can't take you with me." He wants to go on to say something else about the way he will live his life, in defiance of his father, because he isn't like his father, or the parade of worthless men who wander into his mother's house looking for whores, or the men at Cheva's who eyed Lucy each time she rose up from her seat. He will have patience for the everyday, the on and on of things. He'll go back to the delivery service. He'll work hard. He'll keep this job for the rest of his life. He'll be bullheaded. *Why not a blind woman?* he asks himself. *Why not start now? Why not save someone who needs saving?* Not Lucy, not Lettie and

Smitty, or Delphine and his mother, or his father, the lost bastard, for that matter, but someone who can be saved, who wants to be saved.

He walks back to his car, puts the nozzle in its tank, and lets it wash down the hose and fill. He fishes in his pocket for enough money. He places glinting coins on the table next to the furry, wasplike man, who is now snoring.

The blind woman says, "I bet you're pretty. I bet you are fine-looking." And she curls forward over the Braille machine, and begins tapping.

He says, "Is he bad to you?"

She raises her head. "He isn't good. He won't come looking for me. He'll be glad to see me go."

Irving looks at the heavy machine on her lap, the thick Bible. He says, "All right, then. Okay. But you've got to come now." He isn't certain, but he doesn't know what else to do. He wants to be a good man, and it seems a good man would have a blind wife.

7

S he will remember that it was night, and it stayed night. The dark chased them. It had eyes, and Lettie could feel them on her. But then it broke, and they seemed blessed, for a short time, like they were on the other side of something.

"I need to get a white dress," Lettie said.

Smitty squinted at the road. The thick smoky air lifted quickly. It was now bright enough that each oncoming car caught sun in its windshield, a jostling rectangle of light. "We'll stop in town, doll. At a fancy shop. And then we'll get us a room after the courthouse. We'll get us a real motel cabin for our honeymoon."

She will remember the windshields, the nearly blazing procession of them. She will remember that the dress he bought her was light blue, not white. And the way he sneered at the salesclerk, "She don't need a *white* wedding dress! Blue will suit her fine." The courthouse will be a blur of wood railings and empty rowed seats. Papers to sign. White concrete steps and the car again. A shiny flask. The motor cabin's dark room. The stained sheets. Dull, dark, muddy stains, but blood clearly enough. The smell of feet, sweat, and in the private bathroom, a sharp biting bleach.

She will always be able to recall that once on the bed, it was like splitting open a wound, wordless. The only sound a rustling of the sheets, the suction and rub of bodies. She thought of the restless caged birds. She tried to pretend she was not there, but in the reverend's house, only listening to birds. But then he rolled her on top of him. It was a break from his weight.

He said, "Put your hands on my throat."

She did so, gently.

"Choke me. Make it so I can barely breathe."

"No, I can't." She was breathless with pain. He was still inside of her.

"Harder," he said. "Harder than that."

She could feel her face tightening. She began to cry, but her hands clasped the cords of his neck, reached around to his sharp Adam's apple. She started to choke him with all of her strength. His eyes went wild. He grabbed her arms, slapped her face so hard that she was knocked from the bed, her body clattering against the floor.

"You trying to kill me, bitch? You bitch." Breathless, he sat on the edge of the bed.

It was quiet. She won't believe that it truly was this quiet. She understood how one person can kill another with barely a sound. She lurched off of the bed, stood, and walked to the bathroom. Her nightgown, wrinkled from riding up around her armpits, wet with sweat.

She will remember this clearly. She pulled the chain on the light. She looked in the mirror. Her neck was red with his handprints. There was a cut from his ring on her cheek. She took toilet paper and blotted the blood. She stared at the bright red on the white paper and sank to the floor, reaching up only to lock the door. The floor looked like water to her suddenly, the swirling water of her dream; the hand reaching out to her was her own hand and her own face underwater looking up. She reached for her hand, but then the image was gone. The floor was simply the bathroom floor, tiled, cool, the grout blackened with dirt.

He knocked softly on the door, saying, "Dollbaby, come on out. Come on out. Don't be this way, doll."

But now she was in the bathroom in his seedy apartment. She was touching her puffed lip, shaking because he had held the gun to her face, the gun from his belt hung on the back of their door, and he'd said, *Bang, bang, bang*. He didn't like the way she looked around like nothing was good enough for her. She comes from a goddamn whorehouse, and nothing's good enough for her?

It was a sweet little place in a run-down row. She told him again and again that it suited her just fine, that she adored it. But she hated the rush of days, a murky haze of scrubbing floors, of lurking in the kitchen, the gauzy blur of time, the grind of labor to keep busy, to keep out of his sight. The neighbor women talked while stringing laundry, but Lettie shied away from them. The women were garrulous, rowdier even than the women in her mother's whorehouse, angrier, more worn. They hissed at her about her bruises, told her to fix it, put him in his place with a kettle of boiling water poured on him while he slept.

She remembers icing a cake, that the icing clumped on her knife, and it made her so nervous that he would beat her for it—he was in a mood—that she wretched in the kitchen sink. And he slapped her for the wretching. The nights were worse, disorienting. He would come home, lights suddenly ablaze in each room. A wild lust. The drunken, loping, arching hunt of his body for hers.

Wasn't it the day of the cake that she was in the bathroom again when there was a distant knock? Her mother's voice. *Open up this goddamn door. You hear me? Smitty, you let her come home with me. You are some son of a bitch to pull this.*

She heard the door open, Smitty saying, *Are you disturbing the peace, Alma? I could have you arrested for that.*

Lettie slipped out of the bathroom. She stood next to a chair, hoping to see her mother. *I could have you arrested for beating on your wife.*

No, Smitty told her. *And you know what else? You can't do a damn thing about anything. Because she is my wife. You understand me? Do I have to call the police? Oh, no—my, my—I am the police.*

But after he shut the door on her mother, he turned on Lettie with a wholly new viciousness, a betrayed man, and she didn't have enough time to run back to the bathroom and lock the door. He grabbed her by the waist. He beat her, saying, *Why did you go and tell family? We're family now. What there is stays between us, and we are tied together forever.* He beat loyalty into her, and then left her there on the floor. He was going out to get a drink.

She will remember how she set to work, methodically, but quick. The sky was heavy with rain. She took the bullets out of his gun and put them in her pocket, where they clicked together. She picked up his clothes from their drawers, from the closet, from the suitcase he'd been rummaging through for a week or more. They smelled like him, sour, dank. She dumped armfuls into the bathtub. She struck a match and then another and another, watched just long enough to see them catch, the fire to rise up. She took her own suitcase and walked out the back door, a flimsy wood door with a loose screen. The neighbor—was her name Alice?—looked up at her lazily. A cigarette hanging from the sticky inside of her lip. But Alice didn't say anything. Lettie climbed over fences, took off her ring and thew it into a patch of trees, and the bullets, too. They pattered against trees and onto the ground. The suitcase was too heavy. It pulled her arm. She dropped it, and started running, each bruise ringing through her body. The sky opened, a crack of light, and then rain, too. She felt like she was floating, like she was swept up in a tide. She found her way to the pocked road. Puddles filled the dips, colliding circles. Cars slowed and then passed her. She listed toward home, her body buoying, drifting, until finally she saw the hedgerow, and then her yard, the house growing straight up out of the ground, and there was her mother, windblown and soaking, ripping clothes off the line, her mother, a crazy woman, a screeching gull, drowning, crying out, the sheets wet and swelling as sails.

8

*A*lma must think, and yet she's distracted. Her body, rain-wet, slick, her knees muddy from falling while pulling clothes from the line, doesn't feel like her own. It was anger and hate. Didn't she throw herself into the full, windy sheet? Didn't she want it to lift her? But it snapped off the line, and she fell into it. The sun is loud, broken through the sky, but low, about to set. It clamors, pouring in the kitchen windows in great wide, dross-laced streams. It is disorienting to Alma. When she heard Lettie had run off, the sun was roiled in sooty clouds, a constant night, and then there is this new light. Now, she cannot shake the new gratitude she has for the sun. She had taken it for granted, as she had her daughter. Who'd been taken. The flies bash themselves against the panes. Lettie is back.

The three of them sit around the table, Lettie in the middle, Roxy and Delphine on either side, holding her daughter's hands, keeping her pinned to earth. She looks as if she would drift up without them, and rise away. The light, they're golden from it, drenched in sun. She loves them. Her heart grieves.

Roxy says, "I'll kill him."

Delphine hushes. "You'll scare her."

But Roxy is right. Alma has already decided to kill Smitty, although she doesn't know how. It shocks her how quickly the notion came to her and how it's taken hold, become unshakable. The murder exists like a stone inside of her that she won't be free of, until she hoists it out by the killing. She isn't afraid as much as she is disturbingly calm. She knows it won't be hard for her. When she became a mother, she felt what an animal must feel, the deep pain calcifying into an animalistic protectiveness. It was after giving birth, holding her children, that she felt the most tender and the most capable of murder. Men are no good at killing. They murder the wrong ones, for the wrong reasons. Her father, with his bitten, hissing tongue, didn't ask anyone to kill the Prophet. Her father was already gone by then. And God is no better at choosing who should live and die. Her baby was born dead, wrapped in a sheet and taken away, her mother, too.

"He'll come for me," Lettie says through jerking sobs. "He'll stay out all night tonight. When he's this bad off, he doesn't come home until he's slept it off. He'll come home in the morning and he'll find I'm not there. And straightaway, he'll show up at this door. Tomorrow morning. By ten in the morning, he'll be knocking on that door, ready to break it down."

Alma feels like a general, beleaguered, smoldering. The army isn't unified, the soldiers don't even always know they are soldiers, and some women don't even seem to know there is a war. She doesn't understand them, dainty, gloved, naturally refined, sacrificial, yielding. The problem is that each fight is private. Mrs. Bass, for example, her own stern fortress. Pearly, a defeated queen. Even Roxy's mother, years ago, her death a revolt. She could go on and on, counting every woman she knows. She thinks back on the stockings in the hosiery mill, woman after woman, their silent charges, captures, defeats.

The light is steady. Alma has never noticed before the way it slides across the floor, and rises, sun squares, in the house while the sun sets. It inches up her legs, her hips as she washes dishes in the sink, circling a bowl with a bristle, again and again. When she steps away, light has pooled in the scrubbed bowl in the sink. It gleams like cat's milk. If she could, she would lift the bowl to her lips and swallow the light. They are waiting for her to say something. She can feel them, staring at her back, just as she can feel the bees boring into her wooden eaves. In two days, it will be Sunday again. She wonders if Irving will come for dinner. She will ask him to tar the bees' holes. Sometimes it is clear that Lettie is the only one left to save. She watches the bowl empty, fill with shadow. She thinks of the nun, the dark bowl of her skirt, that her legs beneath it once were a girl's legs, scissoring through water.

She says, "Can he swim?"

And Lettie gives out a slow breath. Alma turns and watches her daughter soften. Her eyes fill with tears. She blinks, and the word escapes from her, more than it is said. "No."

Lettie is inside of the office for the first time in her life, and it's better than being left behind. She is within the dream now. Each turn is a recognition, the way as a little girl on the ride home from her grandmother's house in the country, she would fall asleep wedged between her brothers in the backseat but would always wake up as they neared home because somewhere deep inside, her body knew this pattern of turns and dips, the familiar bump over a lip as they pulled into the driveway. *This is the way it goes. This is the way it goes.* Even the sweet soapiness of her freshly washed hair seems true to the dream now.

Sister Margaret strides into the room. An hour ago, Lettie was sitting in her mother's parlor, and now the plan is in motion. There's a furiousness in Sister Margaret, but it isn't exactly anger, more bustle and business. Lettie is afraid of her and yet at the same time, there's some comfort. Her chest is broad and flat, and Lettie remembers holding onto her shoulders, pulling herself to the scratchy wool of her habit. It couldn't have been a dream. It was Sister Margaret who carried her from the small chapel back to her bed the night she followed the mouse. Sister Margaret rounds her desk. She looks up as she sits in her chair, pulling herself to her desk, first at Alma and then Lettie, her face still swollen, blue. The nun swallows, stiffens. "What happened here?" She is angry.

Her mother says, "We need your help." She tells the nun about the reverend. She says, "I thought he was the miracle I'd prayed for." Lettie is surprised to hear that her mother prays. She can't imagine a soft conversation or her mother begging on her knees to anyone. Her mother tells the nun how the reverend came back to the house early one morning, alone, the car empty, and told her that Lettie was gone. Every day, the three of them—Alma, Roxy, even Delphine—kept coming back to Smitty's apartment to take Lettie home. Lettie imagines Delphine in the sunlight, her weak eyes, so pale, blinking in the brightness of day. Irving is gone. He's disappeared, it seems. The laundry truck stolen, with its wash loads still in it. His rent is late, and Alma paid it for him. He doesn't come back to his apartment. In retelling this part of the story to the nun, Lettie's mother nearly begins crying, but instead she stiffens. She has said to Lettie that she fears Irving is gone for good, and Lettie has told her no, that Irving is good. He will return. Her mother tells the nun that finally they were back, Smitty and Lettie, but he wouldn't let them take her. And then her daughter finally escaped. Alma doesn't tell the nun that they were both deranged. Her mother weeping in the rain, yanking clothes from the line, and screaming out, not words, just squalling. And Lettie, too, she was insane. She thinks she still is, wonders if she will always feel this crazy and yet there's a solid march, an end, inevitable, undeniable. "He'll beat on her until one day she'll die of it, if we let him. So, I came to you."

There is an exchange between her mother and the nun. Lettie knows that there is more to this conversation than she understands. "What do you intend to do to stop him?" Sister Margaret asks.

Her mother says, "We're going to drown him. An accident. He'll be drunk. All we need is a body of water and a good witness." The nun stands up and begins to pace. "He'll be coming for her soon. And we won't be able to stop him. He's a police officer."

Sister Margaret stares at her sharply. It gives her a moment's pause.

"The police won't trust us. Not any of us. But they will believe you, Sister. And we have to move quickly. There isn't any time to waste here."

Sister Margaret walks to her window. She lifts the curtain. She is staring far off, and then she begins, "I can see the dock from here. Maybe you'll have a picnic, come to see your brother. Willard can't watch, though. He'll be called in to help lift something heavy in the kitchen. He can get the dessert. And everyone, the children, the other sisters will be at a special mass, but I will fall ill at the last minute. I'm just a lonely nun. I'll be watching from here. I can see you all on the dock, and how he jumps in or stumbles off the downstream side. I can see you reaching to help him, all of you women on the dock, reaching to pull him up. But you're not strong enough, any of you."

"We need it to happen tomorrow," her mother says.

The nun looks up at her, narrows her eyes, nods.

And so the dream is recited, takes on the leadenness of words. Lettie can smell the cake, its whipped white icing. *This is the way it goes. This is the way it goes.* It's a song that she's never heard, yet she knows it.

Her mother says, "How can we be strong enough? We're just women." Her mother is like this. She isn't sure how, but she says things and you know she means something brutish. She is the one with the fire in her, not Lettie, not even Delphine anymore. Delphine is just smoke. Her mother has a fire, a lit coke oven in her chest, and Lettie decides that once it was filled with love, something near to pure. Her mother had once been a girl filled with notions. She can nearly imagine the girl that toughened into this fiery, rugged figure, this heavy magnet, Lettie is drawn to. Life is demanding, Lettie can feel the surge of it, and her mother grapples, doesn't allow anything to budge her. If Lettie is to become a woman in the world, she has to learn something from her mother, but just a squared inch of knowledge, not so much so that she can't desire. There is the deep pull of her mother's full body, but Lettie will edge away. There will be a dock, a hand. *This is the way it goes.*

And she knows that at the end of it all, after it has all played out, she will fall asleep and there will be no dream, no absolute, unyielding premonition, no presence of a future ambling toward her. Her life will stretch before her like a green field that shifts and rolls, that is so unpredictable and mutable it barely holds onto its greenness.

Delphine has her head on Roxy's shoulder, stiffly muscled as the side of a horse. They sit on side-by-side chairs in the kitchen. The house is quiet. It's morning, the room softly lit with sun. Delphine isn't sure she can usher Smitty to his death. She asks Roxy, "Do you think I can do it the right way, the way Alma needs me to?" She wants to say, *I can't. I cannot be relied upon.*

But Roxy says, "Of course you can. You have got to."

And Delphine thinks of all of the men she's ushered to bed, and isn't sex a lot like death? She's always felt as if she were practicing dying, letting go of the body, allowing it to be a body, a release to animalness, thoughtlessness, a giving in, a handing over. If this is so, then she will die beautifully one day, and she'll know just how to lead Smitty to it.

It's nearly ten o'clock in the morning, and Smitty arrives just as Lettie said he would. He knocks at the door with the butt of his fist, and although Delphine expects him, she feels the knock in her stomach, a jolt. She wants to be in her bed-room smoking pills. She can taste the smoke in her mouth, her throat, and the buzz of her mind as it turns over to its gentleness, its slowing tirade, and final loss of time. She can hear voices today—her mother, for example, still screaming for her in the front yard. It is a sharpened echo in her head.

Roxy says, "Answer it." She sits forward with her elbows on her knees, her hands clasped together.

Delphine says, "Do you love me?"

Roxy tilts her head. She's caught off-guard. "You are per-fect. Of course I love you."

It pains her, Roxy's love, even though she desires it. Delphine says, "Stop it. Hush. You know I don't like that gushing. Go on upstairs. You'll only scare him."

And Roxy stands up. She walks to the top of the stairs. "I'll be up here. Just holler if you need me, and when it's time to go, I'll appear, like a chauffeur, and drive out to the orphanage."

When Delphine looks out through the screen, Smitty is in the yard, looking up at the windows. She says, "It's been a long time, Smitty." And it has been. She remembers him as a boy, looking out at her from his shadowed eyes, his need so large, so sickening, she could barely touch him, and that was all he wanted. She remembers once how she picked him up to carry him to a back room where it was quieter. She carried him like a baby, and he woke up and said, "Stay with me here. Hold me just like this while I sleep." And she did. She hummed for him. But at nineteen, she couldn't be his mother. She wasn't even able to take care of herself. She wonders if she could have been better to him, if he isn't somehow a sin of her own.

He charges back up the porch steps. "Where is she? Where is she at?"

"She's at the orphanage, visiting Willard."

"Let me in." He barges past Delphine and looks around the parlor, wildly. "Who burned up all my clothes? There's a blackened tub in my house—my clothes burned to nothing but a lump of char."

"Alma lost her mind. Lettie loves you, and you know what? Alma has learned that now. She's come around. She'll buy you all new clothes. You need a drink. You want a drink?"

He stares at her now for the first time. She rubs her dress, smooths it out over her hips. "You know that girl loves you. And I can see how. Her mama did the burning. Alma was upset. But Lettie just told her how much she loved you and how she was set on you." She pours him a drink, hands it to him.

He stares at the drink in his hand. "I'm an officer of the law now. I can't take this drink."

She looks around. "Well, I don't see your captain."

He shoots the drink to the back of his throat.

She says, "Sit down. We'll drive out in a bit. I know where they are. Lettie is visiting with her brother. They're family. Like us, Smitty. We're family, right? We go back a long way, don't we?" She stares at him coolly and then smiles. "There's no rush to it. Let's have a few drinks first." After enough drinks, she'll let it slip that there's to be a picnic, and then she'll admit that it's an attempt to call a truce.

He sits down on the sofa. And she sits beside him. She refreshes his drink and her own. She sips it, savoring the hot burn in her throat. She puts her hand on his knee. She says, "You and me go back a long, long, long way."

He looks down at her hand. It's the one with the scar across her knuckles. Smitty runs his finger along it, suddenly gentle. He says, "You know he loved us both." He looks up into her eyes. He says, "He could have run it cross your throat—you know that. It was an act of kindness."

Delphine reaches up. She kisses his sweaty cheek. He is her own ugly child, raised from the rot of her neglect. He leans toward her, to kiss her lips. She's a whore. She is nobody's mother. She could have sex with him. She could kill him. There's a rip inside of her. It makes no difference.

Except that Roxy is on the stairs. Roxy is hovering on the landing. It would pain her, and there is too much pain in the world, too much brash light and heat and noise. She doesn't think she can live much longer like this. A whore, a mother, a lover, tender and grieving and joyful, the sick mix of love and hate that this world demands. She is surprised suddenly at how easy it becomes to do her part in the killing. She will carry him like a part of herself to his death. It is a kindness, a gentle act of love. One day, she hopes, someone will do the same for her.

Sister Margaret lies in the tub. A glimpse. A moment, only, to pause here. The nuns are preparing the children for chapel, but she has told them that she's sick. She needs to be washed clean. She usually closes her eyes to her own nakedness, especially when she's menstruating, as she is now. It seems a waste of blood. Her womb is pointless. She shouldn't have to forgo this womanly burden.

She usually steps into the tub and enters the dark, knowing her body during these brisk weekly dips only by soapy washrag. But today she is dizzy. Her hand slips off the washrag, the soap dips underwater. The room is unsteady. She is afraid suddenly that someone is there, watching her. Her grandmother, she suddenly imagines the woolly woman poised above her, old, senile, nearly blind and deaf. She opens her eyes, but the room is small, private, the door locked with a hook.

And once her eyes are open, she cannot close them again. She looks at her long legs, the bony hinges of her knees, her ribs like thick spokes. It's as if her body has just arrived. It doesn't belong to her after all. It is God's body. Her body became an instrument, and she was saved from herself. She wonders if Alma's prostitutes feel disconnected from their bodies, as she does. To go on, to do what they do, to persist, they must learn that the body is only a body, a useful tool.

She thinks of those women often, although she knows none of them. Perhaps they know better than anyone that the soul exists elsewhere. Perhaps they could have more faith that the young man who will arrive for a picnic and drown is only a body, dying.

Her backbone is stiff, her knees bare and cool. The small window is open. She watches the drawn curtain kick, puffing breaths of light. Soon Alma will be in the yard, snapping the tablecloth so that it falls open on the grass, and Sister Margaret will look down as he struggles, as his soul spirals up from this earth. Blood, it spirals up, too, from between her legs. It clouds red, dissipates, pinking. *I am a lowly handmaid of the Lord. I am a whore. Who could be more a servant than that?* This is what she thinks. A loud voice in her head. The words, unmistakable. And although she tries to push it from her mind—*blessed art thou among women*—it seems like she has become stronger. As if she's asked for some gift of faith, and it has arrived. She stands, naked, tall. Her body, long and beautiful. It seems to stretch on beneath her forever.

9

*L*ettie is here, a collection of tender bruises. She's distant, edging the corners of things. Alma saw her flinch at a bird's open-winged shadow gliding across the grass. Willard is here, too. She needs him. He is the sum of any goodness she has ever had. He is the part of her that doesn't think all of the time, that isn't so knotted by these visions that sweep across her mind as if tidal. She is trying now, as she has for years, not to recount them, a lifetime of things she's seen and tried to unsee, but in doing so only calls them up in horrible detail. She is trying to fool herself for the moment that there is going to be a real picnic. She sets out the potato salad, meats, a stack of plates on a tablecloth from the convent, white, bought for a visit from the bishop, who has never returned and who isn't expected to. The foods will gray with a film of ash, and be eaten, calmly, happily by her picnickers.

Willard says, "I wish Lettie didn't hurt herself."

"I fell down, Willard," Lettie says. "I told you that."

He looks away from her as a distraction. He's nervous, too, because he knows in his own way that it isn't a normal picnic. He crosses his arms on his chest, breasty with fat. "The sky is bluer."

"Yes," Alma says. "It is a little." But still it is a gray blue. There is no blue like the sky over the oil-stained, rusty, dank Miami docks.

Lettie glances up fearfully as if expecting something to fall from it.

The car appears, Smitty's, but Roxy is behind the wheel. Doors pop open, and Delphine and Smitty seem to fall out as if pushed. Roxy walks ahead in overalls, her man's shirt with its cuffed sleeves, and Delphine and Smitty follow, arms clasped, bobbling against each other. They hoot and laugh.

Lettie walks up to Alma and shakes her head. "No, no. It's not playing out just right. Things have shifted. In my dream, I'm wearing the apron, not you."

But Alma takes her daughter's arm and grips it firmly. There's no time for talk about her awful dreams just now. They walk together toward Smitty, Alma steering Lettie's arm, as rigid as a rudder.

Roxy says, "We're here, Alma."

And Delphine calls out, "Hidy-ho!" She is spirited,

and Alma is relieved to see that she's playing the role. Delphine sits on the tablecloth, pats her knees. "It's all so nice!"

Roxy is nervous. She glances around. "Yes," she says, distractedly. "It is nice."

Smitty says, "Well, now, here's my bride."

"Yes," Alma says. "I hope that we can make things right between us."

"I see you have got a picnic."

"Can I eat now, Momma?" Willard asks. "Can I eat now that Smitty is here?"

"Sure you can," Alma says. "We should all eat, before the food loses its chill."

Willard kneels, denting the blanket, and begins to dip up potato salad. Smitty walks up close to Alma, his face inches from hers. There's a small sway to his body. He says, "I think I'll drink lunch. You are a snakish woman, Alma. I wouldn't be surprised if you poisoned my food." Alma imagines his mouth filling with water. His arms flailing, the panicked churn of his legs. He knows only survival. He'll open his eyes underwater and look up to see the sun, reaching for it. The whole entire world has wanted him to die. He was born only in that hope by some desperate woman who cast him out. He will be difficult to kill.

Alma cocks her head. "Now, Smitty—I'm here to put things right."

"That's right. That's right." He pulls Lettie from Alma's

arm, picks her up, and staggers in a circle. Alma can see her daughter wince with pain.

"Why don't you two take a walk along the dock?" Alma says. "And Willard, you go on and get the cake. A nun will be in the kitchen to help you with it. Carry it on back."

Willard stands up. He's nervous now. He stammers and claps his hands twice, angrily, a gesture he might have picked up from a nun trying to get his attention.

"Go on, now," Alma says in a low voice, urgently.

"Well, somebody's got a sweet tooth that doesn't like to be put off," Smitty says. He takes Lettie's hand, and they head off to the dock.

Willard looks at his mother, sorrowful almost. And then he turns and runs across the field, his heft jostling. "Don't run," Alma calls out. "Or you will fall and hurt yourself." He stops and looks over his shoulder, now lumbering through the clipped grass, his back sweat-stained.

The three women are alone. "Eat," Alma says. "It's a picnic." She looks up at Sister Margaret's window. The curtain is raised, and she can see the black habit, the long, white oval of her face.

Willard is now out of sight. "Don't look," she says to Delphine and Roxy. "Keep your heads down." They both do what she says, picking at their plates, shifting through congealed potato salad with fork tines. Alma wonders how long Delphine and Roxy will stay with her in the house. She imagines them leaving her sometime, maybe because of this day. It will prove too much, and Roxy will get her way. They'll move to some quiet town and pretend to be old-maid sisters. They could be invited to picnics, real picnics, and they could sit together as they now do, eating potato salad like normal women, or perhaps, not. They could also stay as they are forever, a mismatched pair, living together in the bedroom across the hall. The routine of dusk and men with their bucking, their spits of cum. (She has never before thought of a woman's body as a gracious spittoon.) And then early morning sleep, the day sprawling before them. A life as willful as Alma's.

Alma cranes her neck to see the dock. Her daughter is down on her hands and knees, and Smitty is standing above her, his hands on his bony hips. Lettie is patting the wood planks with her hands, nervously, like a blind person. Alma is scared. What is Lettie doing on the ground? What could she be looking for? Her daughter lacks the strength. Alma charges toward the dock.

"What are you lovebirds doing? There's food to eat." She tries to chirp sweetly.

Smitty walks around Lettie. She's still on the ground, now behind him, at his heels. "Goddamn it if she didn't lose her wedding ring!"

Now time slows, because Lettie lifts her eyes. She looks at her mother through Smitty's parted legs. Alma lowers her shoulder. She begins to run toward him. He doesn't have time to say anything. Her shoulder lands squarely in his chest. His feet catch on Lettie crouched behind him. He tips backward, losing his balance, and Alma pushes him over the hip-high railing. She can feel the give of his muscles. His body flips, and then catches. He has a fistful of Alma's apron. His hand clutched, and he is suspended there. Alma bends her knees. She's being pulled, her waist pressed against the railing, her hands gripping the wood to keep herself from going with him. She can feel Lettie's fast hands, the quick work behind her back, untying the apron. It finally snaps off, a white shimmer before he falls into the water.

Alma can hear him. "Get a stick. Give me something to grab hold of! I can't swim." She watches his strong hands, batting, his face bobbing and disappearing and bobbing up again. The river is greedy. It pulls him in hungrily. Alma feels momentarily as if this has nothing to do with killing. It's more a momentary generosity, like she's given the starving river something to feed on.

Lettie is kneeling on the dock, her voice, calm now. "The apron becomes the wings. See it twisting in the water."

His head dips under the water, and then there's only his hand, opening and closing on nothing, and then it too disappears, swallowed by the choppy waves. Alma hears the distant singing of children in the halls on their way to chapel. She looks down at her daughter, fresh and whole, quite miraculously alive. Alma looks out across the field. Soon Willard will appear, proud, his cheeks glowing with sun, carrying a white sheet cake. And she can feel the nun, looking down from the window.

It is done, and yet not done. There is only a small splintering in her chest, like ice across the surface of a lake. She nearly sighs, but the breath stalls in her lungs. They need to find the body. She walks off the dock and calls to Delphine and Roxy and Lettie to come downstream. Only Lettie doesn't. She drifts off, and Alma lets her.

"The body," she says to Roxy and Delphine. "Do you see it?" They huddle together, moving slowly.

Roxy says, "I should wade in and see what I see." And so she does, her legs slowed by the water like dream-walking, long, lurching steps. Delphine and Alma watch Roxy from shore. It's too much for her daughter. The water collapses in on itself, swirls, roils on, washing through the rusty rocks on the bank. The rush is loud, constant. Alma is looking for the churn of limbs, an arm like a fish rolling toward the surface. But there aren't any flashes of white.

She hears an animal noise. Her head snaps in the direction of Lettie, standing near the bank. Alma says, "Stay here," to Delphine, and she nods, her eyes fixed on the water.

Alma turns and sees Lettie bending toward a shape, ragged and dark, on the bank. At first she hopes it to be a raccoon, a beaver, but no, it is Smitty's wet head, his mouth lifted, gasping, retching, one pale outstretched hand gripping a rock. Alma doesn't scream. She lifts her skirt and walks swiftly. She doesn't want to alarm Lettie, who seems only remotely interested like a child peering at worms under an upturned rock. Alma thinks of picking up one of the heavy rounded rocks and lowering it on his head. She can nearly imagine the thud of rock and skull and how it would have its own echo of memory in her hands as it was with slicing the rattlesnake. But that isn't the plan. She refuses to panic. He's supposed to drown, and that is what he will do.

She's close enough now to see his soaked shirt, which billows and clings to his knotty back, his stocking feet bob in the water behind him. Lettie now moves closer, scoots down on the rocks, pushes his shoulder with the heel of her shoe to cast him loose.

Alma calls out to her, "No, no."

But it's too late. Smitty lifts his face. He looks at Lettie with something near to a mixed expression of fear and love, and then with sudden quickness, he grabs her bony ankle and pulls her down the rocky bank, hand over hand up her leg, yanking violently on her skirts. Lettie tries to scramble up. Her knees knock against the rocks. It happens too quickly. Lettie is now in the water with him, her skirt billows, dry in a puff around her momentarily, until water seeps up, pulling the skirt down.

Alma doesn't think. She jumps in, her arms and legs turning wildly in the air before her body plunges into the water, cold. She feels swallowed by it. She paddles awkwardly toward her daughter, whose face dips suddenly underwater. Smitty is underwater, too. Alma swims toward him. She is a choppy swimmer. Her feet kick beneath her. She grabs a handful of Smitty's hair and forces him to stay down. She can see only Lettie's hair, splayed, pluming like seaweed. The water is thick, Alma's clothes heavy, her shoes like strapped stones. Smitty strains to tilt his head back so that he is staring up. Alma can see the white glow of his face, his eyes wide. But she does not give. She digs her fingernails into the slick skin of his arm, tries to unlock his hold on Lettie's waist. Bubbles rise. He thrashes. The surface becomes an explosion of water. His hair is slick and short and hard to hold. Lettie appears, her stringy hair streaking her face. She is carried on a current toward the bank. Alma's head is still up, above the water, her chin raised, the back of her hair already wet. She can see across to the other side of the river now, a calm sloping hillside in the distance. The far bank is dotted with jewelweed and monkey flowers. The broad field's green face gazes, the weary sun, too. All so out of place with the hysteria beneath her, the tight muscle of her arms, the strained heat in her face, it shocks her. The instant memory of her father leaning over this very water to show her how to light a bubbled line of natural gas and watch it catch, miraculously flare.

But then there is another pull, as if Smitty has changed his mind and decided not to try to come to the surface but to pull Alma down with him. Her head goes under. Her eyes are wide, but the water is grayed by bubbles and thick with silt, swirling muddied clouds. She holds onto the shoulders of his shirt, but he has her now. His arms clasp her waist, an embrace, like the end of a lurid, disastrous affair. His body arches like a fish, swift and unpredictable. She could die. They could drown together and then swirl in an awkward, passionate lock until they bump up against a stony bank. They would say she was trying to save him, that he was trying to save her. In the confusion, both seem possible. The struggles blur. She lets air slip from her mouth; it fills with water. She imagines Henry's face in the window of the car, the reverend, the small swollen bite on his cheek, and one by one, her children as children, nearly babies, sweaty and pink with sleep. Her lungs will fill tightly and she will die. She's sure of it now. It seems fitting that her anger, her protectiveness, her desire to keep safe what is hers would be the death of her. But there is a small give in Smitty's arms. She has his wrists. The grip loosens on the fabric at the small of her back. She slips away and beats to the bright sheen of water, breaking the surface, her lungs rung out, gasping. Smitty rolls away from her, his arms tumbling around his head, as if he's dancing.

Alma looks to shore, and there stands the nun, nearly naked, her shoes and black habit, her wimple, lay in a pile. She is wearing only her black stockings, pinching her long, narrow waist, and a thick strapped camisole, one strap safely pinned where it snapped loose. Her hair is thin and short, cropped at odd angles. Lettie is there at her feet, dragged out, nearly limp, but breathing. Alma paddles weakly to shore. Delphine and Roxy are still downstream. Not much time has passed after all. The nun is tall but thicker than Alma imagined. She is so very human, achingly real, down to the detail of her longer second toe, nudging out of a hole in her stockings. Sister Margaret edges down on the rocks, holds out her hand, and pulls Alma in. They are both breathless.

"Were you going to come in?" Alma's voice is raw, her throat burning.

Sister Margaret doesn't nod. She is shy and pale like this, ashamed. It's hard to say why. She steps into her dress and begins zipping it up the back. She arranges her wimple, which attaches with little fuss. She steps into her shoes. She wipes her hands on her skirt. She says, "Follow his body downstream as far as you can. Let the fish feed on it some. And then draw it out. I will call the police from my office. It will be simple. Keep the story very simple."

"Were you going to save me?"

"I was praying for your soul."

"But you were undressing to swim. Didn't you trust God to answer your prayers?"

"I am an instrument of God," she says. "I do his will. You should understand this, Alma."

"I should understand what?"

But Sister Margaret doesn't answer. She turns and walks back toward the convent, her skirt grazing grass tips. She moves with such fluidity, such ample grace, comfortable, it seems, hauling around contradiction. It's as if she, too, is being swept off by a strong, ceaseless current.

Alma steps outside of herself, this drenched woman, her dress pressing wet to her breasts, hips. She allows the moment to expand and expand. The nun can be an instrument of God, if she wants. But Alma is simply a woman. She asked for a miracle. It didn't work the way she'd wanted it to, and so she knew it was necessary to create her own, an accident. It will fade. She knows how quickly they will all return to their daily habits. Soon she will go home, and perhaps Irving will be there awaiting a good meal. He will not have abandoned her like his father. He missed last Sunday, but he'll be back for it, won't he? Perhaps he'll bring Lucy, and Alma will try to hold her tongue. She will ask him to tar the bee holes, and she might tell him that Smitty drowned, but not even mention that there was ever a marriage. He wouldn't have to know. But quickly she changes her mind. Even this soon, she can feel another version rising up. Yes, she will have to acknowledge the marriage, so that Lettie, for her sake, can become a tragic young widow. *Her husband died just days after the wedding. Drowned at a picnic, a celebration. He couldn't swim, you see.* The nun is on her way to call the police and then, no doubt, to perform some perfunctory part of her day for which she's late, a tardy instrument of God. It all seems quite ordinary and disorienting.

Alma tilts her head back to open her throat and take in deeper breaths. The air is cindery, the sky pale with fleet, untrussed clouds, a bunker of them, now darkening, low bellied, like the lone cow, milk-swollen, heavy with its own curdle. It is good to be a murderer, Alma decides. She already finds herself keeping track of all she has stolen from Smitty. Each moment of life, the trees filled with twittering birds, the river's agitated surface of water spiders and mosquitoes, the sky. It is what he would have taken from Lettie, from her, too, if he'd gotten the chance to kill them, her daughter slowly over years, herself dragged to the bottom of the river. It's better this way.

She turns. Yes, there is Willard, carrying the cake. He'll remember the body later, pulled up from the river. He'll talk on and on about dead Smitty and she'll have to explain it to him again and again. For years to come, he will turn to her on any given day, and ask her why he was blue like that and why he drowned. And she will say that he didn't have enough air. He couldn't swim. From here, Alma can already see Willard's lips white with tongue-smeared icing. She has stolen even this small sweetness, Willard's mouth, from Smitty, but she is good with figures, with keeping track.

Time clips. Roxy lunges through the water and pulls Smitty's body up as best she can, dragging it up the rocks. She sets it down, an odd angle of bones, one arm pinned behind his back, his chest hefted forward. His skin is luminescent, so fine it seems his blood shines up blue beneath it. Willard eats cake. The clouds pass. Delphine and Roxy hover like the clouds. Lettie sits, agog and dreamy, knees to chest, tightening. The captain arrives—a gouty waddle, the beefy mound of his sweat-soaked back. He gets his boys to lay the body properly on the grass, white on green, arms to sides.

The captain says, "It was just you women here. Is that right? And he was drunk, you say?"

She hears herself retelling the story, a voice that swims in her chest, words rising up from her mouth. The captain tugs his belt, looks at his shoes, old and toe-warped.

Lettie says, mournfully, "He wasn't strong in water."

The captain repeats, "And Willard wasn't here. It was just you all women. Just you old sorry, whoring women. Is that right?"

She is the nigger-lover's daughter, a madam of a whorehouse, a murderer.

"No." Sister Margaret is here now. "No," she says. "I was the one to call you. I saw it all from my window. He was drunk. It was an accident."

The captain apologizes for his language, his cheeks slack, a humbled reddening. He's disappointed but dutiful. He harbors a deep cowardice known to Alma. She recalls the shame-faced way he tucked in his wilted penis. This is his expression now. He has a notebook, a pencil, to write it down. He nods, unwilling to challenge, taking it all in word for word.

Alma feels like she is finally giving in to the world, her imagined self. She feels like a woman who sets out to collect each oily peanut bag, each button, each sun-filled bowl, and she caresses her things, even Smitty pulled from the river, his eyes nibbled at by bottom fish—she will keep him, too, so beautifully blue. She will polish, polish each memory with the quick hissing strokes of her mind, a sweet penance. Her heart begins its clangor. The Prophet, her father's tongue, the girls with sticks, her imagined baby, dead in its sheet, and also a miracle, squalling, with its many arms and many legs, the Mule-Faced Woman reading with her ankles crossed, Mrs. Bass's hunched backbone. Her children, circling, circling, innocently, before the consumption, the fire. She recalls the nest squirming with baby rats, the moths rising from the open trunk, the dog in the trap, and Henry, whom she doesn't expect to ever see again, not ever, although she would like to know where he buried the dead baby. Finally, she recalls finding her mother in bed, the stench of the body's difficult final resolute task of returning to dust and the durable, inexhaustible brass buttons of her coat. Everything returns to her in a blurred rush motored by the intricate mechanisms of her raucous heart, and she gives in to it, although she doesn't understand it, doesn't have a name to call it. The coal—its fine dust raining down, its constant blessing—covers everything, all of them with its gritty veil of absolution. The orphans are ringing their little bells.

Afterword

$\mathcal{I}$rving guides the blind woman across the yard. "There's a hedgerow and wild flowers, an empty laundry line. An empty grazing field. There are porch steps here. One, two, three, four. We're alone. Everyone is out." Her eyes sometimes reveal a milkiness, as if she's filled with it, and at the top there's risen cream. He says, "Let me take you to my old room. There was a bear once who stayed in it, and Mr. Bucci. But the bear died. It was old." He counts going up the staircase. She has her arm curled around his. They have been traveling together in the laundry truck. He has learned to narrate landscapes, and now it's time to come home.

She says, "I'd learned mister's story. I needed a new one. I confess I'm addicted to this, being led through rooms on a strong arm."

He hopes that she won't ever leave him, that she won't

one day ask a stranger to take her with him—perhaps while he's sleeping like the furry, waspish service station owner— and, if she does, he hopes that the stranger is a better man than he is. He is disastrous at being good. He can feel himself failing even while he prides himself on being the strong arm. He can hear his own tinny voice rising up: *How is this good? Stealing a blind woman from a service station to make love to her in your mother's house? Never returning to your job, because you see fit to show someone the world you know?* And yet he is desperately trying. Mostly, he has much to say, so much his heart aches in his chest. It isn't love but the urging toward release. He leads her down the hall. There's a douche bag hanging on a hook behind the door, iodine and vinegar bottles on a table. The room holds the yeasty ferment of bodies, sweat, the weeping ocean scent of sex, and deep in the room's cankerous history, the bear's fur and breath, Mr. Bucci's small gas burner. He'll get to his father, his mother, Willard, Lettie, the show people, the whores. He feels embattled, a casualty and yet resolved.

He will get to everything he knows and form from dust what he doesn't. But he'll begin here, undoing the small, chipped buttons on her sleeve's cuff that loosen at her thin wrist, and inch his way, painstakingly, irrefutably, into the swollen, swelling past.